The White Moll

Frank L. Packard

Contents

THE WHITE MOLL

BY

Frank L. Packard

I. NIGHT IN THE UNDERWORLD

It was like some shadowy pantomime: The dark mouth of an alleyway thrown into murky relief by the rays of a distant street lamp...the swift, forward leap of a skulking figure...a girl's form swaying and struggling in the man's embrace. Then, a pantomime no longer, there came a half threatening, half triumphant oath; and then the girl's voice, quiet, strangely contained, almost imperious:

"Now, give me back that purse, please. Instantly!" The man, already retreating into the alleyway, paused to fling back a jeering laugh.

"Say, youse've got yer nerve, ain't youse!"

The girl turned her head so that the rays of the street lamp, faint as they were, fell full upon her, disclosing a sweet, oval face, out of which the dark eyes gazed steadily at the man.

And suddenly the man leaned forward, staring for an instant, and then his hand went awkwardly to touch his cap.

"De White Moll!" he mumbled deferentially. He pulled the peak of his cap down over his eyes in a sort of shame-faced way, as though to avoid recognition, and, stepping nearer, returned the purse.

"'Scuse me, miss," he said uneasily. "I didn't know it was youse--honest to Gawd, I didn't! 'Scuse me, miss. Good-night!"

For a moment the girl stood there motionless, looking down the alleyway after the retreating figure. From somewhere in the distance came the rumble of an elevated train. It drowned out the pound of the man's speeding footsteps; it died away itself--and now there was no other sound. A pucker, strangely wistful, curiously perturbed, came and furrowed her forehead into little wrinkles, and then she turned and walked slowly on along the deserted street.

The White Moll! She shook her head a little. The attack had not unnerved her. Why should it? It was simply that the man had not recognized her at first in the darkness. The White Moll here at night in one of the loneliest, as well as one of the most vicious and abandoned, quarters of New York, was as safe and inviolate as--as--She shook her head again. Her mind did not instantly suggest a comparison that seemed wholly adequate. The pucker deepened, but the sensitive, delicately chiseled lips parted now in a smile. Well, she was safer here than anywhere else in the world, that was all.

It was the first time that anything like this had happened, and, for the very reason that it was unprecedented, it seemed to stir her memory now, and awaken a dormant train of thought. The White Moll! She remembered the first time she had ever been called by that name. It took her back almost three years, and since that time, here in this sordid realm of crime and misery, the name of Rhoda Gray, her own name, her actual identity, seemed to have become lost, obliterated in that of the White Moll. A "dip" had given it to her, and the underworld, quick and trenchant in its "monikers," had instantly ratified it. There was not a crook or denizen of crimeland, probably, who did not know the White Moll; there was, probably, not one to-day who knew, or cared, that she was Rhoda Gray!

She went on, traversing block after block, entering a less deserted, though no less unsavory, neighborhood. Here, a saloon flung a sudden glow of yellow light athwart the sidewalk as its swinging doors jerked apart; and a form lurched out into the night; there, from a dance-hall came the rattle of a tinny piano, the squeak of a raspy violin, a high-pitched, hectic burst of laughter; while, flanking the street on each side, like interjected inanimate blotches, rows of squalid tenements and cheap, tumble-down frame houses silhouetted themselves in broken, jagged points against the sky-line. And now and then a man spoke to her--his untrained fingers fumbling in clumsy homage at the brim of his hat.

How strange a thing memory was! How strange, too, the coincidences that sometimes roused it into activity! It was a man, a thief, just like the man to-night, who had first brought her here into this shadowland of crime. That was just before her father had died. Her father had been a mining engineer, and, though an American, had been for many years resident in South America as the representative of a large English concern. He had been in ill health for a year down there, when, acting on his physician's advice, he had come to New York for consultation, and she had accompanied him. They had taken a little flat, the engineer had placed himself in the hands of a famous specialist, and an operation had been decided upon. And then, a few days prior to the date set for the operation and before her father, who was still able to be about, had entered the hospital, the flat had been broken into during the early morning hours. The thief, obviously not counting on the engineer's wakefulness, had been caught red-handed. At first defiant, the man had finally broken down, and had told a miserable story. It was hackneyed possibly, the same story told by a thousand others as a last defense in the hope of inducing leniency through an appeal to pity, but somehow to her that night the story had rung true. Pete McGee, alias the Bussard, the man had said his name was. He couldn't get any work; there was the shadow of a long abode in Sing Sing that lay upon him as a curse--a job here to-day, his record discovered to-morrow, and the next day out on the street again. It was very old, very threadbare, that story; there were even the sick wife, the hungry, unclothed children; but to her it had rung true. Her father had not placed the slightest faith in it, and but for her intervention the Bussard would have been incontinently consigned to the mercies of the police.

Her face softened suddenly now as she walked along. She remembered well that scene, when, at the end, she had written down the address the man had given her.

"Father is going to let you go, McGee, because I ask him to," she had said. "And to-morrow morning I will go to this address, and if I find your story is true, as I believe it is, I will see what I can do for you."

"It's true, miss, so help me God!" the man had answered brokenly. "Youse come an' see. I'll be dere-an'-an'-God bless youse, miss!"

And so they had let the man go free, and her father, with a whimsical, tolerant smile, had shaken his head at her. "You'll never find that address, Rhoda-or our friend the Bussard, either!"

But she had found both the Bussard and the address, and destitution and a squalor unspeakable. Pathetic still, but the vernacular of the underworld where men called their women by no more gracious names than "molls" and "skirts" no longer strange to her ears, there came to her again now the Bussard's words in which he had paid her tribute on that morning long ago, and with which he had introduced her to a shrunken form that lay upon a dirty cot in the barefloored room:

"Meet de moll I was tellin' youse about, Mag. She's white--all de way up. She's white, Mag; she's a white moll--take it from me."

The White Moll!

The firm little chin came suddenly upward; but into the dark eyes unbidden came a sudden film and mist. Her father's health had been too far undermined, and he had been unable to withstand the shock of the operation, and he had died in the hospital. There weren't any relatives, except distant ones on her mother's side, somewhere out in California, whom she had never seen. She and her father had been all in all to each other, chums, pals, comrades, since her mother's death many years ago. She had gone everywhere with him save when the demands of her education had necessarily kept them apart; she had hunted with him in South America, ridden with him in sections where civilization was still in the making, shared the crude, rough life of mining camps with him--and it had seemed as though her life, too, had gone out with his.

She brushed her hand hastily across her eyes. There hadn't been any friends either, apart from a few of her father's casual business acquaintances; no one else--except the Bussard. It was very strange! Her reward for that one friendly act had come in a manner little expected, and it had come very quickly. She had sought and found a genuine relief from her own sorrow in doing what she could to alleviate the misery in that squalid, one-room home. And then the sphere of her activities had broadened, slowly at first, not through any preconceived intention on her part, but naturally, and as almost an inevitable corollary consequent upon her relations with the Bussard and his ill-fortuned family.

The Bussard's circle of intimates was amongst those who lay outside the law, those who gambled for their livelihood by staking their wits, to win against the toils of the police; and so, more and more, she had come into close and intimate contact with the criminal element of New York, until to-day, throughout its length and breadth, she was known, and, she had reason to believe, was loved and trusted by every crook in the underworld. It was a strange eulogy, self-pronounced! But it was none the less true. Then, she had been Rhoda Gray; now, even the Bussard, doubtless, had forgotten her name in the one with which he himself, at that queer baptismal font of crimeland, had christened her--the White Moll. It even went further than that. It embraced what might be called the entourage of the underworld, the police and the social workers with whom she inevitably came in contact. These, too, had long known her as the White Moll, and had come, since she had volunteered no further information, tacitly to accept her as such, and nothing more.

Again she shook her head. It wasn't altogether a normal life. She was only a woman, with all the aspirations of a woman, with all the yearning of youth for its measure of gayety and pleasure. True, she had not made a recluse of herself outside her work; but, equally, on the other hand, she had not made any intimate friends in her own station in life. She had never purposed continuing indefinitely the work she was doing, nor did she now; but, little by little, it had forced its claims upon her until those claims were not easy to ignore. Even though the circumstances in which her father had left her were barely more than sufficient for a modest little flat uptown, there was still always a little surplus, and that surplus counted in certain quarters for very much indeed. But it wasn't only that. The small amount of money that she was able to spend in that way had little to do with it. The bonds which linked her to the sordid surroundings that she had come to know so well were stronger far than that. There wasn't any money involved in this visit, for instance, that she was going now to make to Gypsy Nan. Gypsy Nan was...

Rhoda Gray had halted before the doorway of a small, hovel-like, two-story building that was jammed in between two tenements, which, relatively, in their own class, were even more disreputable than was the little frame house itself. A secondhand-clothes store occupied a portion of the ground floor, and housed the proprietor and his family as well, permitting the rooms on the second floor to be "rented out"; the garret above was the abode of Gypsy Nan.

There was a separate entrance, apart from that into the secondhand-clothes store, and she pushed this door open and stepped forward into an absolutely black and musty-smelling hallway. By feeling with her hands along the wall she reached the stairs and began to make her way upward. She had found Gypsy Nan last night huddled in the lower doorway, and apparently in a condition that was very much the worse for wear. She had stopped and helped the woman upstairs to her garret, whereupon Gypsy Nan, in language far more fervent than elegant, had ordered her to begone, and had slammed the door in her face.

Rhoda Gray smiled a little wearily, as, on the second floor now, she groped her way to the rear, and began to mount a short, ladder-like flight of steps to the attic.

Gypsy Nan's lack of cordiality did not absolve her, Rhoda Gray, from coming back to-night to see how the woman was--to crowd one more visit on her already over-expanded list. She had never had any personal knowledge of Gypsy Nan before, but, in a sense, the woman was no stranger to her. Gypsy Nan was a character known far and wide in the under-world as one possessing an insatiable and unquenchable thirst. As to who she was, or what she was, or where she got her money for the gin she bought, it was not in the ethics of the Bad Lands to inquire. She was just Gypsy Nan. So that she did not obtrude herself too obviously upon their notice, the police suffered her; so that she gave the underworld no reason for complaint, the under-world accepted her at face value as one of its own!

There was no hallway here at the head of the ladder-like stairs, just a sort of narrow platform in front of the attic door. Rhoda Gray, groping out with her hands again, felt for the door, and knocked softly upon it. There was no answer. She knocked again. Still receiving no reply, she tried the door, found it unlocked, and, opening it, stood for an instant on the threshold. A lamp, almost empty, ill-trimmed and smoking badly, stood on a chair beside a cheap iron bed; it threw a dull, yellow glow about its immediate vicinity, and threw the remainder of the garret into deep, impenetrable shadows; but also it disclosed the motionless form of a woman on the bed.

Rhoda Gray's eyes darkened, as she closed the door behind her, and stepped quickly forward to the bedside. For a moment she stood looking down at the recumbent figure; at the matted tangle of gray-streaked brown hair that straggled across a pillow which was none too clean; at the heavy-lensed, old-fashioned, steel-bowed spectacles, awry now, that were still grotesquely perched on the woman's nose; at the sallow face, streaked with grime and dirt, as though it had not been washed for months; at a hand, as ill-cared for, which lay exposed on the torn blanket that did duty for a counterpane; at the dirty shawl that enveloped the woman's shoulders, and which was tightly fastened around Gypsy Nan's neck-and from the woman her eyes shifted to an empty bottle on the floor that protruded from under the bed.

"Nan!" she called sharply; and, stooping over, shook the woman's shoulder. "Nan!" she repeated. There was something about the woman's breathing that she did not like, something in the queer, pinched condition of the other's face that suddenly frightened her. "Nan!" she called again.

Gypsy Nan opened her eyes, stared for a moment dully, then, in a curiously quick, desperate way, jerked herself up on her elbow.

"Youse get t'hell outer here!" she croaked. "Get out!"

"I am going to," said Rhoda Gray evenly. "And I'm going at once." She turned abruptly and walked toward the door. "I'm going to get a doctor. You've gone too far this time, Nan, and--"

"No, youse don't!" Gypsy Nan s voice rose in a sudden scream. She sat bolt upright in bed, and pulled a revolver out from under the coverings. "Youse don't bring no doctor here! See! Youse put a finger on dat door, an' it won't be de door youse'll go out by!"

Rhoda Gray did not move.

"Nan, put that revolver down!" she ordered quietly. "You don't know what you are doing."

"Don't!" leered Gypsy Nan. The revolver held, swaying a little unsteadily, on Rhoda Gray. There was silence for a moment; then Gypsy Nan spoke again, evidently through dry lips, for she wet them again and again with her tongue: "Say, youse are de White Moll, ain't youse?"

"Yes," said Rhoda Gray.

Gypsy Nan appeared to ponder this for an instant.

"Well den, come back here an' sit down on de foot of de bed," she commanded finally.

Rhoda Gray obeyed without hesitation. There was nothing to do but humor the woman in her present state, a state that seemed one bordering on delirium and complete collapse.

"Nan," she said, "you--"

"De White Moll!" mumbled Gypsy Nan. "I wonder if de dope dey hands out about youse is all on de level? My Gawd, I wonder if wot dey says is true?"

"What do they say?" asked Rhoda Gray gently.

Gypsy Nan lay back on her pillow as though her strength, over-taxed, had failed her; her hand, though it still clutched the revolver, seemed to have been dragged down by the weapon's weight, and now rested upon the blanket.

"Dey say," said Gypsy Nan slowly, "dat youse knows more on de inside here dan anybody else--t'ings youse got from de spacers' molls, an' from de dips demselves when youse was lendin' dem a hand; dey say dere ain't many youse couldn't send up de river just by liftin' yer finger, but dat youse're straight, an' dat youse've kept yer map closed, an' dat youse' re safe."

Rhoda Gray's dark eyes softened, as she leaned forward and laid a hand gently over the one of Gypsy Nan that held the revolver.

"It couldn't be any other way, could it, Nan?" she said simply.

"Wot yer after?" demanded Gypsy Nan, with sudden mockery. "De gun? Well, take it!" She let go her hold of the weapon. "But don't kid yerself dat youse're kiddin' me into givin' it to youse because youse have got a pretty smile an' a sweet voice! Savvy? I"--she choked suddenly, and caught at her throat--"I guess youse're de only chance I got-dat's all."

"That's better," said Rhoda Gray encouragingly. "And now you'll let me go and get a doctor, won't you, Nan?"

"Wait!" said Gypsy Nan hoarsely. "Youse're de only chance I got. Will youse swear youse won't t'row me down if I tells youse somet'ing? I ain't got no other way. Will youse swear youse'll see me through?"

"Of course, Nan," said Rhoda Gray soothingly. "Of course, I will, Nan. I promise."

Gypsy Nan came up on her elbow.

"Dat ain't good enough!" she cried out. "A promise ain't good enough! For Gawd's sake, come across all de way! Swear youse'll keep mum an' see me through!"

"Yes, Nan"--Rhoda Gray's eyes smiled reassurance--"I swear it. But you will be all right again in the morning."

"Will I? You think so, do you? Well, I can only say that I wish I did!"

Rhoda Gray leaned sharply forward, staring in amazement at the figure on the bed. The woman's voice was the same, it was still hoarse, still heavy, and the words came with painful effort; but the English was suddenly perfect now.

"Nan, what is it? I don't understand!" she said tensely. "What do you mean?"

"You think you know what's the matter with me." There was a curious mockery in the weak voice. "You think I've drunk myself into this state. You think I'm on the verge of the D.T.'s now. That empty bottle under the bed proves it, doesn't it? And anybody around here will tell you that Gypsy Nan has thrown enough empties out of the window there to stock a bottle factory for years, some of them on the flat roof just outside the window, some of them on the roof of the shed below, and some of them down into the yard, just depending on how drunk she was and how far she could throw. And that proves it, too, doesn't it? Well, maybe it does, that's what I did it for; but I never touched the stuff, not a drop of it, from the day I came here. I didn't dare touch it. I had to keep my wits. Last night you thought I was drunk when you found me in the doorway downstairs. I wasn't. I was too sick and weak to get up here. I almost told you then, only I was afraid, and--and I thought that perhaps I'd be all right to-day."

"Oh, I didn't know!" Rhoda Gray was on her knees beside the bed. There was no room to question the truth of the woman's words, it was in Gypsy Nan's eyes, in the struggling, labored voice.

"Yes." Gypsy Nan clutched at the shawl around her neck, and shivered. "I thought I might be all right to-day, and that I'd get better. But I didn't. And now I've got about a chance in a hundred. I know. It's my heart."

"You mean you've been alone here, sick, since last night?" There was anxiety, perplexity, in Rhoda Gray's face. "Why didn't you call some one? Why did you even hold me back a few minutes ago, when you admit yourself that you need immediate medical assistance so badly?"

"Because," said Gypsy Nan, "if I've got a chance at all, I'd finish it for keeps if a doctor came here. I--I'd rather go out this way than in that horrible thing they call the 'chair.' Oh, my God, don't you understand that! I've seen pictures of it! It's a horrible thing--a horrible thing--horrible!"

"Nan"--Rhoda Gray steadied her voice--"you re delirious. You do not know what you are saying. There isn't any horrible thing to frighten you. Now you just lie quietly here. I'll only be a few minutes, and--" She stopped abruptly as her wrists were suddenly imprisoned in a frantic grip.

"You swore it!" Gypsy Nan was whispering feverishly. "You swore it! They say the White Moll never snitched. That's the one chance I've got, and I'm going to take it. I'm not delirious--not yet. I wish to God it was nothing more than that! Look!"

With a low, startled cry, Rhoda Gray was on her feet. Gypsy Nan was gone. A sweep of the woman's hand, and the spectacles were off, the gray-streaked hair a tangled wig upon the pillow--and Rhoda Gray found herself staring in a numbed sort of way at a dark-haired woman who could not have been more than thirty, but whose face, with its streaks of grime and dirt, looked grotesquely and incongruously old.

II. SEVEN--THREE--NINE

For a moment neither spoke, then Gypsy Nan broke the silence with a bitter laugh. She threw back the bedclothes, and, gripping at the edge of the bed, sat up.

"The White Moll!" The words rattled in her throat. A fleck of blood showed on her lips. "Well, you know now! You're going to help me, aren't you? I--I've got to get out of here--get to a hospital."

Rhoda Gray laid her hands firmly on the other's shoulders.

"Get back into bed," she said steadily. "Do you want to make yourself worse? You'll kill yourself!"

Gypsy Nan pushed her away.

"Don't make me use up what little strength I've got left in talking," she cried out piteously, and suddenly wrung her hands together. "I'm wanted by the police. If I'm caught, it's--it's that 'chair.' I couldn't have a doctor brought here, could I? How long would it be before he saw that Gypsy Nan was a fake? I can't let you go and have an ambulance, say, come and get me, can I, even with the disguise hidden away? They'd say this is where Gypsy Nan lives. There's something queer here. Where is Gypsy Nan? I've got to get away from here--away from Gypsy Nan--don't you understand? It's death one way; maybe it is the other, maybe it'll finish me to get out of here, but it's the only thing left to do. I thought some one, some one that I could trust, never mind who, would have come to-day, but-but no one came, and--and maybe now it s too late, but there's just the one chance, and I've got to take it." Gypsy Nan tore at the shawl around her throat as though it choked her, and flung it from her shoulders. Her eyes were gleaming with an unhealthy, feverish light. "Don't you see? We get out on the street. I collapse there. You find me. I tell you my name is Charlotte Green. That's all you know. There isn't much chance that anybody at the hospital would recognize me. I've got money. I take a private room. Don't you understand?"

Rhoda Gray's face had gone a little white. There was no doubt about the woman's serious condition, and yet--and yet--She stood there hesitant. There must be some other way! It was not likely even that the woman had strength enough to walk down the stairs to begin with. Strange things had come to her in this world of shadow, but none before like this. If the law got the woman it would cost the woman her life; if the woman did not receive immediate and adequate medical assistance it would cost the woman her life. Over and over in her brain, like a jangling refrain, that thought repeated itself. It was not like her to stand hesitant before any emergency, no matter what that emergency might be. She had never done it before, but now...

"For God's sake," Gypsy Nan implored, "don't stand there looking at me! Can't you understand? If I'm caught, I go out. Do you think I'd have lived in this filthy hole if there had been any other way to save my life? Are you going to let me die here like a dog? Get me my clothes; oh, for God's sake, get them, and give me the one chance that's left!"

A queer little smile came to Rhoda Gray's lips, and her shoulders straightened back.

"Where are your clothes?" she asked.

"God bless you!" The tears were suddenly streaming down the grimy face. "God bless the White Moll! It's true! It's true--all they said about her!" The woman had lost control of herself.

"Nan, keep your nerve!" ordered Rhoda Gray almost brutally. It was the White Moll in another light now, cool, calm, collected, efficient. Her eyes swept Gypsy Nan. The woman, who had obviously flung herself down on the bed fully dressed the night before, was garbed in coarse, heavy boots, the cheapest of stockings which were also sadly in need of repair, a tattered and crumpled skirt of some rough material, and, previously hidden by the shawl, a soiled, greasy and spotted black blouse. Rhoda Gray's forehead puckered into a frown. "What about your hands and face--they go with the clothes, don't they?"

"It'll wash off," whispered Gypsy Nan. "It's just some stuff I keep in a box--over there--the ceiling-" Her voice trailed off weakly, then with a desperate effort strengthened again. "The door! I forgot the door! It isn't locked! Lock the door first! Lock the door! Then you take the candle over there on the washstand, and--and I'll show you. You--you get the things while I'm undressing. I--I can help myself that much."

Rhoda Gray crossed quickly to the door, turned the key in the lock, and re-traced her steps to the washstand that stood in the shadows against the wall on the opposite side from the bed, and near the far end of the garret. Here she found the short stub of a candle that was stuck in the mouth of a gin bottle, and matches lying beside it. She lighted the candle, and turned inquiringly to Gypsy Nan.

The woman pointed to the end of the garret where the roof sloped sharply down until, at the wall itself, it was scarcely four feet above the floor.

"Go down there. Right to the wall--in the center," instructed Gypsy Nan weak-ly. And then, as Rhoda Gray obeyed: "Now push up on that wide board in the ceil-ing."

Rhoda Gray, already in a stooped position, reached up, and pushed at a rough, unplaned board. It swung back without a sound, like a narrow trap-door, until it rested in an upright position against the outer frame of the house, disclosing an aperture through which, by standing erect, Rhoda Gray easily thrust her head and shoulders.

She raised the candle then through the opening--and suddenly her dark eyes widened in amazement. It was a hiding place, not only ingenious, but exceedingly generous in expanse. As far as one could reach the ceiling metamorphosed itself into a most convenient shelf. And it had been well utilized! It held a most astounding collection of things. There was a cashbox, but the cashbox was apparently wholly inadequate--there must have been thousands of dollars in those piles of banknotes that were stacked beside it! There was a large tin box, the cover off, containing some black, pastelike substance--the "stuff," presumably, that Gypsy Nan used on her face and hands. There was a bunch of curiously formed keys, several boxes of revolver cartridges, an electric flashlight, and a great quantity of the choicest brands of tinned and bottled fruits and provisions--and a little to one side, evidently kept ready for instant use, a suit of excellent material, underclothing, silk stockings shoes and hat were neatly piled together.

Rhoda Gray took the clothing, and went back to the bedside. Gypsy Nan had made little progress in disrobing. It seemed about all the woman could do to cling to the edge of the cot and sit upright.

"What does all this mean, Nan," she asked tensely; "all those things up there-- that money?"

Gypsy Nan forced a twisted smile.

"It means I know how bad I am, or I wouldn't have let you see what you have," she answered heavily. "It means that there isn't any other way. Hurry! Get these things off! Get me dressed!"

But it took a long time. Gypsy Nan seemed with every moment to grow weaker. The lamp on the chair went out for want of oil. There was only the guttering candle in the gin bottle to give light. It threw weird, flickering shadows around the garret; it seemed to enhance the already deathlike pallor of the woman, as, using the pitcher of water and the basin from the washstand now, Rhoda Gray removed the grime from Gypsy Nan's face and hands.

It was done at last--and where there had once been Gypsy Nan, haglike and repulsive, there was now a stylishly, even elegantly, dressed woman of well under middle age. The transformation seemed to have acted as a stimulant upon Gypsy Nan. She laughed with nervous hilarity she even tried valiantly to put on a pair of new black kid gloves, but, failing in this, pushed them unsteadily into the pocket of her coat.

"I'm--I'm all right," she asserted fiercely, as Rhoda Gray, pausing in the act of gathering up the discarded garments, regarded her anxiously. "Bring me a package of that money after you've put those things away--yes, and you'll find a flashlight there. We'll need it going down the stairs."

Rhoda Gray made no answer. There was no hesitation now in her actions, as, to the pile of clothing in her arms, she added the revolver that lay on the blanket, and, returning to the little trap-door in the ceiling, hid them away; but her brain was whirling again in a turmoil of doubt. This was madness, utter, stark, blind madness, this thing that she was doing! It was suicide, literally that, nothing less than suicide for one in Gypsy Nan's condition to attempt this thing. But the woman would certainly die here, too, with out medical assistance--only there was the police! Rhoda Gray's face, as she stood upright in the little aperture again, throwing the wavering candle-rays around her, seemed suddenly to have grown pinched and wan.

The police! The police! It was her conscience, then, that was gnawing at her--because of the police! Was that it? Well, there was also, then, another side. Could she turn informer, traitor, become a female Judas to a dying woman, who had sobbed and thanked her Maker because she had found some one whom she believed she could trust? That was a hideous and an abominable thing to do! "You swore it! You swore you'd see me through!"--the words came and rang insistently in her ears. The sweet, piquant little face set in hard, determined lines. Mechanically she picked up the flashlight and a package of the banknotes, lowered the board in the ceiling into place, and returned to Gypsy Nan.

"I'm ready, if there is no other way," she said soberly, as she watched the other tuck the money away inside her waist. "I said I would see you through, and I will. But I doubt if you are strong enough, even with what help I can give you, to get down the stairs, and even if you can, I am afraid with all my soul of the consequences to you, and--"

Gypsy Nan blew out the candle, and staggered to her feet.

"There isn't any other way." She leaned heavily on Rhoda Gray's arm. "Can't you see that? Don't you think I know? Haven't you seen enough here to convince you of that? I--I'm just spilling the dice for--for perhaps the last time--but it's the only chance--the only chance. Go on!" she urged tremulously. "Shoot the glim, and get me to the door. And--and for the love of God, don't make a sound! It's all up if we're seen going out!"

The flashlight's ray danced in crazy gyrations as the two figures swayed and crept across the garret. Rhoda Gray unlocked the door, and, as they passed out, locked it again on the outside.

"Hide the key!" whispered Gypsy Nan. "See--that crack in the floor under the partition! Slip it in there!"

The flashlight guiding her, Rhoda Gray stooped down to where, between the rough attic flooring and the equally rough boarding of the garret partition, there was a narrow space. She pushed the key in out of sight; and then, with her arm around Gypsy Nan's waist, and with the flashlight at cautious intervals winking ahead of her through the darkness, she began to descend the stairs.

It was slow work, desperately slow, both because they dared not make the slightest noise, and because, too, as far as strength was concerned, Gypsy Nan was close to the end of her endurance. Down one flight, and then the other, they went, resting at every few steps, leaning back against the wall, black shadows that merged with the blackness around them, the flashlight used only when necessity compelled it, lest its gleam might attract the attention of some other occupant of the house. And at times Gypsy Nan's head lay cheek to Rhoda Gray's, and the other's body grew limp and became a great weight, so heavy that it seemed she could no longer support it.

They gained the street door, hung there tensely for a moment to make sure they were not observed by any chance passer-by, then stepped out on the sidewalk. Gypsy Nan spoke then:

"I--I can't go much farther," she faltered. "But--but it doesn't matter now we're out of the house--it doesn't matter where you find me--only let's try a few steps more."

Rhoda Gray had slipped the flashlight inside her blouse.

"Yes," she said. Her breath was coming heavily. "It's all right, Nan. I understand."

They walked on a little way up the block, and then Gypsy Nan's grasp suddenly tightened on Rhoda Gray's arm.

"Play the game!" Gypsy Nan's voice was scarcely audible. "You'll play the game, won't you? You'll--you'll see me through. That's a good name--as good as any--Charlotte Green--that's all you know--but--but don't leave me alone with them--you--you'll come to the hospital with me, won't you--I--"

Gypsy Nan had collapsed in a heap on the sidewalk.

Rhoda Gray glanced swiftly around her. In the squalid tenement before which she stood there would be no help of the kind that was needed. There would be no telephone in there by means of which she could summon an ambulance. And then her glance rested on a figure far up the block under a street lamp--a policeman. She bent hurriedly over the prostrate woman, whispered a word of encouragement, and ran in the officer's direction.

As she drew closer to the policeman, she called out to him. He turned and came running toward, and, as he reached her, after a sharp glance into her face, touched his helmet respectfully.

"What's wrong with the White Moll to-night?" he asked pleasantly.

"There's--there's a woman down there"--Rhoda Gray was breathless from her run--"on the sidewalk. She needs help at once."

"Drunk?" inquired the officer laconically.

"No, I'm sure it's anything but that," Rhoda Gray answered quickly. "She appears to be very sick. I think you had better summon an ambulance without delay."

"All right!" agreed the officer. "There's a patrol box down there in the direction you came from. We'll have a look at her on the way." He started briskly forward with Rhoda Gray beside him. "Who is she d'ye know?" he asked.

"She said her name was Charlotte Green," Rhoda Gray replied. "That's all she could, or would, say about herself."

"Then she ain't a regular around here, or I guess you'd know her!" grunted the policeman.

Rhoda Gray made no answer.

They reached Gypsy Nan. The officer bent over her, then picked her up and carried her to the tenement doorway.

"I guess you're right, all right! She's bad! I'll send in a call," he said, and started on the run down the street.

Gypsy Nan had lost consciousness. Rhoda Gray settled herself on the doorstep, supporting the woman's head in her lap. Her face had set again in grim, hard, perplexed lines. There seemed something unnatural, something menacingly weird, something even uncanny about it all. Perhaps it was because it seemed as though she could so surely foresee the end. Gypsy Nan would not live through the night. Something told her that. The woman's masquerade, for whatever purpose it had been assumed, was over. "You'll play the game, won't you? You'll see me through?" There seemed something pitifully futile in those words now!

The officer returned.

"It's all right," he said. "How's she seem?"

Rhoda Gray shook her head.

A passer-by stopped, asked what was the matter--and lingered curiously. Another, and another, did the same. A little crowd collected. The officer kept them back. Came then the strident clang of a gong and the rapid beat of horses' hoofs. A white-coated figure jumped from the ambulance, pushed his way forward, and bent over the form in Rhoda Gray's lap. A moment more, and they were carrying Gypsy Nan to the ambulance.

Rhoda Gray spoke to the officer:

"I think perhaps I had better go with her."

"Sure!" said the officer.

She caught snatches of the officer's words, as he made a report to the doctor:

"Found her here in the street...Charlotte Green...nothing else...the White Moll, straight as God makes 'em...she'll see the woman through." He turned to Rhoda Gray. "You can get in there with them, miss."

It took possibly ten minutes to reach the hospital, but, before that time, Gypsy Nan, responding in a measure to stimulants, had regained consciousness. She insisted on clinging to Rhoda Gray's hand as they carried in the stretcher.

"Don't leave me!" she pleaded. And then, for the first time, Gypsy Nan's nerve seemed to fail her. "I--oh, my God--I--I don't want to die!" she cried out.

But a moment later, inside the hospital, as the admitting officer began to ask questions of Rhoda Gray, Gypsy Nan had apparently recovered her grip upon herself.

"Ah, let her alone!" she broke in. "She doesn't know me any more than you do. She found me on the street. But she was good to me, God bless her!"

"Your name's Charlotte Green? Yes?" The man nodded. "Where do you live?"

"Wherever I like!" Gypsy Nan was snarling truculently now. "What's it matter where I live? Don't you ever have any one come here without a letter from the pastor of her church!" She pulled out the package of banknotes. "You aren't going to get stuck. This'll see you through whatever happens. Give me a--a private room, and"--her voice was weakening rapidly--"and"--there came a bitter, facetious laugh--"the best you've got." Her voice was weakening rapidly.

They carried her upstairs. She still insisted on clinging to Rhoda Gray's hand.

"Don't leave me!" she pleaded again, as they reached the door of a private room, and Rhoda Gray disengaged her hand gently.

"I'll stay outside here," Rhoda Gray promised. "I won't go away without seeing you again."

Rhoda Gray sat down on a settee in the hall. She glanced at her wrist watch. It was five minutes of eleven. Doctors and nurses came and went from the room.

Then a great quiet seemed to settle down around her. A half hour passed. A doctor went into the room, and presently came out again. She intercepted him as he came along the corridor.

He shook his head.

She did not understand his technical explanation. There was something about a clot and blood stoppage. But as she resumed her seat, she understood very fully that the end was near. The woman was resting quietly now, the doctor had said, but if she, Rhoda Gray, cared to wait, she could see the other before leaving the hospital.

And so she waited. She had promised Gypsy Nan she would.

The minutes dragged along. A quarter of an hour passed. Still another. Midnight came. Fifteen minutes more went by, and then a nurse came out of the room, and, standing by the door, beckoned to Rhoda Gray.

"She is asking for you," the nurse said. "Please do not stay more than a few minutes. I shall be outside here, and if you notice the slightest change, call me instantly."

Rhoda Gray nodded.

"I understand," she said.

The door closed softly behind her. She was smiling cheerily as she crossed the room and bent over Gypsy Nan.

The woman stretched out her hand.

"The White Moll!" she whispered. "He told the truth, that bull did--straight as they make 'em, and--"

"Don't try to talk," Rhoda Gray interrupted gently. "Wait until you are a little stronger."

"Stronger!" Gypsy Nan shook her head. "Don't try to kid me! I know. They told me. I'd have known it anyway. I'm going out."

Rhoda Gray found no answer for a moment. A great lump had risen in her throat. Neither would she have needed to be told; she, too, would have known it anyway--it was stamped in the gray pallor of the woman's face. She pressed Gypsy Nan's hand.

And then Gypsy Nan spoke again, a queer, yearning hesitancy in her voice:

"Do--do you believe in God?"

"Yes," said Rhoda Gray simply.

Gypsy Nan closed her eyes.

"Do--do you think there is a chance--even at the last--if--if, without throwing down one's pals, one tries to make good?"

"Yes," said Rhoda Gray again.

"Is the door closed?" Gypsy Nan attempted to raise herself on her elbow, as though to see for herself.

Rhoda Gray forced the other gently back upon the pillows.

"It is closed," she said. "You need not be afraid."

"What time is it?" demanded Gypsy Nan.

Rhoda Gray looked at her watch.

"Twenty-five minutes after twelve," she answered.

"There's time yet, then," whispered Gypsy Nan. "There's time yet." She lay silent for a moment, then her hand closed tightly around Rhoda Gray's. "Listen!" she said. "There's more about--about why I lived like that than I told you. And--and I can't tell you now--I can't go out like a yellow cur--I'm not going to snitch on anybody else just because I'm through myself. But--but there's something on to-night that I'd--I'd like to stop. Only the police, or anybody else, aren't to know anything about it, because then they'd nip my friends. See? But you can do it--easy. You can do it alone without anybody knowing. There's time yet. They weren't going to pull it until halfpast one--and there won't be any danger for you. All you've got to do is get the money before they do, and then see that it goes back where it belongs to-morrow. Will you? You don't want to see a crime committed to-night if--if you can stop it, do you?"

Rhoda Gray's face was grave. She hesitated for a moment.

"I'll have to know more than that before I can answer you, Nan," she said.

"It's the only way to stop it!" Gypsy Nan whispered feverishly. "I won't split on my pals--I won't--I won't! But I trust you. Will you promise not to snitch if I tell you how to stop it, even if you don't go there yourself? I'm offering you a chance to stop a twenty-thousand-dollar haul. If you don't promise it's got to go through, because I've got to stand by the ones that were in it with me. I--I'd like to make good--just--once. But I can't do it any other way. For God's sake, you see that, don't you?"

"Yes," said Rhoda Gray in a low voice; "but the promise you ask for is the same as though I promised to try to get the money you speak of. If I knew what was going on, and did nothing, I would be an accomplice to the crime, and guilty myself."

"But I can't do anything else!" Gypsy Nan was speaking with great difficulty. "I won't get those that were with me in wrong--I won't! You can prevent a crime to-night, if you will--you--you can help me to--to make good."

Rhoda Gray's lips tightened, "Will you give me your word that I can do what you suggest--that it is feasible, possible?"

"Yes," said Gypsy Nan. "You can do it easily, and--and it's safe. It--it only wants a little nerve, and--and you've got that."

"I promise, then," said Rhoda Gray.

"Thank God!" Gypsy Nan pulled fiercely at Rhoda Gray's wrist. "Come nearer-nearer! You know Skarbolov, old Skarbolov, who keeps the antique store--on the street--around the corner from my place?" Rhoda Gray nodded.

"He's rich!" whispered Gypsy Nan. "Think of it! Him--rich! But he gets the best of the Fifth Avenue crowd just because he keeps his joint in that rotten hole. They think they're getting the real thing in antiques! He's a queer old fool. Afraid people would know he had money if he kept it in the bank--afraid of a bank, too. Understand? We found out that every once in a while he'd change a lot of small bills for a big one--five-hundred-dollar bills--thousand-dollar bills. That put us wise. We began to watch him. It took months to find where he hid it. We've spent night after night searching through his shop. You can get in easily. There's no one there--upstairs is just a storage place for his extra stock. There's a big padlock on the back door, but there's a false link in the chain--count three links to the right from the padlock--we put it there, and--"

Gypsy Nan's voice had become almost inaudible. She pulled at Rhoda Gray's wrist again, urging her closer.

"Listen--quick! I--my strength!" she panted. "An antique he never sells--old escritoire against rear wall--secret drawer--take out wide middle drawer--reach in and rub your hand along the top--you'll feel the spring. We waited to--to get--get counterfeits--put counterfeits there--understand? Then he'd never know he'd been robbed--not for a long time anyway--discovered perhaps when he was dead--old wife--suffer then--I--got to make good--make good--I--" She came up suddenly on both her elbows, the dark eyes staring wildly. "Yes, yes!" she whispered. "Seven-three-nine! Look out!" Her voice rang with sudden terror, rising almost to a scream. "Look out! Can't you understand, you fool! I've told you! Seven-three-nine! Seven-three..."

Rhoda Gray's arms had gone around the other's shoulders. She heard the door open-and then a quick, light step. There wasn't any other sound now. She made way mechanically for the nurse. And then, after a moment, she rose from her knees. The nurse answered her unspoken question.

"Yes; it's over."

III. ALIAS GYPSY NAN

Rhoda Gray went slowly from the room. In a curiously stunned sort of way she reached the street, and for a few blocks walked along scarcely conscious of the direction she was taking. Her mind was in turmoil. The night seemed to have been one of harrowing hallucination; it seemed as though it were utterly unreal, like one dreaming that one is dreaming. And then, suddenly, she looked at her watch, and the straight little shoulders squared resolutely back. The hallucination, if she chose to call it that, was not yet over! It was twenty minutes of one, and there was still Skarbolov's--and her promise.

She quickened her pace. She did not like this promise that she had made; but, on the other hand, she had not made it either lightly or impulsively. She had no regrets on that score. She would make it again under the same conditions. How could she have done otherwise? It would have been to stand aside and permit a crime to be committed which she was assured was easily within her power to prevent. What excuse could she have had for that? Fear wasn't an excuse. She did not like the thought of entering the back door of a store in the middle of the night like a thief, and, like a thief, taking away that hidden money. She knew she was going to be afraid, horribly afraid--it frightened her now--but she could not let that fear make a moral coward of her.

Her hands clenched at her sides. She would not allow herself to dwell upon that phase of it! She was going to Skarbolov's, and that was all there was to it. The only thing she really had to fear was that she should lose even a single unnecessary moment in getting there. Halfpast one, Gypsy Nan had said. That should give her ample time; but the quicker she went, the wider the margin of safety.

Her thoughts reverted to Gypsy Nan. What had the woman meant by her last few wandering words? They had nothing to do with Skarbolov's, that was certain;

but the words came back now insistently. "Seven-three-nine." What did "seven-three-nine" mean? She shook her head helplessly. Well, what did it matter? She dismissed further consideration of it. She repeated to herself Gypsy Nan's directions for finding the spring of the secret drawer. She forced herself to think of anything that would bar the entry of that fear which stood lurking at the threshold of her mind.

From time to time she consulted her watch--and each time hurried the faster.

It was five minutes past one when, stealing silently along a black lane, and counting against the skyline the same number of buildings she had previously counted on the street from the corner, she entered an equally black yard, and reached the back door of Skarbolov's little store. She felt out with her hands and found the padlock, and her fingers pressed on the link in the chain that Gypsy Nan had described. It gave readily. She slipped it free, and opened the door. There was faint, almost inaudible, protesting creak from the hinges. She caught her breath quickly. Had anybody heard it? It--it had seemed like a cannon shot. And then her lips curled in sudden self-contempt. Who was there to hear it?

She stepped forward, closed the door silently behind her, and drew out her flashlight. The ray cut through the blackness. She was in what seemed like a small, outer storeroom, that was littered with an untidy collection of boxes, broken furniture, and odds and ends of all sorts. Ahead of her was an open door, and, through this, the flashlight disclosed the shop itself. She switched off the light now as she moved forward-there were the front windows, and, used too freely, the light might by some unlucky chance be noticed from the street.

And now, in the darkness again, she reached the doorway of the shop. She had not made any noise. She assured herself of that. She had never known that she could move so silently before--and--and--Yes, she would fight down this panic that was seizing her! She would! It would only take a minute now--just another minute--if--if she would only keep her head and her nerve. That was what Gypsy Nan had said. She only needed to keep her nerve. She had never lost it in the face of many a really serious danger when with her father--why should she now, when there was nothing but the silence and the darkness to be afraid of!

The flashlight went on again, its ray creeping inquisitively now along the rear wall of the shop. It held finally on an escritoire over in the far corner at her right.

Once more the light went out. She moved swiftly across the floor, and in a moment more was bending over the escritoire. And now, with her body hiding the flashlight's rays from the front windows, she examined the desk. It was an old-fashioned, spindle-legged affair, with a nest of pigeonholes and multifarious little drawers. One of the drawers, wider than any of the others, and in the center, was obviously the one to which Gypsy Nan referred. She pulled out the drawer, and in the act of reaching inside, suddenly drew back her hand. What was that? Instinctively she switched off the flashlight, and stood tense and rigid in the darkness.

A minute passed-another. Still she listened. There was no sound--unless--unless she could actually hear the beating of her heart. Fancy! Imagination! The darkness played strange tricks! It--it wasn't so easy to keep one' s nerve. She could have sworn that she had heard some sort of movement back there down the shop.

Angry with herself, she thrust her hand into the opening now and felt hurriedly around. Yes, there it was! Her fingers touched what was evidently a little knob or button. She pressed upon it. There was a faint, answering click. She turned on the flashlight again. What had before appeared to be nothing but one of the wide, pearl inlaid partitions between two of the smaller drawers, was protruding invitingly outward now by the matter of an inch or so. Rhoda Gray pulled it open. It was very shallow, scarcely three-quarters of an inch in depth, but it was quite long enough, and quite wide enough for its purpose! Inside, there lay a little pile of banknotes, banknotes of very large denomination--the one on top was a thousand-dollar bill.

She reached in and took out the money-and then from Rhoda Gray's lips there came a little cry, the flashlight dropped from her hand and smashed to the floor, and she was clinging desperately to the edge of the escritoire for support. The shop was flooded with light. Over by the side wall, one hand still on the electric-light switch, the other holding a leveled revolver, stood a man.

And then the man spoke--with an oath--with curious amazement:

"My God--a woman!"

She did not speak, or stir. It seemed as though not fear, but horror now, held her powerless to move her limbs. Her first swift brain-flash had been that it was one of Gypsy Nan's accomplices here ahead of the appointed time. That would have given her cause, all too much of cause, for fear; but it was not one of Gypsy Nan's accomplices, and, far worse than the fear of any physical attack upon her, was the sense of ruin and disaster that the realization of a quite different and more desperate situation brought her now. She knew the man. She had seen those square, heavy, clamped jaws scores of times. Those sharp, restless black eyes under over-hanging, shaggy eyebrows were familiar to the whole East Side. It was Rorke--"Rough" Rorke, of headquarters.

He came toward her, and halfway across the room another exclamation burst from his lips; but this time it held a jeer, and in the jeer a sort of cynical and savage triumph.

"The White Moll!"

He was close beside her now, and now he snatched from her hand the banknotes that, all unconsciously, she had still been clutching tightly.

"So this is what all the sweet charity's been about, eh?" he snapped. "The White Moll, the Little Saint of the East Side, that lends a helping hand to the crooks to get 'em back on the straight and narrow again! The White Moll-hell! You crooked little devil!"

Again she did not answer. Her mind was clear now, brutally clear, brutally keen, brutally virile. What was there for her to say? She was caught here at one o'clock in the morning after breaking into the place, caught red-handed in the very act of taking the money. What story could she tell that would clear her of that! That she had taken it so that it wouldn't be stolen, and that she was going to give it back in the morning? Was there anybody in the world credulous enough to believe anything like that! Tell Gypsy Nan's story, all that had happened to-night? Yes, she might have told that to-morrow, after she had returned the money, and been believed. But now-no! It would even make her appear in a still worse light. They would credit her with being a member of this very gang to which Gypsy Nan belonged, one in the secrets of an organized band of criminals, who was trying to clear her own skirts at the expense of her confederates. Everything, every act of hers to-night, pointed to that construction being placed upon her story, pointed to duplicity. Why had she hidden the identity of Gypsy Nan? Why had she not told the police that a crime was to be committed, and left it to the police to frustrate it? It would fit in with the story, of course--but the story was the result of having been caught in the act of stealing twenty thousand dollars in cash! What was there to say--and, above all, to this man, whose reputation for callous brutality in the handling of those who fell into his hands had earned him the sobriquet of "Rough" Rorke? Sick at heart, desperate, but with her hands clenched now, she stood there, while the man felt unceremoniously over her clothing for a concealed weapon.

Finding none, he stooped, picked up the flashlight, tested it, and found it broken from its fall.

"Too bad you bust this, we'll have to go out in the dark after I switch off the light," he said with unpleasant facetiousness. "I didn't have one with me, or time to get one, when I got tipped off there was something doing here to-night." He caught her ungently by the arm. "Well, come along, my pretty lady! This'll make a stir, this will! The White Moll!" He led her to the electric-light switch, turned off the light, and, with his grasp tight upon her, made for the front door. He chuckled in a sinister manner. "Say, you're a prize, you are! And pretty clever, too, aren't you? I wasn't looking for a woman to pull this. The White Moll! Some saint!"

Rhoda Gray shivered. Disgrace, ruin, stared her in the face. A sea of faces in a courtroom, morbid faces, hideous faces, leered at her. Gray walls rose before her, walls that shut out sunshine and hope, pitiless, cold things that seemed to freeze the blood in her veins. And to-night, in just a few minutes more--a cell!

From the street outside came the sound of some one making a cheery, but evidently a somewhat inebriated, attempt to whistle some ragtime air. It seemed to enhance her misery, to enhance by contrast in its care-free cheeriness the despair and misery that were eating into her soul. Her hands clenched and unclenched. If there were only a chance--somewhere--somehow! If only she were not a woman! If she could only fight this hulking form that gripped so brutally at her arm!

Rough Rorke opened the door, and pulled her out to the street. She shrank back instinctively. It was quite light here from a nearby street lamp, and the owner of the whistle, a young man, fashionably dressed, decidedly unsteady on his legs, and just opposite the door as they came out, had stopped both his whistle and his progress along the street to stare at them owlishly.

"'Ullo!" said the young man thickly. "What'sh all this about--eh? What'sh you two doing in that place this time of night--eh?"

"Beat it!" ordered Rough Rorke curtly.

"That'sh all right." The young man came nearer. He balanced himself with difficulty, but upon him there appeared to have descended suddenly a vast dignity.

"I'm--hic--law--'biding citizen. Gotta know. Gotta show me. Damn funny--coming out of there this time of night! Eh--what'sh the idea?"

Rough Rorke, with his free hand, grabbed the young man by the shoulder angrily.

"Mind your own business, or you'll get into trouble!" he rasped out. "I'm an officer, and this woman is under arrest. Beat it! D'ye hear? Beat it--or I'll run you in, too!"

"Is that'sh so!" The young man's tones expressed a fuddled defiance. He rocked on his feet and stared from one to the other. "Shay, is that'sh so! You will--eh? Gotta show me. How do I know you're--hic--officer? Eh? More likely damned thief yourself! I--"

The young man lurched suddenly and violently forward, breaking Rough Rorke's grip on Rhoda Gray--and, as his arms swept out to grasp at the detective in an apparently wild effort to preserve his balance, Rhoda Gray felt a quick, significant push upon her shoulder.

For the space of time it takes a watch to tick she stood startled and amazed, and then, like a flash, she was speeding down the street. A roar of rage, a burst of unbridled profanity went up from Rough Rorke behind her; it was mingled with equally angry vituperation in the young man's voice. She looked behind her. The two men were swaying around crazily in each other's arms. She ran on--faster than she had ever run in her life. The corner was not far ahead. Her brain was working with lightning speed. Gypsy Nan's house was just around the corner. If she could get out of sight--hide--it would...

She glanced behind her again, as her ears caught the pound of racing feet. The young man was sitting in the middle of the sidewalk, shaking his fist; Rough Rorke, perhaps a bare fifty yards away, was chasing her at top speed.

Her face set hard. She could not out-run a man! There was only one hope for her--just one--to gain Gypsy Nan's doorway before Rorke got around the corner.

A yard--another--still another! She swerved around the corner. And, as she turned, she caught a glimpse of the detective. The man was nearer--much nearer. But it was only a little way, just a little way, to Gypsy Nan's--not so far as the distance between her and Rorke--and--and if the man didn't gain too fast, then--then--A little cry of dismay came with a new and terrifying thought. Quite apart from

Rorke, some one else might see her enter Gypsy Nan's! She strained her eyes in all directions as she ran. There wasn't any one--she didn't see any one--only Rorke, around the corner there, was bawling out at the top of his voice, and--and...

She flung herself against Gypsy Nan's door, stumbled in, and, closing it, heard Rorke just swinging around the corner. Had he seen her? She didn't know. She was panting, gasping for her breath. It seemed as though her lungs would burst. She held her hand tightly to her bosom as she made for the stairs--she mustn't make any noise--they mustn't hear her breathing like that--they--they mustn't hear her going up the stairs.

How dark it was! If she could only see--so that she would be sure not to stumble! She couldn't go fast now--she would make a noise if she did. Stair after stair she climbed stealthily. Perhaps she was safe now--it had taken her a long time to get up here to the second floor, and there wasn't any sound yet from the street below.

And now she mounted the short, ladder-like steps to the attic, and, feeling with her hand for the crack in the flooring under the partition, reached in for the key. As her fingers closed upon it, she choked back a cry. Some one had been here! A piece of paper was wrapped around the key. What did it mean? What did all these strange, yes, sinister, things that had happened to-night mean? How had Rorke known that a robbery was to be committed at Skarbolov's? Who was that man who had effected her escape, and who, she knew now, was no more drunk than she was? Fast, quick, piling one upon the other, the questions raced through her mind.

She fought them back. There was no time for speculation now! There was only one question that mattered: Was she safe?

She stood up, thrust the paper for safe-keeping into her bosom, and unlocked the door. If--if Rorke did not know that she had entered this house here, she could remain hidden for a few hours; it would give her time to think, and...

It came this time, no strength of will would hold it back, a little moan. The front door below had opened, a heavy footstep sounded in the lower hall. She couldn't see, of course. But she knew. It was Rorke! She heard him coming up the stairs.

And then, in a flash, it seemed, her brain responded to her despairing cry. There was still a way--a desperate one--but still a way--if there was time! She darted inside the garret, locked the door, found the matches and candle, and, running silently to the rear wall, pushed up the board in the ceiling. In frantic haste she tore off her outer garments, her stockings and shoes, pulled on the rough stockings and coarse boots that Gypsy Nan had worn, slipped the other's greasy, threadbare skirt over her head, and pinned the shawl tight about her shoulders. There was a big, voluminous pocket in the skirt, and into this she dropped Gypsy Nan's revolver, and the paper she had found wrapped around the key.

She could hear a commotion from below now. It was the one thing she had counted upon. Rough Rorke might know she had entered the house, but he could not know whereabouts in the house she was, and he would naturally search each room as he came to it on the way up. She fitted the gray-streaked wig of tangled, matted hair upon her head, plunged her hand into the box that Gypsy Nan used for her make-up and daubed some of the grime upon both hands and face, adjusted the spectacles upon her nose, hid her own clothing, closed the narrow trap-door in the ceiling, and ran back, carrying the candle, to the washstand.

Here, there was a small and battered mirror, and more coolly, more leisurely now, for the commotion still continued from the floor below, she spread and rubbed in, as craftily as she could, the grime streaks on her face and hands. It was neither artistic nor perfect, but in the meager, flickering light now the face of Gypsy Nan seemed to stare reassuringly back at her. It might not deceive any one in daylight-- she did not know, and it did not matter now--but with only this candle to light the garret, since the lamp was empty, she could fairly count on her identity not being questioned.

She blew out the candle, left it on the washstand, because, if she could help it, she did not want to risk having it lighted near the bed or door, and, tiptoeing now, went to the door, unlocked it, then threw herself down upon the bed.

Possibly a minute went by, possibly two, and then there was a quick step on the ladder-like stairs, the door handle was rattled violently, and the door was flung open and slammed shut again.

Rhoda Gray sat upright on the bed. It was her wits now, her wits against Rough Rorke's; nothing else could save her. She could not even make out the man's form, it was so dark; but, as he had not moved, she was quite well aware that he was standing with his back to the door, evidently trying to place his surroundings.

It was Gypsy Nan, not Rhoda Gray, who spoke.

"Who's dere?" she screeched. "D'ye hear, blast youse, who's dere?"

Rough Rorke laughed gratingly.

"That you, Nan, my dear?"

"Who d'youse t'ink it is-me gran'mother?" demanded Rhoda Gray caustically. "Who are youse?"

"Rorke," said Rorke shortly. "I guess you know, don't you?"

"Is dat so?" snorted Rhoda Gray. "Well den, youse can beat it--hop it--on de jump! Wot t'hell right have youse got bustin' into me room at dis time of night--eh? I ain't done nothin'!"

Rough Rorke, his feet scuffling to feel the way, came forward.

"Cut it out!" he snarled. "I ain't the only visitor you've got! It's not you I want; it's the White Moll."

"Wot's dat got to do wid me?" Rhoda Gray flung back hotly. "She ain't here, is she?"

"Yes, she's here!" Rough Rorke's voice held an ugly menace. "I lost her around the corner, but a woman from a window across the street, who heard the row, saw her run into this house. She ain't downstairs--so you can figure the rest out the same way I do."

"De woman was kiddin' youse!" Rhoda Gray, alias Gypsy Nan, cackled derisively. "Dere ain't nobody here but me."

"We'll see about that!" said Rough Rorke shortly. "Strike a light!"

"Aw, strike it yerself!" retorted Rhoda Gray. "I ain't yer servant! Dere's a candle over dere on de washstand against de wall, if youse wants it."

A match crackled and spurted into flame; its light fell upon the lamp standing on the chair beside the bed. Rough Rorke stepped toward it.

"Dere ain't any oil in dat," croaked Rhoda Gray. "Didn't I tell youse de candle was over dere on de washstand, an'--"

The words seemed to freeze in her throat, the chair, the lamp, the shadowy figure of the man in the match flame to swirl before her eyes, and a sick nausea to come upon her soul itself. With a short, triumphant oath, Rough Rorke had stopped suddenly and reached in under the chair. And now he was dangling a new, black kid glove in front of her. Caught! Yes, she was caught! She remembered Gypsy Nan's attempt to put on her gloves--one must have fallen to the floor unnoticed by either of them when Gypsy Nan had thought to put them in her pocket! The man's voice came to her as from some great distance:

"So, she ain't here--ain't she! I'll teach you to lie to me! I'll--" The match was dying out. Rorke raised it higher, and with the last flicker located the washstand, and made toward it, obviously for the candle.

Her wits against Rough Rorke's! Nothing else could save her! Failing to find any one here but herself, certain now that the White Moll was here, only a fool could have failed in his deduction--and Rough Rorke was not a fool. Her wits against Rough Rorke's! There was the time left her while the garret was still in darkness, just that, no more!

With a quick spring she leaped from the bed, seized the chair, sending the lamp to the floor, and, dragging the chair after her to make as much noise and confusion as she could, she rushed for the door, screeching at the top of her voice:

"Run, dearie, run! Run!" She was scuffling with her feet, clattering the chair, as she wrenched the door open. And then, in her own voice: "Nan, I won't! I won't let you stand for this, I--"

Then as Gypsy Nan again: "Run, dearie! Don't youse mind old Nan!" She banged the door shut, locked it, and whipped out the key. It had taken scarcely a second. She was still screeching at the top of her voice to cover the absence of flying footers on the stairs. "Run, dearie, run! Run!"

And then, in the darkness, the candle still unlighted, Rough Rorke was on her like a madman. With a sweep of his arm he sent her crashing to the floor, and wrenched at the door. The next instant he was on her again.

"The key! Give me that key!" he roared.

For answer she flung it from her. It fell with a tinkle on the floor at the far end of the garret. The man was beside himself with rage.

"Damn you, if I had time, I'd wring your neck for this, you she-devil!" he bawled-and raced back, evidently for the candle on the washstand.

Rhoda Gray, sprawled on the floor where he had thrown her, did not move-except to take the revolver from the pocket of her dress. She was crooning queerly to herself, as she watched Rough Rorke light the candle and grope around on the floor:

"She was good to me, de White Moll was. Jellies an' t'ings she brought me, she did. An' Gypsy Nan don't ferret. Gypsy Nan don't--"

She sat up suddenly, snarling. Rorke had found the key, left the bottle with the short stub of guttering candle standing on the floor, and was back again.

"By God!" he gritted through his teeth, as he jabbed the key with frantic haste into the lock. "I'll fix you for this!" He made a clutch at her throat, as he swung the door open.

She jerked herself backward, eluding him, her revolver leveled.

"Youse keep yer dirty paws off me!" she screamed. "Yah, wot can youse do! Wot do I care! She was good to me, she was, an--"

Rough Rorke was gone-taking the stairs three and four at a time. Then she heard the street door slam.

She rose slowly to her feet--and suddenly reached out, grasping at the door to steady herself. It seemed as though every muscle had gone limp, as though her limbs had not strength to support her. And for a moment she hung there, then she locked the door, staggered back, sank down on the edge of the bed, and, with her chin in her hands, stared at the guttering stub of candle. And presently, in an almost aimless, mechanical way, she felt in her pocket for the piece of paper that she had found wrapped around the key, and drew it out. There were three figures scrawled upon it--nothing else.

7   3   9

She dropped her chin in her hands again, and stared again at the candle. And after a while the candle went out.

IV. THE ADVENTURER

Twenty-Four hours had passed. Twenty four hours! Was it no more than that since--Rhoda Gray, in the guise of Gypsy Nan, as she sat on the edge of the disreputable, poverty-stricken cot, grew suddenly tense, holding her breath as she listened. The sound reached the attic so faintly that it might be but the product solely of the imagination. No--it came again! And it even defined itself now--a stealthy footstep on the lower stairs.

A small, leather-bound notebook, in which she had been engrossed, was tucked instantly away under the soiled blanket, and she glanced sharply around the garret. A new candle, which she had bought in the single excursion she had ventured to make from the house during the day, was stuck in the neck of the gin bottle, and burned now on the chair beside her. She had not bought a new lamp--it gave too much light! The old one, the pieces of it, lay over there, brushed into a heap in the corner on the floor.

The footstep became more audible. Her lips tightened a little. The hour was late. It must be already after eleven o'clock. Her eyes grew perturbed. Perhaps it was only one of the unknown tenants of the floor below going to his or her room; but, on the other hand, no one had come near the garret since last night, when that strange and, yes, sinister trick of fate had thrust upon her the personality of Gypsy Nan, and it was hoping for too much to expect such seclusion to obtain much longer. There were too many who must be interested, vitally interested, in Gypsy Nan! There was Rough Rorke, of headquarters; he had given no sign, but that did not mean he had lost interest in Gypsy Nan. There was the death of the real Gypsy Nan, which was pregnant with possibilities; and though the newspapers, that she, Rhoda Gray, had bought and scanned with such tragic eagerness, had said nothing about the death of one Charlotte Green in the hospital, much less had given any hint that the identity Gypsy Nan had risked so much to hide had been discovered, it did not mean that the police, with their own ends in view, might not be fully informed, and were but keeping their own counsel while they baited a trap.

Also, and even more to be feared, there were those of this criminal organization to which Gypsy Nan had belonged, and to which she, Rhoda Gray, through a sort of hideous proxy, now belonged herself! Sooner or later, they must show their hands, and the test of her identity would come. And here her danger was the greater because she did not know who any of them were, unless the man who had stepped in between Rough Rorke and herself last night was one of them--which was a question that had harassed her all day. The man had been no more drunk than she had been, and he had obviously only played the part to get her out of the clutches of Rough Rorke; but, against this, he had seen her simply as herself then, the White Moll, and what could the criminal associates of Gypsy Nan have cared as to what became of the White Moll?

A newspaper, to procure which had been the prime motive that had lured her out of her retreat that afternoon, caught her eye now, and she shivered a little as, from where it lay on the floor, the headlines seemed to leer up at her, and mock, and menace her. "The White Moll....The Saint of the East Side Exposed....Vicious Hypocrisy....Lowly Charity for Years Cloaks a Consummate Thief..." They had not spared her!

Her lips firmed suddenly, as she listened. The stealthy footfall had not paused in the hall below. It was on the short, ladder-like steps now, leading up here to the garret--and now it had halted outside her door, and there came a low, insistent knocking on the panels.

"Who's dere?" demanded Rhoda Gray, alias Gypsy Nan, in a grumbling tone, as, getting up from the bed, she moved the chair noiselessly a few feet farther away, so that the bed would be beyond the immediate radius of the candle light. Then she shuffled across the floor to the door. "Who's dere?" she demanded again, and her hand, deep in the voluminous pocket of Gypsy Nan's greasy skirt, closed tightly around the stock of Gypsy Nan's revolver.

The voice that answered her expostulated in a plaintive whisper:

"My dear lady! And after all the trouble I have taken to reach here without being either seen or heard!"

For an instant Rhoda Gray hesitated--there seemed something familiar about the voice--then she unlocked the door, and retreated toward the bed.

The door opened and closed softly. Rhoda Gray, reaching the edge of the bed, sat down. It was the fashionably-attired, immaculate young man, who had saved her from Rough Rorke last night. She stared at him in the faint light without a word. Her mind was racing in a mad turmoil of doubt, uncertainty, fear. Was he one of the gang, or not? Was she, in the role of Gypsy Nan, supposed to know him, or not? Did he know that the real Gypsy Nan, too, had but played a part, and, therefore, when she spoke must it be in the vernacular of the East Side--or not? And then sudden enlightenment, with its incident relief, came to her.

"My dear lady"--the young man's soft felt hat was under his arm, and he was plucking daintily at the fingers of his yellow gloves as he removed them--"I beg you to pardon the intrusion of a perfect stranger. I offer you my very genuine apologies. My excuse is that I come from a--I hope I am not overstepping the bounds in using the term--mutual friend." Rhoda Gray snorted disdainfully.

"Aw, cut out de boudoir talk, an' get down to cases!" she croaked. "Who are youse, anyway?"

The young man had gray eyes--and they lighted up now humorously.

"Boudoir? Ah--yes! Of course! Awfully neat!" His eyes, from the chair that held the candle, strayed around the scantily furnished, murky garret as though in search of a seat, and finally rested inquiringly on Rhoda Gray.

"Youse can put de candle on de floor, if youse like," she said grudgingly. "Dat's de only chair dere is."

"Thank you!" he said.

Rhoda Gray watched him with puckered brow, as he placed the gin bottle with its candle on the floor, and appropriated the chair. He might, from his tone, have been thanking her for some priceless boon. He wore a boutonniere. His clothes fitted him like gloves. He exuded a certain studied, almost languid fastidiousness--that was wholly out of keeping with the quick, daring, agile wit that he had exhibited the night before. She found her hand toying unconsciously with the weapon in her pocket. She was aware that she was fencing with unbuttoned foils. How much did he know--about last night?

"Well, why don't youse spill it?" she invited curtly. "Who are youse?"

"Who am I?" He lifted the lapel of his coat, carrying the boutonniere to his nose. "My dear lady, I am an adventurer."

"Youse don't say!" observed Rhoda Gray, alias Gypsy Nan. "An' wot's dat w' en it's at home?"

"In my case, first of all a gentleman, I trust," he said pleasantly; "after that, I do not quarrel with the accepted definition of the term--though it is not altogether complimentary."

Rhoda Gray scowled. As Rhoda Gray, she might have answered him; as Gypsy Nan, it was too subtle, and she was beyond her depth.

"Youse look to me like a slick crook!" she said bluntly.

"I will admit," he said, "that I have at times, perhaps, taken liberties with the law."

"Well, den," she snapped, "cut out de high-brow stuff, an' come across wid wot brought youse here. I ain't holdin' no reception. Who's de friend youse was talkin' about?"

The Adventurer looked around him, and lowered his voice.

"The White Moll," he said.

Rhoda Gray eyed the man for a long minute; then she shook her head.

"I take back wot I said about youse bein' a slick crook," she announced coolly. "I guess youse're a dick from headquarters. Well, youse have got de wrong number--see? Me fingers are crossed. Try next door!"

The Adventurer's eyes were fixed on the newspaper headlines on the floor. He raised them now significantly to hers.

"You helped her to get away from Rough Rorke last night," he said gently. "Well, so did I. I am very anxious to find the White Moll, and, as I know of no other way except through you, I have got to make you believe in me, if I can. Listen, my dear lady--and don't look at me so suspiciously. I have already admitted that I have taken liberties with the law. Let me add now that last night there was a little fortune of quite a few thousand dollars that I had already made up my mind was as good as in my pocket. I was on my way to get it--the newspaper will already have given you the details--when I found that I had been forestalled by the young lady, who, the papers say, is known as the White Moll." He smiled whimsically. "Even though one might be a slick crook as you suggest, it is no reason why he should fail in his duty to himself--as a gentleman. What other course was open to me? I discovered a very charming young lady in the grip of a hulking police brute. She also, apparently, took liberties with the law. There was a bond between us. I--er--took it upon myself to do what I could. And, besides, I was not insensible to the fact that I was under a certain obligation to her, quixotic as it may sound, in view of the fact that we were evidently competitors after the same game. You see, if she had not forestalled me and been caught herself, I should most certainly have walked into the trap that our friend of headquarters had prepared. I--er--as I say, did what I could. She got away; but somehow Rough Rorke later discovered her here in this room, I understand that he was not happy over the result; that, thanks to you, she escaped again, and has not been heard of since."

Rhoda Gray dropped her chin in her grime-smeared hand, staring speculatively at the other. The man sat there, apparently a self-confessed crook and criminal, but, also, he sat there as the man to whom she owed the fact that at the present moment she was not behind prison bars. He proclaimed himself in the same breath both a thief and a gentleman, as far as she could make out. They were characteristics which, until now, she had never associated together; but now, curiously enough, they did not seem so utterly at variance. Of course they were at variance, must of necessity be so; but in the personality of this man the incongruity seemed somehow lost. Perhaps it was a sense of gratitude toward him that modified her views. He looked a gentleman. There was something about him that appealed. The gray eyes seemed full of cool, confident, self-possession; and, quiet as his manner was, she sensed a latent dynamic something lurking near the surface all the time--that she was conscious she would much prefer to have enlisted on her behalf than against her. The strong, firm chin bore this out. He was not handsome, but--with a sort of mental jerk, she forced her mind back to the stark realities of her surroundings. She could not thank him for what he had done last night. She could not tell him that she was the White Moll. She could only play out the role of Gypsy Nan until--until--Her hand tightened with a fierce, involuntary pressure upon her chin until it brought a physical hurt. Until what? God alone knew what the end of this miserable, impossible horror, in which she found herself engulfed, would be!

Her eyes sought his face again. The Adventurer was tactfully engaged in carefully smoothing out the fingers of his yellow gloves. Thief and gentleman, whatever he might be, whatever he might choose to call himself, what, exactly, was it that had brought him here to-night? The White Moll, he had said; but what did he want with the White Moll?

He answered her unspoken question now, almost as though he had read her thoughts.

"She is very clever," he said quietly. "She must be exceedingly clever to have beaten the police the way she has for the last few years; and--er--I worship at the shrine of cleverness--especially if it be a woman's. The idea struck me last night that if she and I should--er--pool our resources, we should not have to complain of the reward."

"Oh, so youse wants to work wid her, eh?" sniffed Rhoda Gray. "So dat's it, is it?"

"Partially," he said. "But, quite apart from that, the reason I want to find her is because she is in very great danger. Clever as she is, it is a very different matter to-day now that the police have found her out. She has been forced into hiding, and, if alone and without any friend to help her, her situation, to put it mildly, must be desperate in the extreme. You befriended her last night, and I honor you for the unselfishness with which you laid yourself open to the future attentions of that animal Rorke, but that very fact has deprived her of what might otherwise have been a refuge and a quite secure retreat here with you. I do not wish to intrude, or force myself upon her, but I believe I could be of very material help, and so I have come to you, as I have said, because you are the only source through which I can hope to find her, and because, through your act of last night, I know you to be a trustworthy, and, perhaps, even an intimate, friend of hers."

"Aw, go on!" said Rhoda Gray, alias Gypsy Nan, deprecatingly. "Dat don't prove nothin'! I'd have done as much for a stray cat if de bulls was chasm' her. See? I told youse once youse had de wrong number. She didn't leave no address. Dat's flat, an' dat's de end of it."

"I'm sorry," said the Adventurer gravely. "Perhaps I haven't made out a good enough case. Or perhaps, even believing me, you consider that the White Moll, and not yourself, should be the judge as to whether my services are acceptable or not?"

"Youse can dope it out any way youse likes," said Rhoda Gray indifferently. "Me t'roat's gettin' hoarse tellin' youse dere's nothin' doin'!"

"I'm sorry," said the Adventurer again. He smiled suddenly, and tucking his gloves into his pocket, leaned forward and tore off a small piece from the margin of the newspaper on the floor--but his head the while was now cocked in a curious listening attitude in the direction of the door. "You will pardon me, my dear lady, if I confess that, in spite of what you say, I still harbor the belief that you know where to reach the White Moll; and so--" He stopped abruptly, and she found his glance, sharp and critical, upon her. "You are expecting a visitor, perhaps?" he inquired softly.

Rhoda Gray stared in genuine perplexity.

"Wot's de answer?" she demanded.

"There is some one on the stairs," replied the Adventurer.

Rhoda Gray listened--and her perplexity deepened. She could hear nothing.

"Youse must have good ears!" she scoffed.

"I have," returned the Adventurer coolly. "My hearing is one of the resources that I wanted to pool with the White Moll."

"Well, den, mabbe it's Rough Rorke." Her tone still held its scoffing note; but her words voiced the genuine enough, that had come flashing upon her. "An' if it is, after last night, an' he finds youse an' me together, dere'll be--"

"My dear lady," interposed the Adventurer calmly, "if there were the remotest possibility that it could be Rough Rorke, I would not be here."

"Wot do youse mean?" She had unconsciously towered her voice.

The Adventurer shrugged his shoulders whimsically. He had laid the piece of paper on his knee, and, with a small gold pencil which he had taken from his pocket, was writing something upon it.

"The fact that I can assure you that, whoever else it may be, the person outside there cannot be Rough Rorke, is simply a proof that, if I had the opportunity, I could be of real assistance to the White Moll," he said imperturbably. "Well"--a grim little smile flickered suddenly across his lips--"do you hear any one now?"

Quite low, but quite unmistakably, the short, ladder-like steps just outside the door were voicing a creaky protest now as some one mounted them. Rhoda Gray did not move. It seemed as though she could hear the sudden thumping of her own heart. Who was it this time? How was she to act? What was she to say? It was so easy to make the single little slip of word or manner that would spell ruin and disaster.

"Rubber heels and rubber soles," murmured the Adventurer. "But, at that, it is extremely well done." He held out the torn piece of paper to Rhoda Gray.

"If"--he smiled significantly--"if, by any good fortune, you see the White Moll again, please give her this and let her decide for herself. It is a telephone number. She can always reach me there by asking for--the Adventurer." He was still extending the piece of paper. "Quick!" he whispered, as the door knob rattled.

V. A SECOND VISITOR

Mechanically Rhoda Gray thrust the paper into the pocket of her skirt. The door swung open. A tall man, well dressed, as far as could be seen in the uncertain light, a slouch hat pulled far down over his eyes, stood on the threshold, surveying the interior of the garret.

The Adventurer rose composedly to his feet--and moved slightly back out of the direct radius of the candlelight.

There was silence for a moment, and then the man in the doorway laughed unpleasantly.

"Hello!" he flung out harshly. "Who's the dude, Nan?"

Rhoda Gray, on the edge of the bed, shrugged her shoulders. The Adventurer was standing quite at his ease, his soft hat tucked under his right arm, his hand thrust into the side pocket of his coat. She could no longer see his face distinctly.

"Well?" There was a snarl in the man's voice as he advanced from the doorway. "You heard me, didn't you? Who is he?"

"Why don't youse ask him yerself?" inquired Rhoda Gray truculently. "I dunno."

"You don't, eh?" The man had halted close to where the candle stood on the floor between himself and the Adventurer. "Well, then, I guess we'll find out!" He was peering in the Adventurer's direction, and now there came a sudden savage scowl to his face. "It seems to me I've seen those clothes somewhere before, and I guess now we'll take a look at your face so that there won't be any question about recognition the next time we meet."

The Adventurer laughed softly.

"There will be none on my part," he said calmly. "It's Danglar, isn't it? I am surely not mistaken. Parson Danglar, alias--ah! Please don't do that!"

It seemed to Rhoda Gray that it happened in the space of time it might take a watch to tick: The newcomer stooping to the floor, and lifting the candle with the obvious intention of thrusting it into the Adventurer's face--a glint of metal, as the Adventurer whipped a revolver from the side pocket of his coat--and then, how they got there she could not tell, it was done so adroitly and swiftly, the thumb and forefinger of the Adventurer's left hand had closed on the candle wick and snuffed it out, and the garret was in darkness.

There was a savage oath, a snarl of rage from the man whom the Adventurer had addressed as Danglar; then an instant s silence; and then the Adventurer's voice--from the doorway:

"I beg of you not to vent your disappointment on the lady--Danglar. I assure you that she is in no way responsible for my visit here, and, as far as that goes, never saw me before in her life. Also, it is only fair to tell you, in case you should consider leaving here too hurriedly, that I am really not at all a bad shot--even in the dark. I bid you good-night, Danglar--and you my dear lady!"

Danglar's voice rose again in a flood of profane rage. He stumbled and moved around in the dark.

"Damn it!" he shouted. "Where are the matches? Where's the lamp? This cursed candle's put enough to the bad already! Do you hear? Where's the lamp?"

"It's over dere on de floor, bust to pieces," mumbled Rhoda Gray. "Youse'll find the matches on de washstand, an--"

"What's the idea?" There was a sudden, steel-like note dominating the angry tones. "What are you handing me that hog-wash language for? Eh? It's damned queer! There's been damned queer doings around here ever since last night! See? What's the idea?"

Rhoda Gray felt her face whiten in the darkness. It was the slip she had feared; the slip that she had had to take the chance of making, and which, if it were not retrieved, and instantly retrieved, now that it was made, meant discovery, and after that--She shivered a little.

"You needn't lose your head, just because you've lost your temper!" she said tartly, in a guarded whisper. "The door into the hall is still wide open, isn't it?"

"Oh, all right!" he said, his tones a sort of sullen admission that her retort was justified. "But even now your voice sounds off color."

Rhoda Gray bridled.

"Does it?" she snapped at him. "I've got a cold. Maybe you'd get one too, and maybe your voice would be off color, if you had to live in a dump like this, and--"

"Oh, all right, all right!" he broke in hurriedly. "For Heaven's sake don't start a row! Forget it! See? Forget it!" He walked over to the door, peered out, swore savagely to himself, shut the door, held the candle up to circle the garret, and scowled as its rays fell upon the shattered pieces of the lamp in the corner then, returning, he set the candle down upon the chair and began to pace restlessly, three or four steps each way, up and down in front of the bed.

Rhoda Gray, from the edge of the bed, shifted back until her shoulders rested against the wall. Danglar, too, was dressed like a gentleman--but Danglar's face was not appealing. The little round black eyes were shifty, they seemed to possess no pupils whatever, and they roved constantly; there was a hard, unyielding thinness about the lips, and the face itself was thin, almost gaunt, as though the skin had had to accommodate itself to more than was expected of it, and was elastically stretched over the cheek-bones.

"Well, I'm listening!" jerked out the man abruptly. "You knew our game at Skarbolov's was queered. You got the 'seven-three-nine,' didn't you?"

"Yes, of course, I got it," answered Rhoda Gray. "What about it?"

"For two weeks now, yes, more than two weeks"--the man's voice rasped angrily--"things have been going wrong, and some one has been butting in and getting away with the goods under our noses. We know now, from last night, that it must have been the White Moll, for one, though it's not likely she worked all alone. Skeeny dropped to the fact that the police were wise about Skarbolov's, and that's why we called it off, and the 'seven-three-nine' went out. They must have got wise through shadowing the White Moll. See? Then they pinch her, but she makes her get-away, and comes here, and, if the dope I've got is right, you hand Rough Rorke one, and help her to beat it again. It looks blamed funny--doesn't it?--when you come to consider that there's a leak somewhere!"

"Is that so!" Rhoda Gray flashed back. "And did you know before last night that it was the White Moll who was queering our game?"

"If I had," the man gritted between his teeth, "I'd--"

"Well, then, how did you expect me to know it?" demanded Rhoda Gray heatedly. "And if the White Moll happens to know Gypsy Nan, as she knows everybody else through her jellies and custards and fake charity, and happens to be near here when she gets into trouble, and beats it for here with the police on her heels, and asks for help, what do you expect Gypsy Nan's going to do if she wants to stand any chance of sticking around these parts--as Gypsy Nan?"

The man paused in his walk, and, jerking back his hat, drew his hand nervously across his forehead.

"You make me tired!" said Rhoda Gray wearily. "Do you think you could find the door without too much trouble?"

Danglar resumed his pacing back and forth, but more slowly now.

"Oh, I know! I know, Bertha!" he burst out heavily. "I'm talking through my hat. You've got the roughest job of any of us, old girl. Don't mind what I'm saying. Something's badly wrong, and I'm half crazy. It's certain now that the White Moll's the one that's been doing us, and what I really came down here for to-night was to tell you that your job from now on was to get the White Moll. You helped her last night. She doesn't know you are anybody but Gypsy Nan, and so you're the one person in New York she'll dare try to communicate with sooner or later. Understand? That's what I came for, not to talk like a fool--but that fellow I found here started me off. Who is he? What did he want?"

"He wanted the White Moll, too," said Rhoda Gray, with a short laugh.

"Oh, he did, eh!" Danglar's lips twisted into a sudden, merciless smile. "Well, go on! Who is he?"

"I don't know who he is," Rhoda Gray answered a little impatiently. "He said he was an adventurer--if you can make anything out of that. He said he got the White Moll away from Rough Rorke last night, after Rorke had arrested her; and then he doped the rest out the same as you have--that he could find the White Moll again through Gypsy Nan. I don't know what he wanted her for."

"That's better!" snarled Danglar, the merciless smile still on his lips. "I thought she must have had a pal, and we know now who her pal is. It's open and shut that she's sitting so tight she hasn't been able to get into touch with him, and that's what's worrying Mr. Adventurer."

Rhoda Gray, save for a nod of her head, made no answer.

Danglar laughed suddenly, as though in relief; then, coming closer to the bed, plunged his hand into his coat pocket, and tossed handful of jewelry carelessly into Rhoda Gray's lap.

"I feel better than I did!" he said, and laughed again. "It's a cinch now that we'll get them both through you, and it s a cinch that the White Moll won't cut in to-night. Put those sparklers away with the rest until we get ready to 'fence' them."

Rhoda Gray did not speak. Mechanically, as though she were living through some hideous nightmare, she began to scoop up the gems from her lap and allow them to trickle back through her fingers. They flashed and scintillated brilliantly, even in the meager light. They seemed alive with some premonitory, baleful fire.

"Yes, there's some pretty slick stuff there," said Danglar, with an appraising chuckle; "but there'll be something to-night that'll make all that bunch look like chicken-feed. The boys are at work now, and we'll have old Hayden-Bond's necklace in another hour. Skeeny's got the Sparrow tied up in the old room behind Shluker's place, and once we're sure there's no back-fire anywhere, the Sparrow will chirp his last chirp." He laughed out suddenly, and, leaning forward, clapped Rhoda Gray exultantly on the shoulder. "It was like taking candy from a kid! The Sparrow and the old man fell for the sick-mother, needing-her-son-all-night stuff without batting a lid; but the Sparrow hasn't been holding the old lady's hand at the bedside yet. We took care of that."

Again Rhoda Gray made no comment. She wondered, as she gripped at the rings and brooches in hand, so fiercely that the settings pricked into the flesh, if her face mirrored in any way the cold, sick misery that had suddenly taken possession of her soul. The Sparrow! She knew the Sparrow; she knew the Sparrow's sick mother. That part of it was true. The Sparrow did have an old mother who was sick. A fine old lady--finer than the son--Finch, her name was. Indirectly, she knew old Hayden-Bond, the millionaire, and--Almost subconsciously she was aware that Danglar was speaking again.

"I guess luck's breaking our way again," he grinned. "The old boy paid a hundred thousand cold for that necklace. You know how long we've been waiting to get our hooks on it, and we've never had our eyes off his house for two months. Well, it pays to wait, and it pays to do things right. It broke our way at last to-night, all right, all right! To-day's Saturday--and the safety deposit vaults aren't open on Sunday. Mrs. Hayden-Bond's been away all week visiting, but she comes back to-morrow, and there's some swell society fuss fixed for to-morrow night, and she wants her necklace to make a splurge, so she writes Mr. H-hyphen-B, and out it comes from the safety deposit vault, and into the library safe. The old man isn't long on social stunts, and he's got pretty well set in his habits; one of those must-have-nine-hours'-sleep bugs, and he's always in bed by ten--when his wife'll let him. She being away to-night, the boys were able to get to work early. They ought to be able to crack that box without making any noise about it in an hour and a half at the outside." He pulled out his watch-and whistled low under his breath. "It's a quarter after eleven now," he said hurriedly, and moved abruptly toward the door. "I can't stick around here any longer. I've got to be on deck where they can slip me the 'white ones,' and then there's Skeeny waiting for the word to bump off the Sparrow." He jerked his hand suddenly toward the jewels in her lap. "Salt those away before any more adventurers blow in!" he said, half sharply, half jocularly. "And don't let the White Moll slip you--at any cost. Remember! She's bound to come to you again. Play her--and send out the call. You understand, don't you? There's never been a yip out of the police. Our methods are too good for that. Look at the Sparrow to-night. Where there's no chance taken of suspicion going anywhere except where we lead it, there's no chance of any trouble--for us! But this cursed she-fiend's another story. We're not planting plum trees for her to pick any more of the fruit. Understand?"

She answered him mechanically.

"Yes," she said.

"All right, then; that end of it is up to you," he said significantly. "You're clever, clever as the devil, Bertha. Use your brains now--we need 'em. Good-night, old girl. See you later."

"Good-night," said Rhoda Gray dully.

The door closed. The short, ladder-like steps to the hallway below creaked once, and then all was still. Danglar did have on rubber-soled shoes. She sat upright, her hands, clenched now, pressed hard against her throbbing temples. It wasn't true! None of this was true--this hovel of a place, those jewels glinting like evil eyes in her lap; her existence itself wasn't true; it was only her brain now, sick like her soul, that conjured up these ugly phantoms with horrible, plausible ingenuity. And then an inner voice seemed to answer her with a calmness that was hideous in its finality. It was true. All of it was true. Those words of Danglar, and their bald meaning, were true. Men did such things; men made in the image of their Maker did such things. They were going to kill a man to-night--an innocent man whom they had made their pawn.

She swept the jewels from her lap to the blanket, and rising, seized the candle, went to the door, looked out, and, holding the candle high above her head, peered down the stairs. Yes, he was gone. There was no one there.

She locked the door again, returned to the bed, set the candle down upon the chair, and stood there, her face white and drawn, staring with wide, tormented eyes about her. Murder. Danglar had spoken of it with inhuman callousness--and had laughed at it. They were going to take a man's life. And there was only herself, already driven to extremity, already with her own back against the wall in an effort to save herself, only herself to carry the burden of the responsibility of doing something-to save a man's life.

It seemed to plumb the depths of irony and mockery. She could not make a move as Gypsy Nan. It would only result in their turning upon her, of the discovery that she was not Gypsy Nan at all, of the almost certainty that it would cost her her own life without saving the Sparrow's. That way was closed to her from the start. As the White Moll, then? Outside there in the great city, every plain-clothes man, every policeman on every beat, was staring into every woman's face he met-- searching for the White Moll.

She wrung her hands in cruel desperation. Even to her own problem she had found no solution, though she had wrestled with it all last night, and all through the day; no solution save the negative one of clinging to this one refuge that remained to her, such as it was, temporarily. She had found no solution to that; what solution was there to this! She had thought of leaving the city as Gypsy Nan, and then somewhere far away, of sloughing off the character of Gypsy Nan, and of resuming her own personality again under an assumed name. But that would have meant the loss of everything she had in life, her little patrimony, the irredeemable stamp of shame upon the name she once had owned; and also the constant fear and dread that at any moment the police net, wide as the continent was wide, would close around her, as, sooner or later, it was almost inevitable that it would close around her. It had seemed that her only chance was to keep on striving to play the role of Gypsy Nan, because it was these associates of Gypsy Nan who were at the bottom of the crime of which she, Rhoda Gray, was held guilty, and because there was always the hope that in this way, through confidences to a supposed confederate, she could find the evidence that would convict those actually guilty, and so prove her own innocence. But in holding to the role of Gypsy Nan for the purpose of receiving those criminal confidences, she had not thought of this--that upon her would rest the moral responsibility of other crimes of which she would have knowledge, and, least of all, that she should be faced with what lay before her now, to-night, at the first contact with those who had been Gypsy Nan's confederates.

What was she to do? Upon her, and upon her alone, depended a man's life, and, adding to her distraction, she knew the man--the Sparrow, who had already done time; that was the vile ingenuity of it all. And there would le corroborative evidence, of course; they would have seen to that. If the Sparrow disappeared and was never heard of again, even a child would deduce the assumption that the proceeds of the robbery had disappeared with him.

Her brain seemed to grow panicky. She was standing here helplessly. And time, the one precious ally that she possessed, was slipping away from her. She could not go to the police as Gypsy Nan--and, much less, as the White Moll! She could not go to the police in any case, for the "corroborative" evidence, that obviously must exist, unless Danglar and those with him were fools, would indubitably damn the Sparrow to another prison term, even supposing that through the intervention of the police his life were saved. What was she to do?

And then, for a moment, her eyes lighted in relief. The Adventurer! She thrust her hand into the pocket of her skirt, and drew out the torn piece of paper, and studied the telephone number upon it--and slowly the hurt and misery came back into her eyes again. Who was he? He had told her. An adventurer. He had given her to understand that he, if she had not been just a few minutes ahead of him, would have taken that money from Skarbolov's escritoire last night. Therefore he was a crook. Danglar had said that some one had been getting in ahead of them lately and snatching the plunder from under their noses; and Danglar now believed that it had been the White Moll. A wan smile came to her lips. Instead of the White Moll, it appeared to be quite obvious that it was the Adventurer. It therefore appeared to be quite as obvious that the man was a professional thief, and an extremely clever one, at that. She dared not trust him. To enlist his aid she would have to explain the gang's plot; and while the Adventurer might go to the Sparrow's assistance, he might also be very much more interested in the diamond necklace that was involved, and not be entirely averse to Danglar's plan of using the Sparrow as a pawn, who, in that case, would make a very convenient scapegoat for the Adventurer--instead of Danglar! She dared not trust the man. She could not absolve her conscience by staking another's life on a hazard, on the supposition that the Adventurer might do this or that. It was not good enough.

She was quick in her movements now. Subconsciously her decision had been made. There was only one way--only one. She gathered up the jewels from the bed and thrust them, with the Adventurer's torn piece of paper, into her pocket. And now she reached for the little notebook that she had hidden under the blanket. It contained the gang's secret code, and she had found it in the cash box in Gypsy Nan's strange hiding place that evening. Half running now, carrying the candle, she started toward the lower end of the attic, where the roof sloped down to little more than shoulder high. "Seven-Three-Nine!" Danglar had almost decoded the message word for word in the course of his conversation. In the little notebook, set against the figures, were the words: "Danger. The game is off. Make no further move." It was only one of many, that arbitrary arrangement of figures, each combination having its own special significance; but, besides these, there was the key to a complete cipher into which any message might be coded, and--But why was her brain swerving off at inconsequential tangents? What did a coder or code book, matter at the present moment?

She was standing under the narrow trap-door in the low ceiling now, and now she pushed it up, and lifting the candle through the opening, set it down on the inner surface of the ceiling, which, like some vast shelf, Gypsy Nan had metamorphosed into that exhaustive storehouse of edibles, of plunder--a curious and sinister collection that was eloquent of a gauntlet long flung down against the law. She emptied the pocket of her skirt, retaining only the revolver, and substituted the articles she had removed with the tin box that contained the dark compound Gypsy Nan, and she herself, as Gypsy Nan, had used to rob her face of youthfulness, and give it the grimy, dissolute and haggard aspect which was so simple and yet so efficient a disguise.

She worked rapidly now, changing her clothes. She could not go, or act, as Gypsy Nan; and so she must go in her own character, go as the White Moll--because that was the lesser danger, the one that held the only promise of success. There wasn't any other way. She could not very well refuse to risk her capture by the police, could she, when by so doing she might save another's life? She could not balance in cowardly selfishness the possibility of a prison term for herself, hideous as that might be, against the penalty of death that the Sparrow would pay if she remained inactive. But she could not leave here as the White Moll. Somewhere, somewhere out in the night, somewhere away from this garret where all connection with it was severed, she must complete the transformation from Gypsy Nan to the White Moll. She could only prepare for that now as best she could.

And there was not a moment to lose. The thought made her frantic. Over her own clothes she put on again Gypsy Nan's greasy skirt, and drew on again, over her own silk ones, Gypsy Nan's coarse stockings. She put on Gypsy Nan's heavy and disreputable boots, and threw the old shawl again over her head and shoulders. And then, with her hat--for the small shape of which she breathed a prayer of thankfulness!--and her own shoes under her arm and covered by the shawl, she took the candle again, closed the trap-door, and stepped over to the washstand. Here, she dampened a rag, that did duty as a facecloth, and thrust it into her pocket; then, blowing out the candle, she groped her way to the door, locked it behind her, and without any attempt at secrecy made her way downstairs.

VI. THE RENDEZVOUS

Rhoda Gray's movements were a little unsteady as she stepped out on the sidewalk. Gypsy Nan's accepted inebriety was not without its compensation. It enabled her, as she swayed for a moment, to scrutinize the street in all directions. Were any of Rough Rorke's men watching the house? She did not know; she only knew that as far as she had been able to discover, she had not been followed when she had gone out that afternoon. Up the street, to her right, there were a few pedestrians; to her left, as far as the corner, the block was clear. She turned in the latter direction. She had noticed that afternoon that there was a lane between Gypsy Nan's house and the corner; she gained this and slipped into it unobserved.

And now, in the comparative darkness, she hurried her steps. Somewhere here in the lane she would make the transformation from Gypsy Nan to the White Moll complete; it required only some place in which she could with safety leave the garments that she discarded, and--Yes, this would do! A tumble-down old shed, its battered door half open, ample proof that the place was in disuse, intersected the line of high board fence on her right.

She stole inside. It was utterly dark, but she had no need for light. It was a matter of perhaps three minutes; and then, the revolver transferred to the pocket of her jacket, the stains removed from her face by the aid of the damp cloth, her hands neatly gloved in black kid, the skirt, boots, stockings, shawl, spectacles and wig of Gypsy Nan carefully piled together and hidden in a hole under the rotting boards of the floor, behind the door, she emerged as the White Moll, and went on again.

But at the end of the lane, where it met a cross street, and the street lamp flung out an ominous challenge, and, dim though it was, seemed to glare with the brightness of daylight, she faltered for a moment and drew back. She knew where Shluker's place was, because she knew, as few knew it, every nook and cranny in the East Side, and it was a long way to that old junk shop, almost over to the East River, and--and there would be lights like this one here that barred her exit from the lane, thousands of them, lights all the way, and--and out there they were searching everywhere, pitilessly, for the White Moll.

And then, with her lips tightened, the straight little shoulders thrown resolutely back, she slipped from the lane to the sidewalk, and, hugging the shadows of the buildings, started forward.

She was alert now in mind and body, every faculty strained and in tension. It was a long way, and it would take a great while--by wide detours, by lanes and alleyways, for only on those streets that were relatively deserted and poorly lighted would she dare trust herself to the open. And as she went along, now skirting the side of a street, now through some black courtyard, now forced to take a fence, and taking it with the agility born of the open, athletic life she had led with her father in the mining camps of South America, now hiding at the mouth of a lane waiting her chance to cross an intersecting street when some receding footstep should have died away, the terror of delay came gripping at her heart with an icy clutch, submerging the fear of personal peril in the agony of dread that, with her progress so slow, she would, after all, be too late. And at times she almost cried out in her vexation and despair, as once, when crouched behind a door-stoop, a policeman, not two yards from her, stood and twirled his night stick under the street lamp while the minutes sped and raced themselves away.

When she could run, she ran until it seemed her lungs must burst, but it was slow progress at best, and always the terror grew upon her. Had Danglar met the men yet who had looted the millionaire's safe? Had he already joined Skeeny in that old room behind Shluker's place? Had the Sparrow--She would not let her mind frame that question in concrete words. The Sparrow! His real name was Martin, Martin Finch--Marty, for short. Times without number she had visited the sick and widowed mother--while the Sparrow had served a two-years' sentence for his first conviction in safe-breaking. The Sparrow, from a first-class chauffeur mechanic, had showed signs of becoming a first-class cracksman, it was true; but the Sparrow was young, and she had never believed that he was inherently bad. Her opinion had been confirmed when, some six months ago, on his release, listening both to her own pleadings and to those of his mother, the Sparrow had sworn that he would stick to the "straight and narrow." And Hayden-Bond, the millionaire, referred to by a good many people as eccentric, had further proved his claims to eccentricity in the eyes of a good many people by giving a prison bird a chance to make an honest living, and had engaged the Sparrow as his chauffeur. It was a vile and an abominable thing that they were doing, even if they had not planned to culminate it with murder. What chance would the Sparrow have had!

It had taken a long time. She did not know how long, as, at last, she stole unnoticed into a black and narrow driveway that led in, between two blocks of down-at-the-heels tenements, to a courtyard in the rear. Shluker had his junk shop here. Her lips pursed up as though defiant of a tinge of perplexity that had suddenly taken possession of her. She did not know Shluker, or anything about Shluker's place except its locality; but surely "the old room behind Shluker's" was direction enough, and--She had just emerged from the end of the driveway now, and now, startled, she turned her head quickly, as she heard a brisk step turning in from the street behind her. But in the darkness she could see no one, and satisfied, therefore, that she in turn had not been seen, she moved swiftly to one side, and crouched down against the rear wall of one of the tenements. A long moment, that seemed an eternity, passed, and then a man's form came out from the driveway, and started across the courtyard.

She drew in her breath sharply, a curious mingling of relief and a sudden panic fear upon her. It was not so dark in the courtyard as it had been in the driveway, and, unless she were strangely mistaken that form out there was Danglar's. She watched him as he headed toward a small building that loomed up like a black, ir- regular shadow across the courtyard, and which was Shluker's shop--watched him in a tense, fascinated way. She was in time, then--only--only somehow now her limbs seemed to have become weak and powerless. It seemed suddenly as though she craved with all her soul the protecting shadows of the tenement, and that every impulse bade her cling there, flattened against the wall, until she could make her escape. She was afraid now; she shrank from the next step. It wasn't illogical. She had set out with a purpose in view, and she had not been blind to the danger that she ran, but the prospective and mental encounter with danger did not hold the terror that the tangible, concrete and actual presence of that peril did--and that was

Danglar there.

She felt her face whiten, and she felt the tremor of her lips, tightly as they were drawn together. Yes, she was afraid, afraid in every fiber of her being, but there was a difference, wasn't there, between being afraid and being a coward? Her small, gloved hands clenched, her lips parted slightly. She laughed a little now, low, without mirth. Upon what she did or did not do, upon the margin between fear and cowardice as applied to herself, there hung a man's life. Danglar was disappearing around the side of Shluker's shop. She moved out from the wall, and swiftly, silently, crossed the courtyard, gained the side of the junk shop in turn, skirted it, and halted, listening, peering around her, as she reached the rear corner of the building. A door closed somewhere ahead of her; from above, upstairs, faint streaks of light showed through the interstices of a shuttered window.

She crept forward now, hugging the rear wall, reached a door-the one, obviously, through which Danglar had disappeared, and which she had heard as it was closed--tried the door, found it unlocked, and, noiselessly, inch by inch, pushed it open; and a moment later, stepping over the threshold, she closed it softly behind her. A dull glow of light, emanating evidently from an open door above, disclosed the upper portion of a stairway over on her left, but apart from that the place was in blackness, and save that she knew, of course, she was in the rear of Shluker's junk shop, she could form no idea of her surroundings. But she could, at last, hear. Voices, one of which she recognized as Danglar's, though she could not distinguish the words, reached her from upstairs.

Slowly, with infinite care, she crossed to the stairs, and on hands and knees now, lest she should make a sound, began to crawl upward. And a little way up, panic fear seized upon her again, and her heart stood still, and she turned a miserable face in the darkness back toward the door below, and fought against the impulse to retreat again.

And then she heard Danglar speak, and from her new vantage point his words came to her distinctly this time:

"Good work, Skeeny! You've got the Sparrow nicely trussed up, I see. Well, he'll do as he is for a while there. I told the boys to hold off a bit. It's safer to wait an hour or two yet, before moving him away from here and bumping him off."

"Two jobs instead of one!" a surly voice answered. "We might just as well have finished him and slipped him away for keeps when we first got our hooks on him."

"Got a little sick of your wood-carving, while you stuck around by your lone-some and watched him--eh?" Danglar's tones were jocularly facetious. "Don't grouch, Skeeny! We're not killing for fun--it doesn't pay. Supposing anything had broken wrong up the Avenue--eh? We wouldn't have had our friend the Sparrow there for the next time we tried it!"

There was something abhorrently callous in the laugh that followed. It seemed to fan into flame a smoldering fire of passionate anger in Rhoda Gray's soul. And before it panic fled. Her hand felt upward for the next stair-tread, and she crept on again, as a face seemed to rise before her--not the Sparrow's face--a woman's face. It was a face that was crowned with very thin white hair, and its eyes were the sad-dest she had ever seen, and yet they were brave, steady old eyes that had not lost their faith; nor had the old, care-lined face itself, in spite of suffering, lost its gentle-ness and sweetness. And then suddenly it seemed to change, that face, and become wreathed in smiles, and happy tears to run coursing down the wrinkled cheeks. Yes, she remembered! It had brought the tears to her own eyes. It was the night that the wayward Sparrow, home from the penitentiary, on his knees, his head buried in his mother's lap, had sworn that he would go straight.

Fear! It seemed as though she never had known, never could know fear--that only a merciless, tigerish, unbridled fury had her in its thrall. And she went on up, step after step, as Danglar spoke again:

"There's nothing to it! The Sparrow there fell for the telephone when Stevie played the doctor. And old Hayden-Bond of course grants his prison-bird chauf-feur's request to spend the night with his mother, who the doctor says is taken worse, because the old guy knows there is a mother who really is sick. Only Mr. Hayden-Bond, and the police with him, will maybe figure it a little differently in the morning when they find the safe looted, and that the Sparrow, instead of ever going near the poor old dame, has flown the coop and can't be found. And in case there's any lingering doubt in their minds, that piece of paper with the grease-smudges and the Sparrow's greasy finger-prints on it, that you remember we copped a few days ago in the garage, will set them straight. The Cricket slipped it in among the papers he pulled out of the safe and tossed around on the floor. It looks as though a tool had been wiped with it while the safe was being cracked, and that it got covered over by the stuff that was emptied out, and had been forgotten. I guess they won't be long in comparing the finger-prints with the ones the Sparrow kindly left with them when they measured him for his striped suit the time they sent him up the river--eh?"

Rhoda Gray could see now. Her eyes were on a level with the landing, and diagonally across from the head of the stairs was the open doorway of a lighted room. She could not see all of the interior, but she could see quite enough. Two men sat, side face to her, one at each end of a rough, deal table--Danglar, and an ugly, pock-marked, unshaven man, in a peaked cap that was drawn down over his eyes, who whittled at a stick with a huge jack-knife. The latter was Skeeny, obviously; and the jack-knife and the stick, quite as obviously, explained Danglar's facetious reference to wood-carving. And then her eyes shifted, and widened as they rested on a huddled form that she could see by looking under and beyond the table, and that lay sprawled out against the far wall of the room.

Skeeny pushed the peak of his cap back with the point of his knife-blade.

"What's the haul size up at?" he demanded. "Anything in the safe besides the shiners?"

"A few hundred dollars," Danglar replied. "I don't know exactly how much. I told the Cricket to divide it up among the boys who did the rough work. That's good enough, isn't it, Skeeny? It gives you a little extra. You'll get yours."

Skeeny grunted compliance.

"Well, let's have a look at the white ones, then," he said.

Rhoda Gray was standing upright in the little hallway now, and now, pressed close against the wall, she edged toward the door-jamb. And a queer, grim little smile came and twisted the sensitive lips, as she drew her revolver from her pocket. The merciless, pitiless way in which the newspapers had flayed the White Moll was not, after all, to be wholly regretted! The cool, clever resourcefulness, the years of reckless daring attributed to the White Moll, would stand her in good stead now. Everybody on the East Side knew her by sight. These men knew her. It was not merely a woman ambitiously attempting to beard two men who, perhaps, holding her sex in contempt in an adventure of this kind, might throw discretion to the winds and give scant respect to her revolver, for behind the muzzle of that revolver was the reputation of the White Moll. They would take her at face value--as one who not only knew how to use that revolver, but as one who would not hesitate an instant to do so.

From the room she heard Skeeny whistle low under his breath, as though in sudden and amazed delight--and then she was standing full in the open doorway, and her revolver in her outflung, gloved hand covered the two men at the table.

There was a startled cry from Skeeny, a scintillating flash of light as a magnificent string of diamonds fell from his hand to the table. But Danglar did not move or speak; only his lips twitched, and a queer whiteness came and spread itself over his face.

"Put up your hands-both of you!" she ordered, in a low, tense voice.

It was Skeeny who spoke, as both men obeyed her. "The White Moll, so help me!" he mumbled, and swallowed hard.

Danglar's eyes never seemed to leave her face, and they narrowed now, full of hatred and a fury that lie made no attempt to conceal. She smiled at him coldly. She quite understood! He had already complained that evening that the White Moll for the last few weeks had been robbing them of the fruits of their laboriously planned schemes. And now-again! Well, she would not dispel his illusion! He had given the White Moll that role--and it was the safest role to play.

She stepped forward now, and with her free hand suddenly pulled the table toward her out of their reach; and then, as she picked up the necklace, she appeared for the first time to become aware of the presence of the huddled form on the floor near the wall. She could see that the Sparrow was bound and gagged, and as he squirmed now he turned his face toward her.

"Why, it's the Sparrow, isn't it?" she exclaimed sharply; then, evenly, to the two men: "I had no idea you were so hospitable! Push your chairs closer together--with your feet, not your hands! You are easier to watch if you are not too far apart."

Danglar complied sullenly. Skeeny, over the scraping of his chair legs, cursed in a sort of unnerved abandon, as he obeyed her.

"Thank you!" said Rhoda Gray pleasantly--and calmly tucked the necklace into her bodice.

The act seemed to rouse Danglar to the last pitch of fury. The blood rushed in an angry tide to his face, and, suffusing, purpled his cheeks.

"This isn't the first crack you've made!" he flung out hoarsely. "You've been getting wise to a whole lot lately somehow, you and that dude pal of yours, but you'll pay for it, you female devil! Understand? By God, you'll pay for it! I promise you that you'll pray yet on your bended knees for the chance to take your own life! Do you hear?"

"I hear," said Rhoda Gray coldly.

She picked up the jack-knife from the table, and keeping both men covered, stepped backward to the wall. Here, kneeling, she reached behind her with her left hand, and felt for, and cut the heavy cord that bound the Sparrow's arms; then, pushing the knife into the Sparrow's hands that he might free himself from the rest of his bonds, she stood up again.

A moment more, and the Sparrow, rubbing the circulation back into his wrists, stood beside her. There was a look on the young, white face that was not good to see. He circled dry lips with the tip of his tongue and then his thumb began to feel over the blade of the big jack-knife in a sort of horribly supercritical appraisal of its edge. He spoke thickly for the gag that had been in his mouth.

"You dirty skates!" he whispered. "You were going to bump me off, were you? You planted me cold, did you? Oh, hell!" His laugh, like the laugh of one insane, jangling, discordant, rang through the room. "Well, it's my turn now, and"--his body was coiling itself in a slow, curious, almost snake-like fashion--"and you'll--"

Rhoda Gray laid her hand on the Sparrow's arm.

"Not that way, Marty," she said quietly. She smiled thinly at Danglar, who, with genuinely frightened eyes now, seemed fascinated by the Sparrow's movements. "I wouldn't care to have anything happen to Mr. Danglar--yet. He has been invaluable to me, and I am sure he will be again."

The Sparrow brushed his hands across his eyes, and stared at her. He licked his lips again. He appeared to be obsessed with the knife-blade in his hand--dazed in a strange way to all else.

"There's enough cord there for both of them," said Rhoda Gray crisply. "Tie them in their chairs, Marty."

For a moment the Sparrow hesitated; and then, with a sort of queer reluctancy, he dropped the knife on the table, and went and picked up the strands of cord from the floor.

No one spoke. The Sparrow, with twitching lips as he worked, and worked not gently, bound first Danglar and then Skeeny to their respective chairs. Skeeny for the most part kept his eyes on the floor, casting only furtive glances at Rhoda Gray's revolver muzzle. But Danglar was smiling now. He had very white teeth. There was something of primal, insensate fury in the hard-drawn, parted lips. Somehow he seemed to remind Rhoda Gray of a beast, stung to madness, but impotent behind the bars of its cage, as it showed its fangs.

"We'll go now, Marty," she said softly, as the Sparrow finished.

She motioned the Sparrow with an imperious little nod of her head to the door. And then, following the other, she backed to the door herself, and halted an instant on the threshold.

"It has been a very profitable evening, Mr. Danglar," she said coolly. "I have you to thank for it. When your friends come, which I think I heard you say would be in another hour or so, I hope you will not fail to convey to them my--"

"You she-fiend!" Danglar had found his voice again. "You'll crawl for this! Do you understand? and I'll show you inside of twenty-four hours what you're up against, you--you--" His voice broke in its fury. The veins were standing out on the side of his neck like whipcords. He could just move his forearms a little, and his hands reached out toward her, curved like claws. "I'll--"

But Rhoda Gray had closed the door behind her, and, with the Sparrow, was retreating down the stairs.

VII. FELLOW THIEVES

Reaching the courtyard, Rhoda Gray led the way without a word through the driveway, and finding the street clear, hurried on rapidly. Her mind, strangely stimulated, was working in quick, incisive flashes. Her work was not yet done. The Sparrow was safe, as far as his life was concerned; but her possession of even the necklace would not save the Sparrow from the law. There was the money that was gone from the safe. She could not recover that, but--yes, dimly, she began to see a way. She swerved suddenly from the sidewalk as she came to an alleyway--which had been her objective--and drew the Sparrow in with her out of sight of the street.

The Sparrow gripped at her hand.

"The White Moll!" he whispered brokenly. "God bless the White Moll! I ain't had a chance to say it before. You saved my life, and I--I--"

In the semi-darkness she leaned forward and laid her fingers gently over the Sparrow's lips.

"And there's no time to say it now, Marty," she said quickly. "You are not out of this yet."

He swept his hand across his eyes.

"I know it," he said. "I got to get those shiners back up there somehow, and I got to get that paper they planted on me."

She shook her head.

"Even that wouldn't clear you," she said. "The safe has been looted of money, as well; and you can't replace that. Even with only the money gone, who would they first naturally suspect? You are known as a safe-breaker; you have served a term for it. You asked for a night off to stay with your mother who is sick. You left Mr. Hayden-Bond's, we'll say, at seven or eight o'clock. It's after midnight now. How long would it take them to find out that between eight and midnight you had not only never been near your mother, but could not prove an alibi of any sort? If you told the truth it would sound absurd. No one in their sober senses would believe you."

The Sparrow looked at her miserably.

"My God!" he faltered. He wet his lips. "That's true."

"Marty," she said quietly, "did you read in the papers that I had been arrested last night for theft, caught with the goods on me, but had escaped?"

The Sparrow hesitated.

"Yes, I did," he said. And then, earnestly: "But I don't believe it!"

"It was true, though, Marty--all except that I wasn't a thief," she said as quietly as before. "What I want to know is, in spite of that, would you trust me with what is left to be done to-night, if I tell you that I believe I can get you out of this?"

"Sure, I would!" he said simply. "I don't know how you got wise about all this, or how you got to know about that necklace, but any of our crowd would trust you to the limit. Sure, I'd trust you! You bet your life!"

"Thank you, Marty," she said. "Well, then, how do you get into Mr. Hayden-Bond's house when, for instance, you are out late at night?"

"I've got a key to the garage," he answered. "The garage is attached to the house, though it opens on the side street."

She held Out her hand.

The Sparrow fished in his pocket, and extended the key without hesitation.

"It's for the small door, of course," he explained.

"You haven't got a flashlight, I suppose?" she smiled.

"Sure! There's plenty of 'em! Each car's got one with its tools under the back seat."

She nodded.

"And now, the library," she said. "What part of the house is it in? How is it situated?"

"It's on the ground floor at the back," he told her. "The little short passage from the garage opens on the kitchen, then the pantry, and then there's a little cross hallway, and the dining-room is on the left, and the library on the right. But ain't I going with you?"

She shook her head again.

"You're going home, Marty--after you've sent me a taxicab. If you were seen in that neighborhood now, let alone by any chance seen in the house, nothing could save you. You understand that, don't you? Now, listen! Find a taxi, and send it here. Tell the chauffeur to pick me up, and drive me to the corner of the cross street, one block in the rear of Mr. Hayden-Bond's residence. Don't mention Hayden-Bond's name. Give the chauffeur simply street directions. Be careful that he is some one who doesn't know you. Tell him he will be well paid--and give him this to begin with." She thrust a banknote into the Sparrow's hand. "You're sure to find one at some all-night cabaret around here. And remember, when you go home afterward, not a word to your mother! And not a word to-morrow, or ever-to any one! You've simply done as you told your employer you were going to do--spent the night at home."

"But you," he burst out, and his words choked a little. "I--I can't let you go, and--"

"You said you would trust me, Marty," she said. "And if you want to help me, as well, don't waste another moment. I shall need every second I have got. Quick! Hurry!"

"But--"

She pushed him toward the street.

"Run!" she said tensely. "Hurry, Marty, hurry!"

She drew back into the shadows. She was alone now. The Sparrow's racing footsteps died away on the pavement. Her mind reverted to the plan that she had dimly conceived. It became detailed, concrete now, as the minutes passed. And then she heard a car coming along the previously deserted street, and she stepped out on the sidewalk. It was the taxi.

"You know where to go, don't you?" she said to the chauffeur, as the cab drew up at the curb, and the man leaned out and opened the door.

"Yes'm," he said.

"Please drive fast, then," she said, as she stepped in.

The taxi shot out from the curb, and rattled forward at a rapid pace. Rhoda Gray settled back on the cushions. A half whimsical, half weary little smile touched her lips. It was much easier, and infinitely safer, this mode of travel, than that of her earlier experience that evening; but, earlier that evening, she had had no one to go to a cab rank for her, and she had not dared to appear in the open and hail one for herself. The smile vanished, and the lips became, pursed and grim. Her mind was back on that daring, and perhaps a little dangerous, plan, that she meant to put into execution. Block after block was traversed. It was a long way uptown, but the chauffeur's initial and generous tip was bearing fruit. The man was losing no time.

Rhoda Gray calculated that they had been a little under half an hour in making the trip, when the taxi finally drew up and stopped at a corner, and the chauffeur, again leaning out, opened the door.

"Wait for me," she instructed, and handed the man another tip--and, with a glance about her to get her location, she hurried around the corner, and headed up the cross street.

She had only a block now to go to reach the Hayden-Bond mansion on the corner of Fifth Avenue ahead--less than that to reach the garage, which opened on the cross street here. She had little fear of personal identification now. Here in this residential section and at this hour of night, it was like a silent and deserted city; even Fifth Avenue, just ahead, for all its lights, was one of the loneliest places at this hour in all New York. True, now and then, a car might race up or down the great thoroughfare, or a belated pedestrian's footsteps ring and echo hollow on the pavement, where but a few hours before the traffic-squad struggled valiantly, and sometimes vainly, with the congestion--but that was all.

She could make out the Hayden-Bond mansion on the corner ahead of her now, and now she was abreast of the rather ornate and attached little building, that was obviously the garage. She drew the key from her pocket, and glanced around her. There was no one in sight. She stepped swiftly to the small door that flanked the big double ones where the cars went in and out, opened it, closed it behind her, and locked it.

For a moment, her eyes unaccustomed to the darkness, she could see nothing; and then a car, taking the form of a grotesque, looming shadow, showed in front of her. She moved toward it, felt her way into the tonneau, lifted up the back seat, and, groping around, found a flashlight. She meant to hurry now. She did not mean to let that nervous dread, that fear, that was quickening her pulse now, have time to get the better of her. She located the door that led to the house, and in another moment, the short passage behind her, she was in the kitchen, the flashlight winking cautiously around her. She paused to listen here. There was not a sound.

She went on again--through a swinging pantry door with extreme care, and into a small hall. "On the right," the Sparrow had said. Yes, here it was; a door that opened on the rear of the library, evidently. She listened again. There was no sound--save the silence, that seemed to grow loud now, and palpitate, and make great noises. And now, in spite of herself, her breath was coming in quick, hard little catches, and the flashlight's ray, that she sent around her, wavered and was not steady. She bit her lips, as she switched off the light. Why should she be afraid of this, when in another five minutes she meant to invite attention!

She pushed the door in front of her open, found it hung with a heavy portiere inside, brushed the portiere aside, stepped through into the room, stood still and motionless to listen once more, and then the flashlight circled inquisitively about her.

It was the library. Her eyes widened a little. At her left, over against the wall, the mangled door of a safe stood wide open, and the floor for a radius of yards around was littered with papers and documents. The flashlight's ray lifted, and she followed it with her eyes as it made the circuit of the walls. Opposite the safe, and quite near the doorway in which she stood, was a window recess, portiered; diagonally across from her was another door that led, presumably, into the main hall of the house; the walls were tapestried, and hung here and there with clusters of ancient trophies, great metal shields, and swords, and curious arms, that gave a sort of barbaric splendor to the luxurious furnishings of the apartment.

She worked quickly now. In a moment she was at the window portieres, and, drawing these aside, she quietly raised the window, and looked out. The window was on the side of the house away from the cross street, and she nodded her head reassuringly to herself as she noted that it gave on a narrow strip of grass, it could not be called lawn, that separated the Hayden-Bond mansion from the house next door; that the window was little more than shoulder-high from the ground; and that the Avenue was within easy and inviting reach along that little strip of grass between the two houses.

She left the window open, and retraced her steps across the room, going now to the littered mass of papers on the floor near the safe. She began to search carefully amongst them. She smiled a little curiously as she came across the plush-lined jeweler's case that had contained the necklace, and which had evidently been contemptuously discarded by the Cricket and his confederates; but it took her longer to find the paper for which she was searching. And then she came upon it--a grease-smeared advertisement for some automobile appliances, a well-defined greasy finger-print at one edge--and thrust the paper into her pocket.

And now suddenly her heartbeat began to quicken again until its thumping became tumultuous. She was ready now. She looked around her, using the flashlight, and her eyes rested appraisingly on one of the great clusters of shields and arms that hung low down on the wall between the window and the door by which she had entered. Yes, that would do. Her lips tightened. It would have been so easy if there had not been that cash to account for! She could replace the necklace, but she could not replace the cash--and one, as far as the Sparrow was concerned, was as bad as the other. But there was a way, and it was simple enough. She whispered to herself that it was not, after all, very dangerous, that the cards were all in her own hands. She had only to pull down those shields with a clatter to the floor, which would arouse some one of the household, and as that some one reached the library door and opened it, she would be disappearing through the window, and the necklace, as though it had slipped from her pocket or grasp in her wild effort to escape, would be lying behind her on the floor. They would see that it was not the Sparrow; and there would be no question as to where the money was gone, since the money had not been dropped. There was the interval, of course, that must elapse between the accident that knocked the shields from the wall and the time it would take any of the inmates to reach the library, an interval in which a thief might reasonably be expected to have had time enough to get away without being seen; but the possibility that she had not fully accomplished her ends when the accident occurred, and that she had stayed to make frantic and desperate efforts to do so right up to the last moment, would account for that.

She moved now to an electric-light switch, and turned on the light. They must be able to see beyond any question of doubt that the person escaping through the window was not the Sparrow. What was she afraid of now, just at the last! There was an actual physical discomfort in the furious thumping of that cowardly little heart of hers. It was the only way. And it was worth it. And it was not so very dangerous. People, aroused out of bed, could not follow her in their night clothes; and in a matter of but a few minutes, before the police notified by telephone could become a factor in the affair, she would have run the block down the Avenue, and then the other block down the cross street, then back to the taxi, and be whirling safely downtown.

Yes, she was ready! She nodded her head sharply, as though in imperative self-command, and running back, her footfalls soundless on the rich, heavy rug, she picked up the plush-lined necklace case. She dropped this again, open, on the floor, halfway between the safe and the window. With the case apparently burst open as it fell, and the necklace also on the floor, the stage would be set! She felt inside her bodice, drew out the necklace--and as she stood there holding it, and as it caught the light and flashed back its fire and life from a thousand facets, a numbness seemed to come stealing over her, and a horror, and a great fear, and a dismay that robbed her of power of movement until it seemed that she was rooted to the spot, and a low, gasping cry came from her lips. Her eyes, wide with their alarm, were fixed on the window. There was a man's face there, just above the sill--and now a man's form swung through the window, and dropped lightly to the floor inside the room. And she stared in horrified fascination, and could not move. It was the Adventurer.

"It's Miss Gray, isn't it? The White Moll?" he murmured amiably. "I've been trying to find you all night. What corking luck! You remember me, don't you? Last night, you know."

She did not answer. His eyes had shifted from her face to the glittering river of gems in her hand.

"I see," he smiled, "that you are ahead of me again. Well, it is the fortune of war, Miss Gray. I do not complain."

She found her voice at last; and, quick as a flash, as he advanced a step, she dropped the necklace into her pocket, and her revolver was in her hand.

"W--what are you doing here?" she whispered.

He shrugged his shoulders expressively.

"I take it that we are both in the same boat," he said pleasantly.

"In the same boat?" she echoed dully. She remembered his conversation with her a few hours ago, when he had believed he was talking to Gypsy Nan. And now he stood before her for the second time a self-confessed thief. In the same boat-fellow-thieves! A certain cold composure came to her. "You mean you came to steal this necklace? Well, you shall not have it! And, furthermore, you have no right to class me with yourself as a thief."

He had a whimsical and very engaging smile. His eyebrows lifted.

"Miss Gray perhaps forgets last night," he suggested.

"No, I do not forget last night," she said slowly, "And I do not forget that I owe you very much for what you did. And that is one reason why I warn you at once that, as far as the necklace is concerned, it will do you no good to build any hopes on the supposition that we are fellow-thieves, and that I am likely either to part with it, or, through gratitude, share it. In spite of appearances last night, I was not a thief."

"And to-night, Miss Gray--in spite of appearances?" he challenged.

He was regarding her with eyes that, while they appraised shrewdly, held a lurking hint of irony in their depths. And somehow, suddenly, self-proclaimed crook though she held him to be, she found herself seized with an absurd, unreasonable, but nevertheless passionate, desire to make good her words.

"Yes, and to-night, too!" she asserted. "I did not steal this necklace. I--never mind how--I--I got it. It was planned to put the theft on an innocent man's shoulders. I was trying to thwart that plan. Whether you believe me or not, I did not come here to steal the necklace; I came here to return it."

"Quite so! Of course!" acknowledged the Adventurer softly. "I am afraid I interrupted you, then, in the act of returning it. Might I suggest, therefore, Miss Gray, that as it's a bit dangerous to linger around here unnecessarily, you carry out your intentions with all possible haste, and get away."

"And you?" she queried evenly.

"Myself, of course, as well." He shrugged his shoulders philosophically. "Under the circumstances, as a gentleman--will you let me say I prefer that word to the one I know you are substituting for it--what else can I do?"

She bit her lips. Was he mocking her? The gray eyes were inscrutable now.

"Then please do not let me detain you!" she said sharply. "And in my turn, let me advise you to go at once. I intend to knock one of those shields down from the wall before I go, in order to arouse the household. I will, however, in part payment for last night, allow you three full minutes from the time you climb out of that window, so that you may have ample time to get away."

He stared at her in frank bewilderment.

"Good Lord!" he gasped. "You--you're joking, Miss Gray."

"No, I am not," she replied coolly. "Far from it! There was money stolen that I cannot replace, and the theft of the money would be put upon the same innocent shoulders. I see no other way than the one I have mentioned. If whoever runs into this room is permitted to get a glimpse of me, and is given the impression that the necklace, which I shall leave on the floor, was dropped in my haste, the supposition remains that, at least, I got away with the money. I am certainly not the innocent man who has been used as the pawn; and if I am recognized as the White Moll, what does it matter--after last night?"

He took a step toward her impetuously--and stopped quite as impetuously. Her revolver had swung to a level with his head.

"Pardon me!" he said.

"Not at all!" she said caustically.

For the first time, as she watched him warily, the Adventurer appeared to lose some of his self-assurance. He shifted a little uneasily on his feet, and the corners of his eyes puckered into a nest of perturbed wrinkles.

"I say, Miss Gray, you can't mean this!" he protested. "You're not serious!"

"I have told you that I am," she answered steadily. "Those three minutes that I gave you are going fast."

"Then look here!" he exclaimed earnestly. "I'll tell you something. I said I had been trying to find you to-night. It was the truth. I went to Gypsy Nan's--and might have been spared my pains. I told her about last night, and that I knew you were in danger, and that I wanted to help you. I mention this so that you will understand that I am not just speaking on the spur of the moment, now that I have an opportunity of repeating that offer in person."

She looked at him impassively for a moment. He had neglected to state that he had also told Gypsy Nan he desired to enter into a partnership with her--in crime.

"It is very kind of you," she said sweetly. "I presume, then, that you have some suggestion to make?"

"Only what any--may I say it?--gentleman would suggest under the circumstances. It is far too dangerous a thing for a woman to attempt; it would be much less dangerous for me. I realize that you are in earnest now, and I will agree to carry out your plan in every detail once I am satisfied that you are safely away."

"The idea being," she observed monotonously, "that, being safely away, and the necklace being left safely on the floor, you are left safely in possession of--the necklace. Well, my answer is--no!"

His face hardened a little.

"I'm sorry, then," he said. "For in that case, in so far as your project is concerned, I, too, must say--no!"

It was an impasse. She studied his face, the strong jaw set a little now, the lips molded in sterner lines, and for all her outward show of composure, she knew a sick dismay. And for a moment she neither moved nor spoke. What he would do next, she did not know; but she knew quite well that he had not the slightest intention of leaving her here undisturbed to carry out her plan, unless--unless, somehow, she could outwit him. She bit her lips again. And then inspiration came. She turned, and with a sudden leap gained the wall, and the next instant, holding him back with her revolver as she reached up with her left hand, she caught at the great metal shield with its encircling cluster of small arms, and wrenched it from its fastenings. It crashed to the floor with a din infernal that, in the night silence, went racketing through the house like the reverberations of an explosion.

"My God, what have you done!" he cried out hoarsely.

"What I said I'd do!" she answered. She was white-faced, frightened at her own act, fighting to maintain her nerve. "You'll go now, I imagine!" she flung at him passionately. "You haven't much time."

"No!" he said. His composure was instantly at command again. "No," he repeated steadily; "not until after you have gone. I refuse--positively--to let you run any such risk as that. It is far too dangerous."

"Yes, you will!" she burst out wildly. "You will! You must! You shall! I--I--" The house itself seemed suddenly to have awakened. From above doors opened and closed. Indistinctly there came the sound of a voice. She clenched her hand in anguished desperation. "Go, you--you coward!" she whispered frantically.

"Miss Gray, for God's sake, do as I tell you!" he said between his teeth. "You don't realize the danger. It's not the pursuit. They are not coming down here unarmed after that racket. I know that you came in by that door there. Go out that way. I will play the game for you. I swear it!"

There were footsteps, plainly audible now, out in the main hall.

"Quick!" he urged. "Are we both to be caught? See!" He backed suddenly toward the window.

"See! I am too far away now to touch that necklace before they get here. Throw it down, and get behind the portiere of the rear door!"

Mechanically she was retreating. They were almost at the other door now, those footsteps outside in the main hall. With a backward spring she reached the portiere. The door handle across the room rattled. She glanced at the Adventurer. He was close to the window. It was true, he could not get the necklace and at the same time hope to escape. She whipped it from her pocket, tossed it from her to the floor near the plush-lined case--and slipped behind the portiere.

The door opposite to her was wrenched violently open. She could see through the corner of the portiere. There was a sharp, excited exclamation, as a gray-haired man, in pajamas, evidently Mr. Hayden-Bond himself, sprang into the room. He was followed by another man in equal dishabille.

And the Adventurer was leaping for the window.

There was a blinding flash, the roar of a report, as the millionaire flung up a revolver and fired; it was echoed by the splatter and tinkle of falling glass. The Adventurer was astride the window sill now, his face deliberately and unmistakably in view.

"A foot too high, and a bit to the right!" said the Adventurer debonairly--and the window sill was empty.

Rhoda Gray stole silently through the doorway behind her. She could hear the millionaire and his companion, the butler, probably, rush across the library to the window. As she gained the pantry, she heard another shot. Tight-lipped, using her flashlight, she ran through the kitchen. In a moment more, she was standing at the garage door, listening, peering furtively outside. The street itself was empty; there were shouts, though, from the direction of the Avenue. She stepped out on the side street, and walking composedly that she might not attract attention, though very impulse urged her to run with frantic haste, she reached the corner and the waiting taxicab. She gave the chauffeur an address that would bring her to the street in the rear of Gypsy Nan's and within reach of the lane where she had left her clothes, and, with an injunction to hurry, sprang into the cab.

And then for a long time she sat there with her hands tightly clasped in her lap. Her mind, her brain, her very soul itself seemed in chaos and turmoil. There was the Sparrow, who was safe; and Danglar, who would move heaven and hell to get her now; and the Adventurer, who--Her mind seemed to grope around in cycles; it seemed to moil on and on and arrive at nothing. The Adventurer had played the game--perhaps because he had had to; but he had not risked that revolver shot in her stead because he had had to. Who was he? How had he come there? How had he found her there? How had he known that she had entered by that rear door behind the portiere? She remembered how that he had offered not a single explanation.

Almost mechanically she dismissed the taxi when at last it stopped; and almost mechanically, as Gypsy Nan, some ten minutes later, she let herself into the garret, and lighted the candle. She was conscious, as she hid the White Moll's clothes away, that she was thankful she had regained in safety even the questionable sanctuary of this wretched place; but, strangely, thoughts of her own peril seemed somehow to be temporarily relegated to the background.

She flung herself down on the bed--it was not Gypsy Nan's habit to undress--and blew out the light. But she could not sleep. And hour after hour in the darkness she tossed unrestfully. It was very strange! It was not as it had been last night. It was not the impotent, frantic rebellion against the horrors of her own situation, nor the fear and terror of it, that obsessed her to-night. It was the Adventurer who plagued her.

VIII. THE CODE MESSAGE

It was strange! Most strange! Three days had passed, and to Gypsy Nan's lodging no one had come. The small crack under the partition that had been impressed into service as a letter-box had remained empty. There had been no messages--nothing--only a sinister, brooding isolation. Since the night Rhoda Gray had left Danglar, balked, almost a madman in his fury, in the little room over Shluker's junk shop, Danglar had not been seen--nor the Adventurer--nor even Rough Rorke. Her only visitant since then had been an ugly premonition of impending peril, which came and stalked like a hideous ghost about the bare and miserable garret, and which woke her at night with its whispering voice--which was the voice of intuition.

Rhoda Gray drew her shawl closer around her shoulders and shivered, as now, from shuffling down the block in the guise of Gypsy Nan, she halted before the street door of what fate, for the moment, had thrust upon her as a home; and shivered again, as, with abhorrence, she pushed the door open and stepped forward into the black, unlighted hallway. Soul, mind and body were in revolt to-night. Even faith, the simple faith in God that she had known since childhood, was wavering. There seemed nothing but horror around her, a mental horror, a physical horror; and the sole means of even momentary relief and surcease from it had been a pitiful prowling around the streets, where even the fresh air seemed to be denied to her, for it was tainted with the smells of squalor that ruled, rampant, in that neighborhood.

And to-night, stronger than ever, intuition and premonition of approaching danger lay heavy upon her, and oppressed her with a sense of nearness. She was not a coward; but she was afraid. Danglar would leave no stone unturned to get the White Moll. He had said so. She remembered the threat he had made--it had lived in her woman's soul ever since that night. Better anything than to fall into Danglar's hands! She caught her breath a little, and shivered again as she groped her way up the dark stairs. But, then, she never would fall into Danglar's power. There was always an alternative. Yes, it was quite as bad as that--death at her own hands was preferable. Balked, outwitted, the plans of the criminal coterie, of which Danglar appeared to be the head, rendered again and again abortive, and believing it all due to the White Moll, all of Danglar's shrewd, unscrupulous cunning would be centered on the task of running her down; and if, added to this, he discovered that she was masquerading as Gypsy Nan, one of their own inner circle, it mean that--She closed her lips in a hard, tight line. She did not want to think of it. She had fought all day, and the days before, against thinking about it, but premonition had crept upon her stronger and stronger, until to-night, now, it seemed as though her mind could dwell on nothing else.

On the landing, she paused suddenly and listened. The street door had opened and closed, and now a footstep sounded on the stairs behind her. She went on again along the hall, feeling her way; and reaching the short, ladder-like steps to the garret, she began to mount them. Who was it there behind her? One of the unknown lodgers on the lower floor, or--? She could not see, of course. It was pitch black. But she could hear. And as she knelt now on the narrow landing, and felt with her fingers along the floor for the aperture, where, imitating the custom of Gypsy Nan, she had left her key when she went out, she heard the footsteps coming steadily on, passing the doors below her, and making toward the garret ladder. And then, stifling a startled little cry, her hand closed on the key, and closed, as it had closed on that first night when she had returned here in the role of Gypsy Nan, on a piece of paper wrapped around the key. The days of isolation were ended with climacteric effect; the pendulum had swung full the other way--to-night there was both a visitor and a message!

The paper detached from the key and thrust into her bodice, she stood up quickly. A form, looming up even in the darkness, showed on the garret stairs. "Who's dere?" she croaked.

"It's all right," a voice answered in low tones. "You were just ahead of me on the street. I saw you come in. It's Pierre."

Pierre! So that was his name! It was only the voice she recognized. Pierre--

Danglar! She fumbled for the keyhole, found it, and inserted the key. "Well, how's Bertha to-night?"

There seemed to be a strange exhilaration in the man's voice. He was standing beside her now, close beside her, and now his hand played with a curiously caressing motion on her shoulder. The touch seemed to scorch and burn her. Who was this Danglar, who was Pierre to her, and to whom she was Bertha? Her breath came quickly in spite of herself; there came, too, a frenzy of aversion, and impulsively she flung his hand away, and with the door unlocked now, stepped from him into the garret.

"Feeling a bit off color, eh?" he said with a short laugh, as he followed her, and shut the door behind him. "Well, I don't know as I blame you. But, look here, old girl, have a heart! It's not my fault. I know what you're grouching about--it's because I haven't been around much lately. But you ought to know well enough that I couldn't help it. Our game has been crimped lately at every turn by that she-devil, the White Moll, and that dude pal of hers." He laughed out again--in savage menace now. "I've been busy. Understand, Bertha? It was either ourselves, or them. We've got to go under--or they have. And we won't! I promise you that! Things'll break a little better before long, and I'll make it up to you."

She could not see him in the blackness of the garret. She breathed a prayer of gratitude that he could not see her. Her face, in spite of Gipsy Nan's disguising grime, must be white, white as death itself. It seemed to plumb some infamous depth from which her soul recoiled, this apology of his for his neglect of her. And then her hands at her sides curled into tight-clenched little fists as she strove to control herself. His words, at least, supplied her with her cue.

"Of course!" she said tartly, but in perfect English--the vernacular of Gipsy Nan was not for Danglar, for she remembered only too well how once before it had nearly tripped her up. "But you didn't come here to apologize! What is it you want?"

"Ah, I say, Bertha!" he said appeasingly. "Cut that out! I couldn't help being away, I tell you. Of course, I didn't come here to apologize--I thought you'd understand well enough without that. The gang's out of cash, and I came to tap the reserves. Let me have a package of the long green, Bertha."

It was a moment before she spoke. Her woman's instinct prompted her to let down the bars between them in no single degree, that her protection lay in playing up to the full what Danglar, jumping at conclusions, had assumed was a grouch at his neglect. Also, her mind worked quickly. Her own clothes were no longer in the secret hiding place here in the garret; they were out there in that old shed in the lane. It was perfectly safe, then, to let Danglar go to the hiding place himself, assuming that he knew where it was--which, almost of necessity, he must.

"Oh!" she said ungraciously. "Well, you know where it is, don't you? Suppose you go and get it yourself!"

"All right!" returned Danglar, a sullenness creeping into his voice. "Have it your own way, Bertha! I haven't got time to-night to coax you out of your tantrums. That's what you want, but I haven't got time--to-night."

She did not answer.

A match crackled in Danglar's hand; the flames spurted up through the darkness. Danglar made his way over to the rickety washstand, found the candle that was stuck in the neck of the gin bottle, lighted it, held the candle above his head, and stared around the garret.

"Why the devil don't you get another lamp?" he grumbled--and started toward the rear of the garret.

Rhoda Gray watched him silently. She did not care to explain that she had not replaced the lamp for the very simple reason that it gave far too much light here in the garret to be safe--for her! She watched him, with her hand in the pocket of her greasy skirt clutched around another legacy of Gypsy Nan--her revolver. And now she became conscious that from the moment she had entered the garret, her fingers, hidden in that pocket, had sought and clung to the weapon. The man filled her with detestation and fear; and somehow she feared him more now in what he was trying to make an ingratiating mood, than she had feared him in the full flood of his rage and anger that other night at Shluker's place.

She drew back a little toward the cot bed against the wall, drew back to give him free passage to the door when he should return again, her eyes still holding on the far end of the garret, where, with the slope of the roof, the ceiling was no more than shoulder high. There seemed something horribly weird and grotesque in the scene before her. He had pushed the narrow trap-door in the ceiling upward, and had thrust candle and head through the opening, and the faint yellow light, seeping back and downward in flickering, uncertain rays, suggested the impression of a gruesome, headless figure standing there hazily outlined in the surrounding murk. It chilled her; she clutched at her shawl, drew it more closely about her, and edged still nearer to the wall.

And then Danglar closed the trap-door again, and came back with the candle in one hand, and one of the bulky packages of banknotes from the hiding place in the other. He set the candle down on the washstand, and began to distribute the money through his various pockets.

He was smiling with curious complacency.

"It was your job to play the spider to the White Moll if she ever showed up again here in your parlor," he said. "Maybe somebody tipped her off to keep away, maybe she was too wily; but, anyway, since you have not sent out any word, it is evident that our little plans along that line didn't work, since she has failed to come back to pay a call of gratitude to you. I don't suppose there's anything to add to that, eh, Bertha? No report to make?"

"No," said Rhoda Gray shortly. "I haven't any report to make."

"Well, no matter!" said Danglar. He laughed out shortly. "There are other ways! She's had her fling at our expense; it's her turn to pay now." He laughed again--and in the laugh now there was something both brutal in its menace, and sinister in its suggestion of gloating triumph.

"What do you mean?" demanded Rhoda Gray quickly. "What are you going to do?"

"Get her!" said Danglar. The man's passion flamed up suddenly; he spoke through his closed teeth. "Get her! I made her a little promise. I'm going to keep it! Understand?"

"You've been saying that for quite a long time," retorted Rhoda Gray coolly. "But the 'getting' has been all the other way so far. How are you going to get her?"

Danglar's little black eyes narrowed, and he thrust his head forward and out from his shoulders savagely. In the flickering candle light, with contorted face and snarling lips, he looked again the beast to which she had once likened him.

"Never mind how I'm going to get her!" he flung out, with an oath. "I told you I'd been busy. That's enough! You'll see--"

Rhoda Gray, in the semi-darkness, shrugged her shoulders. Was the man, prompted by rage and fury, simply making wild threats, or had he at last some definite and perhaps infallible plan that he purposed putting into operation? She did not know; and, much as it meant to her, she did not dare take the risk of arousing suspicion by pressing the question. Failing, then, to obtain any intimation of what he meant to do, the next thing most to be desired was to get rid of him.

"You've got the money. That's what you came for, wasn't it?" she suggested coldly.

He stared at her for a moment, and then his face gradually lost its scowl.

"You're a rare one, Bertha!" he exclaimed admiringly. "Yes; I've got the money--and I'm going. In fact, I'm in a hurry, so don't worry! You got the dope, like everybody else, for to-night, didn't you? It was sent out two hours ago."

The dope! It puzzled her for the fraction of a second--and then she remembered the paper she had thrust into the bodice of her dress. She had not read it. She lunged a little in the dark.

"Yes," she said curtly.

"All right!" he said-and moved toward the door. "That explains why I'm in a hurry--and why I can't stop to oil that grouch out of you. But I'll keep my promise to you, too, old girl. I'll make up the last few days to you. Have a heart, eh, Bertha! 'Night!"

She did not answer him. It seemed as though an unutterable dread had suddenly been lifted from her, as he passed out of the door and began to descend the steps to the hall below. Her "grouch," he had called it. Well, it had served its purpose! It was just as well that he should think so! She followed to the door, and deliberately slammed it with a bang. And from below, his laugh, more an amused chuckle, echoed back and answered her.

And then, for a long time she stood there by the door, a little weak with the revulsion of relief upon her, her hands pressed hard against her temples, staring unseeingly about the garret. He was gone. He filled her with terror. Every instinct she possessed, every fiber of her being revolted against him. He was gone. Yes, he was gone--for the time being. But--but what was the end of all this to be?

She shook her head after a moment, shook it helplessly and wearily, as, finally, she walked over to the washstand, took the piece of paper from the bodice of her dress, and spread it out under the candle light. A glance showed her that it was in cipher. There was the stub of a pencil, she remembered, in the washstand drawer, and, armed with this, and a piece of wrapping paper that had once enveloped one of Gypsy Nan's gin bottles, she took up the candle, crossed the garret, and sat down on the edge of the cot, placing the candle on the chair in front of her.

If the last three days had been productive of nothing else, they had at least furnished her with the opportunity of studying the notebook she had found in the secret hiding place, and of making herself conversant with the gang's cipher; and she now set to work upon it. It was a numerical cipher. Each letter of the alphabet in regular rotation was represented by its corresponding numeral; a zero was employed to set off one letter from another, and the addition of the numerals between the zeros indicated the number of the letter involved. Also, there being but twenty-six letters in the alphabet, it was obvious that the addition of three nines, which was twenty-seven, could not represent any letter, and the combination of 999 was therefore used to precede any of the arbitrary groups of numerals which were employed to express phrases and sentences, such as the 739 that she had found scrawled on the piece of paper around her key on the first night she had come here, and which, had it been embodied in a message and not preceded by the 999, would have meant simply the addition of seven, three and nine, that is, nineteen--and therefore would indicate the nineteenth letter of the alphabet, S.

Rhoda Gray copied the first line of the message on the piece of wrapping paper:

321010333203202306663103330111102210444202101112052110761

Adding the numerals between the zeros, and giving to each its corresponding letter, she set down the result:

6010110505022090405014030509014
f a k e e v i d e n c e i n

It was then but a matter of grouping the letters into words; and, decoded, the first line read:

Fake evidence in......

She worked steadily on. It was a lengthy message, and it took her a long time. It was an hour, perhaps more, after Danglar had gone, before she had completed her task; and then, after that, she sat for still a long time staring, not at the paper on the chair before her, but at the flickering shadows thrown by the candle on the opposite wall.

Queer and strange were the undercurrents and the cross-sections of life that were to be found, amazingly contradictory, amazingly incomprehensible, once one scratched beneath the surface of the poverty and the squalor, and, yes, the crime, amongst the hiving thousands of New York's East Side! In the days--not so very long ago--when, as the White Moll, she had worked amongst these classes, she had on one occasion, when he was sick, even kept old Viner in food. She had not, at the time, failed to realize that the man was grasping, rapacious, even unthankful, but she had little dreamed that he was a miser worth fifty thousand dollars!

Her mind swerved off suddenly at a tangent. The tentacles of this crime octopus, of which Danglar seemed to be the head, reached far and into most curious places to fasten and hold and feed on the progeny of human foibles! She could not help wondering where the lair was from which emanated the efficiency and system that, as witness this code message to-night, kept its members, perhaps widely scattered, fully informed of its every movement.

She shook her head. That was something she had not yet learned; but it was something she must learn if ever she hoped to obtain the evidence that would clear her of the crime that circumstances had fastened upon her. And yet she had made no move in that direction, because--well, because, so far, it had seemed all she could do to protect and safeguard herself in her present miserable existence and surroundings, which, abhorrent as they were, alone stood between her and a prison cell.

Her forehead gathered into little furrows; and, reverting to the code message, her thoughts harked back to a well-known crime, the authorship of which still remained a mystery, and which had stirred the East Side some two years ago. A man--in the vernacular of the underworld a "stage hand"--by the name of Kroner, credited with having a large amount of cash, the proceeds of some nefarious transaction, in his possession on the night in question, was found murdered in his room in an old and tumble-down tenement of unsavory reputation. The police net had gathered in some of the co-tenants on suspicion; Nicky Viner, referred to in the code message, amongst them. But nothing had come of the investigation. There had been no charge of collusion between the suspects; but Perlmer, a shyster lawyer, had acted for them all collectively, and, one and all, they had been discharged. In what degree Perlmer's services had been of actual value had never been ascertained, for the police, through lack of evidence, had been obliged to drop the case; but the underworld had whispered to itself. There was such a thing as suppressing evidence, and Perlmer was known to have the cunning of a fox, and a code of morals that never stood in the way, or restricted him in any manner.

The code message threw a new light on all this. Perlmer must have known that old Nicky Viner had money, for, according to the code message, Perlmer prepared a fake set of affidavits and forged a chain of fake evidence with which he had blackmailed Nicky Viner ever since; and Nicky Viner, known as a dissolute, shady character, innocent enough of the crime, but afraid because his possession of money if made public would tell against him, and frightened because he had already been arrested once on suspicion for that very crime, had whimpered--and paid. And then, somehow, Danglar and the gang had discovered that the old, seedy, stoop-shouldered, bearded, down-at-the-heels Nicky Viner was not all that he seemed; that he was a miser, and had a hoard of fifty thousand dollars--and Danglar and the gang had set out to find that hoard and appropriate it. Only they had not succeeded. But in their search they had stumbled upon Perlmer's trail, and that was the key to the plan they had afoot to-night. If Perlmer's fake and manufactured affidavits were clever enough and convincing enough to wring money out of Viner for Perlmer, they were more than enough to enable Danglar, employed as Danglar would employ them, to wring from Nicky Viner the secret of where the old miser hid his wealth; for Viner would understand that Danglar was not hampered by having to safeguard himself on account of having been originally connected with the case in a legal capacity, or any capacity, and therefore in demanding all or nothing, would have no cause for hesitation, failing to get what he wanted, in turning the evidence over to the police. In other words, where Perlmer had to play his man cautiously and get what he could, Danglar could go the limit and get all. As it stood, then, Danglar and the gang had not found out the location of that hoard; but they had found out where Perlmer kept his spurious papers--stuffed in at the back of the bottom drawer of his desk in his office, practically forgotten, practically useless to

Perlmer any more, for, having once shown them to Viner, there was no occasion to call them into service again unless Viner showed signs of getting a little out of hand and it became necessary to apply the screws once more.

For the rest, it was a very simple matter. Perlmer had an office in a small building on lower Sixth Avenue, and it was his custom to go to his office in the evenings and remain there until ten o'clock or so. The plan then, according to the code message, was to loot Perlmer's desk some time after the man had gone home for the night, and then, at midnight, armed with the false documents, to beard old Nicky Viner in his miserable quarters over on the East Side, and extort from the old miser the neat little sum that Danglar estimated would amount to some fifty thousand dollars in cash.

Rhoda Gray's face was troubled and serious. She found herself wishing for a moment that she had never decoded the message. But she shook her head in sharp self-protest the next instant. True, she would have evaded the responsibility that the criminal knowledge now in her possession had brought her; but she would have done so, in that case, deliberately at the expense of her own self-respect. It would not have excused her in her own soul to have sat staring at a cipher message that she was satisfied was some criminal plot, and have refused to decode it simply because she was afraid a sense of duty would involve her in an effort to frustrate it. To have sat idly by under those circumstances would have been as reprehensible--and even more cowardly--than it would be to sit idly by now that she knew what was to take place. And on that latter score to-night there was no argument with herself. She found herself accepting the fact that she would act, and act promptly, as the only natural corollary to the fact that she was in a position to do so. Perhaps it was that way to-night, not only because she had on a previous occasion already fought this principle of duty out with herself, but because to-night, unlike that other night, the way and the means seemed to present no insurmountable difficulties, and because she was now far better prepared, and free from all the perplexing, though enormously vital, little details that had on the former occasion reared themselves up in mountainous aspect before her. The purchase of a heavy veil, for instance, the day after the Hayden-Bond affair, would enable her now to move about the city in the clothes of the White Moll practically at will and without fear of detection. And, further, the facilities for making that change, the change from Gypsy Nan to the

White Moll, were now already at hand--in the little old shed down the lane.

And as far as any actual danger that she might incur to-night was concerned, it was not great. She was not interested in the fifty thousand dollars in an intrinsic sense; she was interested only in seeing that old Nicky Viner, unappealing, yes, and almost repulsive both in personality and habits as the man was, was not blackmailed out of it; that Danglar, yes, and hereafter, Perlmer too, should not prey like vultures on the man, and rob him of what was rightfully his. If, therefore, she secured those papers from Perlmer's desk, it automatically put an end to Danglar's scheme to-night; and if, later, she saw to it that those papers came into Viner's possession, that, too, automatically ended Perlmer's persecutions. Indeed, there seemed little likelihood of any danger or risk at all. It could not be quite ten o clock yet; and it was not likely that whoever was delegated by Danglar to rob Perlmer's office would go there much before eleven anyway, since they would naturally allow for the possibility that Perlmer might stay later in his office than usual, a contingency that doubtless accounted for midnight being set as the hour at which they proposed to lay old Nicky Viner by the heels. Therefore, it seemed almost a certainty that she would reach there, not only first, but with ample time at her disposal to secure the papers and get away again without interruption. She might even, perhaps, reach the office before Perlmer himself had left--it was still quite early enough for that--but in that case she need only remain on watch until the lawyer had locked up and gone away. Nor need even the fact that the office would be locked dismay her. In the secret hiding-place here in the garret, among those many other evidences of criminal activity, was the collection of skeleton keys, and--she was moving swiftly around the attic now, physically as active as her thoughts.

It was not like that other night. There were few preparations to make. She had only to secure the keys and a flashlight, and to take with her the damp cloth that would remove the grime streaks from her face, and the box of composition that would enable her to replace them when she came back--and five minutes later she was on the street, making her way toward the lane, and, specifically, toward the deserted shed where she had hidden away her own clothing.

IX. ROOM NUMBER ELEVEN

Another five minutes, and in her own personality now, a slim, trim figure, neatly gloved, the heavy veil affording ample protection to her features, Rhoda Gray emerged from the shed and the lane, and started rapidly toward lower Sixth Avenue. And as she walked, her mind, released for the moment from the consideration of her immediate venture, began again, as it had so many times in the last three days, its striving and its searching after some loophole of escape from her own desperate situation. But only, as it ever did, confusion came--a chaos of things, contributory things and circumstances, and the personalities of those with whom this impossible existence had thrown her into contact. Little by little she was becoming acquainted with the personnel of the gang--in an impersonal way, mostly. Apart from Danglar, there was Shluker, who must of necessity be one of them; and Skeeny, the man who had been with Danglar in Shluker's room; and the Cricket, whom she had never seen; and besides these, there were those who were mentioned in the cipher message to-night, and detailed to the performance of the various acts and scenes that were to lead up to the final climax--which, she supposed, was the object and reason for the cipher message, in order that even those not actually employed might be thoroughly conversant with the entire plan, and ready to act intelligently if called upon. For there were others, of course, as witness herself, or, rather, Gypsy Nan, whose personality she had so unwillingly usurped.

It was vital, necessary, that she should know them all, and more than in that impersonal way, if she counted upon ever freeing herself of the guilt attributed to her. For she could see no other way but one--that of exposing and proving the guilt of this vile clique who now surrounded her, and who had actually instigated and planned the crime of which she was accused. And it was not an easy task!

And then there were those outside this unholy circle who kept forcing their existence upon her consciousness, because they, too, played an intimate part in the sordid drama which revolved around her, and whose end she could not foresee. There was, for instance--the Adventurer. She drew in her breath quickly. She felt the color creep slowly upward, and tinge her throat and cheeks--and then the little chin, strong and firm, was lifted in a sort of self-defiant challenge. True, the man had been a great deal in her thoughts, but that was only because her curiosity was piqued, and because on two occasions now she had had very real cause for gratitude to him. If it had not been for the Adventurer, she would even now be behind prison bars. Why shouldn't she think of him? She was not an ingrate! Why shouldn't she be interested? There was something piquantly mysterious about the man--who called himself an adventurer. She would even have given a good deal to know who he really was, and how he, too, came to be so conversant with Danglar's plans as fast as they were matured, and why, on those two particular occasions, he had not only gone out of his way to be of service to her, but had done so at very grave risk to himself. Of course, she was interested in him--in that way. How could she help it? But in any other way--the little chin was still tilted defiantly upward--even the suggestion was absurd. The man might be chivalrous, courageous, yes, outwardly, even a gentleman in both manner and appearance; he might be all those things, and, indeed, was--but he was a thief, a professional thief and crook. It seemed very strange, of course; but she was judging him, not alone from the circumstances under which they had met and been together, but from what he had given her to understand about himself.

The defiance went suddenly from her face; and, for a moment, her lips quivered a little helplessly. It was all so very strange, and so forbidding, and--and, perhaps she hadn't the stout heart that a man would have--but she did not understand, and she could not see her way through the darkness that was like a pall wrapped about her--and it was hard just to grope out amidst surroundings that revolted her and made her soul sick. It was hard to do this and--and still keep her courage and her faith.

She shook her head presently as she went along, shook it reprovingly at herself, and the little shoulders squared resolutely back. There must be, and there would be, a way out of it all, and meanwhile her position, bad as it was, was not without, at least, a certain compensation. There had been the Sparrow the other night whom she had been able to save, and to-night there was Nicky Viner. She could not be blind to that. Who knew! It might be for just such very purposes that her life had been turned into these new channels!

She looked around her sharply now. She had reached the lower section of Sixth Avenue. Perlmer's office, according to the address given, was still a little farther on. She walked briskly. It was very different to-night, thanks to her veil! It had been horrible that other night, when she had ventured out as the White Moll and had been forced to keep to the dark alleyways and lanes, and the unfrequented streets!

And now, through a jeweler's window, she noted the time, and knew a further sense of relief. It was even earlier than she had imagined. It was not quite ten o'clock; she would, at least, be close on the heels of Perlmer's departure from his office, if not actually ahead of time, and therefore she would be first on the scene, and--yes, this was the place; here was Perlmer's name amongst those on the name-plate at the street entrance of a small three-story building.

She entered the hallway, and found it deserted. It was a rather dirty and unkempt place, and very poorly lighted--a single incandescent alone burned in the hall. Perlmer's room, so the name-plate indicated, was Number Eleven, and on the next floor.

She mounted the stairs, and paused on the landing to look around her again. Here, too, the hallway was lighted by but a single lamp; and here, too, an air of desertion was in evidence. The office tenants, it was fairly obvious, were not habitual night workers, for not a ray of light came from any of the glass-paneled doors that flanked both sides of the passage. She nodded her head sharply in satisfaction. It was equally obvious that Perlmer had already gone. It would take her but a moment, then, unless the skeleton keys gave her trouble. She had never used a key of that sort, but--She moved quietly down the hallway, and, looking quickly about her to assure herself again that she was not observed, stopped before the door of Room Number Eleven.

A moment she hung there, listening; then she slipped the skeleton keys from her pocket, and, in the act of inserting one of them tentatively into the keyhole, she tried the door--and with a little gasp of surprise returned the keys hurriedly to her pocket. The door was unlocked; it had even opened an inch already under her hand.

Again she looked around her, a little startled now; and instinctively her hand in her pocket exchanged the keys for her revolver. But she saw nothing, heard nothing; and it was certainly dark inside there, and therefore only logical to conclude that the room was unoccupied.

Reassured, she pushed the door cautiously and noiselessly open, and stepped inside, and closed the door behind her. She stood still for an instant, and then the round, white ray of her flashlight went dancing inquisitively around the office. It was a medium-sized room, far from ornate in its appointments, bare floored, the furniture of the cheapest--Perlmer's clientele did not insist on oriental rugs and mahogany!

Her appraisal of the room, however, was but cursory. She was interested only in the flat-topped desk in front of her. She stepped quickly around it--and stopped-- and a low cry of dismay came from her as she stared at the floor. The lower drawer had been completely removed, and now lay upturned beside the swivel chair, its contents strewn around in all directions.

And for a moment she stared at the scene, nonplused, discomfited. She had been so sure that she would be first--and she had not been first. There was no need to search amongst those papers on the floor. They told their own story. The ones she wanted were already gone.

In a numbed way, mechanically, she retreated to the door; and, with the flashlight playing upon it, she noticed for the first time that the lock had been roughly forced. It was but corroborative of the despoiled drawer; and, at the same time, the obvious reason why the door had not been relocked when whoever had come here had gone out again.

Whoever had come here! She could have laughed out hysterically. Was there any doubt as to who it was? One of Danglar's emissaries; the Cricket, perhaps-or perhaps even Danglar himself! They had seen to it that lack of prompt action, at least, would not be the cause of marring their plans.

A little dazed, overwrought, confused at the ground being cut from under her where she had been so confident of a sure footing, she made her way out of the building, and to the street--and for a block walked almost aimlessly along. And then suddenly she turned hurriedly into a cross street, and headed over toward the East Side. The experience had not been a pleasant one, and it had upset most thoroughly all her calculations; but it was very far, after all, from being disastrous. It meant simply that she must now find Nicky Viner himself and warn the man, and there was ample time in which to do that. The code message specifically stated midnight as the hour at which they proposed to favor old Viner with their unhallowed attentions, and as it was but a little after ten now, she had nearly a full two hours in which to accomplish what should not take her more than a few minutes.

Rhoda Gray's lips tightened a little, as she hurried along. Old Nicky Viner still lived in the same disreputable tenement in which he had lived on the night of that murder two years ago, and she could not ward off the thought that it had been--yes, and was--an ideal place for a murder, from the murderer's standpoint! The neighborhood was one of the toughest in New York, and the tenement itself was frankly nothing more than a den of crooks. True, she had visited there more than once, had visited Nicky Viner there; but she had gone there then as the White Moll, to whom even the most abandoned would have touched his cap. To-night it was very different--she went there as a woman. And yet, after all--she amended her own thoughts, smiling a little seriously--surely she could disclose herself as the White Moll there again to-night if the actual necessity arose, for surely crooks, pokegetters, shillabers and lags though they were, and though the place teemed with the dregs of the underworld, no one of them, even for the reward that might be offered, would inform against her to the police! And yet--again the mental pendulum swung the other way--she was not so confident of that as she would like to be. In a general way there could be no question but that she could count on the loyalty of those who lived there; but there were always those upon whom one could never count, those who were dead to all sense of loyalty, and alive only to selfish gain and interest--a human trait that, all too unfortunately, was not confined to those alone who lived in that shadowland outside the law. Her face, beneath the thick veil, relaxed a little. Well, she certainly did not intend to make a test case of it and disclose herself there as the White Moll, if she could help it! She would enter the tenement unnoticed if she could, and make her way to Nicky Viner's two miserable rooms on the second floor as secretively as she could. And, knowing the place as she did, she was quite satisfied that, if she were careful enough and cautious enough, she could both enter and leave without being seen by any one except, of course, Nicky Viner.

She walked on quickly. Five minutes, ten minutes passed; and now, in a narrow street, lighted mostly by the dull, yellow glow that seeped up from the sidewalk through basement entrances, queer and forbidding portals to sinister interiors, or filtered through the dirty windows of uninviting little shops that ran the gamut from Chinese laundries to oyster dens, she halted, drawn back in the shadows of a doorway, and studied a tenement building that was just ahead of her. That was where old Nicky Viner lived. A smile of grim whimsicality touched her lips. Not a light showed in the place from top to bottom. From its exterior it might have been uninhabited, even long deserted. But to one who knew, it was quite the normal condition, quite what one would expect. Those who lived there confined their activities mostly to the night; and their exodus to their labors began when the labors of the world at large ended--with the fall of darkness.

For a little while she watched the place, and kept glancing up and down the street; and then, seizing her opportunity when for half a block or more the street was free of pedestrians, she stole forward and reached the tenement door. It was half open, and she slipped quickly inside into the hall.

She stood here for a moment motionless; listening, striving to accommodate her eyes to the darkness, and instinctively her hand went to her pocket for the reassuring touch of her revolver. It was black back there in the hallway of Gypsy Nan's lodging; she had not thought that any greater degree of blackness could exist; but it was blacker here. Only the sense of touch promised to be of any avail. If one could have moved as noiselessly as a shadow moves, one could have passed another within arm's-length unseen. And so she listened, listened intently. And there was very little sound. Once she detected a footstep from the interior of some room as it moved across a bare floor; once she heard a door creak somewhere upstairs; and once, from some indeterminate direction, she thought she heard voices whispering together for a moment.

She moved suddenly then, abruptly, almost impulsively, but careful not to make the slightest noise. She dared not remain another instant inactive. It was what she had expected, what she had counted upon as an ally, this darkness, but she was not one who laughed, even in daylight, at its psychology. It was beginning to attack her now; her imagination to magnify even the actual dangers that she knew to be around her. And she must fight it off before it got a hold upon her, and before panic voices out of the blackness began to shriek and clamor in her ears, as she knew they would do with pitifully little provocation, urging her to turn and flee incontinently.

The staircase, she remembered, was at her right; and feeling out before her with her hands, she reached the stairs, and began to mount them. She went slowly, very slowly. They were bare, the stairs, and unless one were extremely careful they would creak out through the silence with a noise that could be heard from top to bottom of the tenement. But she was not making any noise; she dared not make any noise.

Halfway up she halted and pressed her body close against the wall. Was that somebody coming? She held her breath in expectation. There wasn't a sound now, but she could have sworn she had heard a footstep on the hallway above, or on the upper stairs. She bit her lips in vexation. Panic noises! That's what they were! That, and the thumping of her heart! Why was it that alarms and exaggerated fancies came and tried to unnerve her? What, after all, was there really to be afraid of? She had almost a clear two hours before she need even anticipate any actual danger here, and, if Nicky Viner were in, she would be away from the tenement again in another fifteen minutes at the latest.

Rhoda Gray went on again, and gaining the landing, halted once more. And here she smiled at herself with the tolerant chiding she would have accorded a child that was frightened without warrant. She could account for those whisperings and that footstep now. The door to the left, the one next to Nicky Viner's squalid, two-room apartment, was evidently partially open, and occasionally some one moved within; and the voices came from there too, and, low-toned to begin with, were naturally muffled into whispers by the time they reached her.

She had only, then, to step the five or six feet across the narrow hall in order to reach Nicky Viner's door, and unless by some unfortunate chance whoever was in that room happened to come out into the hall at the same moment, she would-- Yes, it was all right! She was trying Nicky Viner's door now. It was unlocked, and as she opened it for the space of a crack, there showed a tiny chink of light, so faint and meager that it seemed to shrink timorously back again as though put to rout by the massed blackness--but it was enough to evidence the fact that Nicky Viner was at home. It was all simple enough now. Old Viner would undoubtedly make some exclamation at her sudden and stealthy entrance, but once she was inside without those in the next room either having heard or seen her, it would not matter.

Another inch she pushed the door open, another--and then another. And then quickly, silently, she tip-toed over the threshold and closed the door softly behind her. The light came from the inner room and shone through the connecting door, which was open, and there was movement from within, and a low, growling voice, petulant, whining, as though an old man were mumbling complainingly to himself. She smiled coldly. It was very like Nicky Viner--it was a habit of his to talk to himself, she remembered. And, also, she had never heard Nicky Viner do anything else but grumble and complain.

But she could not see fully into the other room, only into a corner of it, for the two doors were located diagonally across from one another, and her hand, in a startled way, went suddenly to her lips, as though mechanically to help choke back and stifle the almost overpowering impulse to cry out that arose within her. Nicky Viner was not alone in there! A figure had come into her line of vision in that other room, not Nicky Viner, not any of the gang--and she stared now in incredulous amazement, scarcely able to believe her eyes. And then, suddenly cool and self-possessed again, relieved in a curious way because the element of personal danger was as a consequence eliminated, she began to understand why she had been forestalled in her efforts at Perlmer's office when she had been so sure that she would be first upon the scene. It was not Danglar, or the Cricket, or Skeeny, or any of the band who had forestalled her--it was the Adventurer. That was the Adventurer standing in there now, side face to her, in Nicky Viner's inner room!

X. ON THE BRINK

Rhoda Gray moved quietly, inch by inch, along the side of the wall to gain a point of vantage more nearly opposite the lighted doorway. And then she stopped again. She could see quite clearly now--that is, there was nothing now to obstruct her view; but the light was miserable and poor, and the single gas-jet that wheezed and flickered did little more than disperse the shadows from its immediate neighborhood in that inner room. But she could see enough--she could see the bent and ill-clad figure of Nicky Viner, as she remembered him, an old, gray-bearded man, wringing his hands in groveling misery, while the mumbling voice, now whining and pleading, now servile, now plucking up courage to indulge in abuse, kept on without even, it seemed, a pause for breath. And she could see the Adventurer, quite unmoved, quite debonair, a curiously patient smile on his face, standing there, much nearer to her, his right hand in the side pocket of his coat, a somewhat significant habit of his, his left hand holding a sheaf of folded, legal-looking documents.

And then she heard the Adventurer speak.

"What a flow of words!" said the Adventurer, in a bored voice. "You will forgive me, my dear Mr. Viner, if I appear to be facetious, which I am not--but money talks."

"You are a thief, a robber!" The old gray-bearded figure rocked on its feet and kept wringing its hands. "Get out of here! Get out! Do you hear? Get out! You come to steal from a poor old man, and--"

"Must we go all over that again?" interrupted the Adventurer wearily. "I have not come to steal anything; I have simply come to sell you these papers, which I am quite sure, once you control yourself and give the matter a little calm consideration, you are really most anxious to buy--at any price.

"It's a lie!" the other croaked hoarsely. "Those papers are a lie! I am innocent. And I haven't got any money. None! I haven't any. I am poor--an old man--and poor."

Rhoda Gray felt the blood flush hotly to her cheeks. Somehow she could feel no sympathy for that cringing figure in there; but she felt a hot resentment toward that dapper, immaculately dressed and self-possessed young man, who stood there, silently now, tapping the papers with provoking coolness against the edge of the plain deal table in front of him. And somehow the resentment seemed to take a most peculiar phase. She resented the fact that she should feel resentment, no matter what the man did or said. It was as though, instead of anger, impersonal anger, at this low, miserable act of his, she felt ashamed of him. Her hand clenched fiercely as she crouched there against the wall. It wasn't true! She felt nothing of the sort! Why should she be ashamed of him? What was he to her? He was frankly a thief, wasn't he? And he was at his pitiful calling now--down to the lowest dregs of it. What else did she expect? Because he had the appearance of a gentleman, was it that her sense of gratitude for what she owed him had made her, deep down in her soul, actually cherish the belief that he really was one--made her hope it, and nourish that hope into belief? Tighter her hand clenched. Her lips parted, and her breath came in short, hard inhalations. Was it true? Was it all only an added misery, where it had seemed there could be none to add to her life in these last few days? Was it true that there was no price she would not have paid to have found him in any role but this abased one that he was playing now?

The Adventurer broke the silence.

"Quite so, my dear Mr. Viner!" he agreed smoothly. "It would appear, then, from what you say that I have been mistaken--even stupidly so, I am afraid. And in that case, I can only apologize for my intrusion, and, as you so delicately put it, get out." He slipped the papers, with a philosophic shrug of his shoulders, into his inside coat pocket, and took a backward step toward the door. "I bid you good-night, then, Mr. Viner. The papers, as you state, are doubtless of no value to you, so you can, of course, have no objection to my handing them over to the police, who--"

"No, no! Wait! Wait!" the other whispered wildly. "Wait!"

"Ah!" murmured the Adventurer.

"I--I'll"--the bent old figure was clawing at his beard--"I'll--"

"Buy them?" suggested the Adventurer pleasantly.

"Yes, I'll--I'll buy them. I--I've got a little money, only a little, all I've been able to save in years, a--a hundred dollars.

"How much did you say?" inquired the Adventurer coldly.

"Two hundred." The voice was a maudlin whine.

The Adventurer took another backward step toward the door.

"Three hundred!"

Another step.

"Five--a thousand!"

The Adventurer laughed suddenly.

"That's better!" he said. "Where you keep a thousand, you keep the rest. Where is the thousand, Mr. Viner?"

The bent figure hesitated a moment; and then, with what sounded like a despairing cry, pointed to the table.

"It's there," he whimpered. "God's curses on you, for the thief you are."

Rhoda Gray found her eyes fixed in sudden, strained fascination on the table-- as, she imagined, the Adventurer's were too. It was bare of any covering, nor were there any articles on its surface, nor, as far as she could see, was there any drawer. And now the Adventurer, his right hand still in his coat pocket, and bulging there where she knew quite well it grasped his revolver, stepped abruptly to the table, facing the other with the table between them.

The bent old figure still hesitated, and then, with the despairing cry again, grasped at the top of the table, and jerked it toward him. The surface seemed to slide sideways a little way, a matter of two or three inches, and then stick there; but the Adventurer, in an instant, had thrust the fingers of his left hand into the crevice. He drew out a number of loose banknotes, and thrust his fingers in again for a further supply.

"Open it wider!" he commanded curtly.

"I--I'm trying to," the other mumbled, and bent down to peer under the table. "It's stuck. The catch is underneath, and--"

It seemed to Rhoda Gray, gazing into that dimly lighted room, as though she were suddenly held spellbound as in some horrible and amazing trance. Like a hideous jack-in-the-box the gray head popped above the level of the table again, and quick as a flash, a revolver was thrust into the Adventurer's face; and the Adventurer, caught at a disadvantage, since his hand in his coat pocket was below the intervening table top, stood there as though instantaneously transformed into some motionless, inanimate thing, his fingers still gripping at another sheaf of banknotes that he had been in the act of scooping out from the narrow aperture.

And then again Rhoda Gray stared, and stared now as though bereft of her senses; and upon her crept, cold and deadly, a fear and a terror that seemed to engulf her very soul itself. That head that looked like a jack-in-the-box was gone; the gray beard seemed suddenly to be shorn away, and the gray hair too, and to fall and flutter to the table, and the bent shoulders were not bent any more, and it wasn't Nicky Viner at all--only a clever, a wonderfully clever, impersonation that had been helped out by the poor and meager light. And terror gripped at her again, for it wasn't Nicky Viner. Those narrowed eyes, that leering, gloating face, those working lips were Danglar's.

And, as from some far distance, dulled because her consciousness was dulled, she heard Danglar speak.

"Perhaps you'll take your hand out of that right-hand coat pocket of yours now!" sneered Danglar. "And take it out--empty!"

The Adventurer's face, as nearly as Rhoda Gray could see, had not moved a muscle. He obeyed now, coolly, with a shrug of his shoulders.

Danglar appeared to experience no further trouble with the surface of the table now. He suddenly jerked it almost off, displaying what Rhoda Gray now knew to be the remainder of the large package of banknotes he had taken from the garret earlier in the evening.

"Help yourself to the rest!" he invited caustically. "There isn't fifty thousand there, but you are quite welcome to all there is--in return for those papers."

The Adventurer was apparently obsessed with an inspection of his finger nails; he began to polish those of one hand with the palm of the other.

"Quite so, Danglar!" he said coolly. "I admit it--I am ashamed of myself. I hate to think that I could be caught by you; but I suppose I can find some self-extenuating circumstances. You seem to have risen to an amazingly higher order of intelligence. In fact, for you, Danglar, it is not at all bad!" He went on polishing his nails. "Would you mind taking that thing out of my face? Even you ought to be able to handle it effectively a few inches farther away."

Under the studied insult Danglar's face had grown a mottled red.

"Damn you!" he snarled. "I'll take it away when I get good and ready; and by that time I'll have you talking out of the other side of your mouth! See? Do you know what you're up against, you slick dude?"

"I have a fairly good imagination," replied the Adventurer smoothly.

"You have, eh?" mimicked Danglar wickedly. "Well, you don't need to imagine anything! I'll give you the straight goods so's there won't be any chance of a mistake. And never mind about the higher order of intelligence! It was high enough, and a little to spare, to make you walk into the trap! I hoped I'd get you both, you and your she-pal, the White Moll; that you'd come here together--but I'm not kicking. It's a pretty good start to get you!"

"Is it necessary to make a speech?" complained the Adventurer monotonously. "I can't help listening, of course."

"You can make up your mind for yourself when I'm through--whether it's necessary or not!" retorted Danglar viciously. "I've got a little proposition to put up to you, and maybe it'll help you to add two and two together if I let you see all the cards. Understand? You've had your run of luck lately, quite a bit of it, haven't you, you and the White Moll? Well, it's my turn now! You've been queering our game to the limit, curse you!" Danglar thrust his working face a little farther over the table, and nearer to the Adventurer. "Well, what was the answer? Where did you get the dope you made your plays with? It was a cinch, wasn't it, that there was a leak somewhere in our own crowd?" He laughed out suddenly. "You poor fool! Did you think you could pull that sort of stuff forever? Did you? Well, then, how do you like the 'leak' to-night? You get the idea, don't you? Everybody, every last soul that is in with us, got the details of what they thought was a straight play to-night--and it leaked to you, as I knew it would; and you walked into the trap, as I knew you would, because the bait was good and juicy, and looked the easiest thing to annex that ever happened. Fifty thousand dollars! Fifty thousand--nothing! All you had to do was to get a few papers that it wouldn't bother any crook to get, even a near--crook like you, and then come here and screw the money out of a helpless old man, who was supposed to have been discovered to be a miser. Easy, wasn't it? Only Nicky Viner wasn't a miser! We chose Nicky because of what happened two years ago. It made things look pretty near right, didn't it? Looked straight, that part about Perlmer, too, didn't it? That was the come-on. Perlmer never saw those papers you've got there in your pocket. I doped them out, and we planted them nice and handy where you could get them without much trouble in the drawer of Perlmer's desk, and--"

"It's a long story," interrupted the Adventurer, with quiet insolence.

"It's got a short ending," said Danglar, with an ugly leer. "We could have bumped you off when you went for those papers, but if you went that far you'd come farther, and that wasn't the place to do it, and we couldn't cover ourselves there the way we could here. This is the place. We brought that trick table here a while ago, as soon as we had got rid of Nicky Viner. That was the only bit of stage setting we had to do to make the story ring true right up to the curtain, in case it was necessary. It wouldn't have been necessary if you and the White Moll had both come together, for then you would neither of you have got any further than that other room. It would have ended there. But we weren't taking any chances. I'll pay you the compliment of admitting that we weren't counting on getting you off your guard any too easily if, as it happened, you came alone, for, being alone, or if either of you were alone, there was that little proposition that had to be settled, instead of just knocking you on the head out there in the dark in that other room; and so, as I say, we weren't overlooking any bets on account of the little trouble it took to plant that table and the money. We tried to think of everything!" Danglar paused for a moment to mock the Adventurer with narrowed eyes. "That's the story; here's the end. I hoped I'd get you both together, you and the White Moll. I didn't. But I've got you. I didn't get you both--and that's what gives you a chance for your life, because she's worth more to us than you are. If you'd been together, you would have gone out-together. As it is, I'll see that you don't do any more harm anyway, but you get one chance. Where is she? If you answer that, you will, of course, answer a minor question and locate that 'leak', for me, that I was speaking about a moment ago. But we'll take the main thing first. And you can take your choice between a bullet and a straight answer. Where is the White Moll?"

Rhoda Gray's hand felt Out along the wall for support. Was this a dream, some ghastly, soul-terrifying nightmare! Danglar! Those working lips! That callous viciousness, that leer in the degenerate face. It seemed to bring a weakness to her limbs, and seek to rob her of the strength to stand. She could not even hope against hope; she knew that Danglar was in deadly earnest. Danglar would not have the slightest compunction, let alone hesitation, in carrying out his threat. Terrified now, her eyes sought the Adventurer. Didn't the Adventurer know Danglar as she knew him, didn't he realize that there was deadly earnestness behind Danglar's words? Was the man mad, that he stood there utterly unmoved, as though he had no consideration on earth other than those carefully manicured finger nails of his!

And then Danglar spoke again.

"Do you notice anything special about this gun I'm holding on you?" he demanded, in low menace.

The Adventurer did not even look up.

"Oh, yes," he said indifferently. "I fancy you got it out of a dime novel, didn't you? One of those silencer things."

"Yes," said Danglar grimly; "one of those silencer things. Where is she?"

The Adventurer made no answer.

The color in Danglar's face deepened.

"I'll make things even a little plainer to you," he said with brutal coolness. "There are two men in our organization from whom it is absolutely impossible that that leak could have come. Those two men followed you from Perlmer's office to this place. They are in the next room now waiting for me to get through with you, and ready for anything if they are needed. But they won't be needed. That's not the way it works out. This gun won't make much noise, and it isn't likely to arouse the inmates of this dive, but even if it does, it doesn't matter very much--we aren't going out by the front door. The two of them, the minute they hear the shot, slip in here, and lock the door--you see it's got a good, husky bolt on it--and then we beat it by the fire escape that runs past that window there. Get the idea? And don't kid yourself into thinking that I am taking any risk with the consequences on account of the coroner having got busy because a man was found here dead on the floor. Nicky Viner stands for that. It isn't the first time he's been suspected of murder. See? Nicky was easy. He'd crawl on his hands and knees from the Battery to Harlem any time if you held a little money in front of his nose. He's been fooled up to the eyes with a faked-up message that he's to deliver secretly to some faked-up crooks out West. He's just about starting away on the train now. And that's where the police nab him--running away from the murder he's pulled in his room here to-night. Looks kind of bad for Nicky Viner--eh? We should worry! It cost a hundred dollars and his ticket. Cheap, wasn't it? I guess you're worth that much to us."

A dull horror seized upon Rhoda Gray. It seemed to clog and confuse her mind. She fought it frantically, striving to think, and to think clearly. Every detail seemed to have been planned with Satanic foresight and ingenuity, and yet--and yet--Yes, in one little thing, Danglar had made a mistake. That was why she was here now; that was why those men in that next room had not been out in the hall on guard, or even out in the street on watch for her. Danglar had naturally gone upon the supposition that the Adventurer and herself worked hand in glove; whereas they were as much in the dark concerning each other's movements as Danglar himself was. Therefore Danglar, and logically enough from his viewpoint, had jumped to the conclusion that, since they had not come together, only one of them, the Adventurer, was acting in the affair to-night, and--Danglar's voice was rasping in her ears.

"I'm not going to stay here all night!" he snarled. "You've got one chance. I've told you what it is. You're lucky to have it. We'd sooner have you out of the way for keeps. I'd rather drop you in your tracks than let you live. Where is the White Moll?"

The Adventurer was side face to the doorway again, and Rhoda Gray saw him smile contemptuously at Danglar now.

"Really," he said blandly, "I haven't the slightest idea in the world."

Danglar laughed ironically.

"You lie!" he flung out hoarsely. "Do you think you can get away with that? Well, think again! Sooner or later, it will be all the same whether you talk or not. We caught you to-night in a trap; we'll catch her in another. Our hand doesn't show here. She'll think that Nicky Viner was a little too much for you, that's all. Come on, now--quick! Are you fool enough to misunderstand? The 'don't know' stuff won't get you by!"

"The misunderstanding seems to be on your side." There was a cold, irritating deliberation in the Adventurer's voice. "I repeat that I do not know where the young lady you refer to could be found; but I did not make that statement with any idea that you would believe it. To a cur, I suppose it is necessary to add that, even if

I did know, I should take pleasure in seeing you damned before I told you."

Danglar's face was like a devil's. His revolver held a steady bead on the Adventurer's head.

"I'll give you a last chance." He spoke through closed teeth. "I'll fire when I count three. One!"

A horrible fascination held Rhoda Gray. If she cried out, it was more likely than not to cause Danglar to fire on the instant. It would not save the Adventurer in any case. It would be but the signal, too, for those two men in the next room to rush in here.

"Two!"

It seemed as though, not in the hope that it would do any good, but because she was going mad with horror, that she would scream out until the place rang and rang again with her outcries. Even her soul was in frantic panic. Quick! Quick! She must act! She must! But how? Was there only one way? She was conscious that she had drawn her revolver as though by instinct. Danglar's life, or the Adventurer's! But she shrank from taking life. Her lips were breathing a prayer. They had called her a crack shot back there in South America, when she had hunted and ridden with her father. It was easy enough to hit Danglar, but that might mean Danglar's life; it was not so easy to hit Danglar's arm, or Danglar's hand, or the revolver Danglar held, and if she risked that and missed, she...

"Thr--"

There was the roar of a report that went racketing through the silence like a cannon shot, and the short, vicious tongue-flame from Rhoda Gray's revolver muzzle stabbed through the black. There was a scream of mingled surprise and fury, and the revolver in Danglar's hand clattered to the floor. She saw the Adventurer spring, quick as a panther, at the other, and saw him whip blow after blow with terrific force full into Danglar's face; she heard a rush of feet coming from the corridor behind her; and she flung herself forward into the inner room, and, panting, snatched at the door and slammed it shut, and groping for the bolt, found it, and shot it home in its grooves.

And she stood there, weak for the moment, and drew her hand across her eyes--and behind her they pounded on the door, and there came a burst of oaths; and in front of her the Adventurer was smiling gravely as he covered Danglar with

Danglar's own revolver; and Danglar, as though dazed and half stunned from the blows he had received, rocked unsteadily upon his feet. And then her eyes widened a little. The pounding on the door, the shouts, the noise, was beginning to arouse what inmates there were in the tenement, and there wasn't an instant to lose--but the Adventurer now was calmly gathering up, to the last one, and pocketing them, the banknotes with which Danglar had baited his trap. And as he crammed the money into his pockets, he spoke to her, with a curious softness, a great, strange gentleness in his voice:

"I owe you my life, Miss Gray. That was a wonderful shot. You knocked the revolver from his hand without even grazing his fingers. A very wonderful shot, and--will you let me say it?--you are a very wonderful woman."

"Oh, quick!" she whispered wildly. "I am afraid this door will not hold."

"There is the window, and the fire escape, so our friend here was good enough to inform me," said the Adventurer, as he composedly pocketed the last dollar. "Will you open the window, Miss Gray, if you please? I am afraid I hit Mr. Danglar a little ungently, and as he is still somewhat groggy, I fancy he will need a little assistance. I imagine"--he caught Danglar suddenly by the collar of his coat as Rhoda Gray ran to the window and flung it up, and rushed the man unceremoniously across the room--"I imagine it would be a mistake to leave him behind. He might open the door, or even be unpleasant enough to throw something down on us from above; also he should serve us very well as a hostage. Will you go first, please, Miss Gray?"

She climbed quickly over the sill to the iron platform. Danglar was dragged through by the Adventurer, mumbling, and evidently still in a half-dazed condition. Windows were opening here and there. From back inside the room, the blows rained more heavily upon the door--and now there came the rip and rend of wood, as though a panel had crashed in.

"Hurry, please, Miss Gray!" prompted the Adventurer.

It was dark, almost too dark to see her footing. She felt her way down. It was only one story above the ground, and it did not take long; but it seemed hours since she had fired that shot, though she knew the time had been measured by scarcely more than a minute. And now, on the lower platform, waiting for that queer, double, twisting shadow of the two men to join her, she heard the Adventurers s voice ring out sharply:

"This is your chance, Danglar! I didn't waste the time to bring you along because it afforded me any amusement. They've found their heads at last, and gone to the next window, instead of wasting time on that door. They can't reach the fire escape there, but if they fire a single shot--you go out! You'd better tell them so-- and tell them quick!"

And then Danglar's voice shrieked out in sudden, "for God's sake, don't fire!"

They were all on the lower platform together now. The Adventurer was pressing the muzzle of his revolver into the small of Danglar's back, and was still supporting the man by the collar of his coat.

"I think," said the Adventurer abruptly, "that we can now dispense with Mr. Danglar's services, and I am sure a little cool night air out here on the fire escape will do him good. Miss Gray--would you mind?--there's a pair of handcuffs in my left-hand coat pocket."

Handcuffs! She could have laughed out idiotically. Handcuffs! They seemed the most incongruous things in the world for the Adventurer to have, and--She felt mechanically in his pocket, and handed them to him.

There was a click as a cuff was snapped over Danglar's wrist, another as the other cuff was snapped shut around the iron hand-railing of the fire escape. The act seemed to arouse Danglar, both mentally and physically. He tore and wrenched at the steel links now, and burst suddenly, raving, into oaths.

"Hold your tongue, Danglar!" ordered the Adventurer in cold menace; and as the other, cowed, obeyed, the Adventurer swung himself over the platform and dropped to the ground. "Come, Miss Gray. Drop! I'll catch you!" he called in a low voice. "One step takes us around the corner of the tenement into the lane, and Mr. Danglar won't let them fire at us before we can make that--when we could still fire at him!"

She obeyed him, swinging at arm's-length. She felt his hands fold about her in a firm grasp as she let go her hold, and she caught her breath suddenly, she did not know why, and felt the hot blood sweep her face--and then she was standing on the ground.

"Now!" he whispered. "Together!"

They sped around the corner of the tenement. A yell from Danglar followed them. An echoing yell from above answered--and then a fusillade of abortive shots, and the sound as of boot heels clattering on the iron rungs of the fire escape; and then, more faintly, for they were putting distance behind them as fast as they could run, an excited outburst of profanity and exclamations.

"They won't follow!" panted the Adventurer. "Those shots of theirs outdoors will have alarmed the police, and they'll try and get Danglar free first. It's lucky your shot inside wasn't heard by the patrolman on the beat. I was afraid of that. But we're safe now--from Danglar's crowd, at least."

But still they ran. They crossed an intersecting street, and continued on along the lane; then swerving into the next intersecting street, moderated their pace to a rapid walk--and stopped finally only as Rhoda Gray drew suddenly into the shadows of another alley-way, and held out her hand. They were both safe now, as he had said. And there were so many reasons why, though her resolution faltered a little, she should go the rest of the way alone. She was not sure that she trusted this strange "gentleman," who was a thief with his pockets crammed even now with the money that had lured him almost to his death; but, too, she was not altogether sure that she distrusted him. But all that was secondary. She must, as soon as she could, get back to Gypsy Nan's garret. Like that other night, she dared not take the risk that Danglar, by any chance, might return there--and find her gone after what had just happened. The man would be beside himself with fury, suspicious of everything-and suspicion would be fatal in its consequences for her. And so she must go. And she could not become Gypsy Nan again with the Adventurer looking on!

"We part here," she said a little unsteadily. "Good-night!"

"Oh, I say, Miss Gray!" he protested quickly. "You don't mean that! Why, look here, I haven't had a chance to tell you what I think, or what I feel, about what you've done to-night--for me."

She shook her head.

"There is nothing you need say," she answered quietly. "We are only quits. You have done quite as much for me."

"But, see here, Miss Gray!" he pleaded. "Can't we come to some understanding? We seem to have a jolly lot in common. Is it quite necessary, really necessary, that you should keep me off at arm's-length? Couldn't you let down the bars just a little? Couldn't you tell me, for instance, where I could find you in case of--real necessity?"

She shook her head again.

"No," she said. "It is impossible."

He drew a little closer. A sudden earnestness deepened his voice, made it rasp a little, as though it were not wholly within control.

"And suppose, Miss Gray, that I refuse to leave you, or to let you go, now that I have you here, unless you give me more of your confidence? What then?"

"The other night," she said slowly, "you informed me, among other things, that you were a gentleman. I believed the other things."

He did not answer for a moment--and then he smiled whimsically.

"You score, Miss Gray," he murmured.

"Good night, then!" she said again. "I will go by the alley here; you by the street."

"No! Wait!" he said gravely. "If nothing will change your mind--and I shall not be importunate, for, as we have met three times now through the same peculiar chain of circumstances, I know we shall meet again--I have something to tell you, before you go. As you already know, I went to Gypsy Nan's the night after I first saw you, because I felt you needed help. I went there in the hope that she would know where to find you, and, failing in that, I left a message for you in the hope that, since she had tricked Rorke in your behalf, you would find means of communicating with her again. But all that is entirely changed now. Your participation in that Hayden-Bond affair the other night makes Gypsy Nan's place the last in all New York to which you should go."

Rhoda Gray stared through the semi-darkness, suddenly startled, searching the Adventurer's face.

"What do you mean?" she demanded quickly.

"Just this," he answered. "That where before I hoped you would go there, I have spent nearly all the time since then in haunting the vicinity of Gypsy Nan's house to warn you away in case you should try to reach her."

"I--I don't understand," she said a little uncertainly.

"It is simple enough," he said. "Gypsy Nan is now one of those you have most to fear. Gypsy Nan is merely a disguise. She is no more Gypsy Nan than you are."

Rhoda Gray caught her breath.

"Not Gypsy Nan!" she repeated--and fought to keep her voice in control. "Who is she, then?"

The Adventurer laughed shortly.

"She is quite closely connected with that gentleman we left airing himself on the fire escape," he said grimly. "Gypsy Nan is Danglar's wife."

It was very strange, very curious--the alleyway seemed suddenly to be revolving around and around, and it seemed to bring her a giddiness and a faintness. The Adventurer was standing there before her, but she did not see him any more; she could only see, as from a brink upon which she tottered, a gulf, abysmal in its horror, that yawned before her.

"Thank you--thank you for the warning." Was that her voice speaking so calmly and dispassionately? "I will remember it. But I must go now. Good-night again!"

He said something. She did not know what. She only knew that she was hurrying along the alleyway now, and that he had made no effort to stop her, and that she was grateful to him for that, and that her composure, strained to the breaking point, would have given away if she had remained with him another instant. Danglar's wife! It was dark here in the alley-way, and she did not know where it led to. But did it matter? And she stumbled as she went along. But it was not the physical inability to see that made her stumble--it was a brain-blindness that fogged her soul itself. His wife! Gypsy Nan was Danglar's wife.

XI. SOME OF THE LESSER BREED

D anglar's wife! It had been a night of horror; a night without sleep; a night, after the guttering candle had gone out, when the blackness of the garret possessed added terrors created by an imagination which ran riot, and which she could not control. She could have fled from it, screaming in panic-stricken hysteria--but there had been no other place as safe as that was. Safe! The word seemed to reach the uttermost depths of irony. Safe! Well, it was true, wasn't it?

She had not wanted to return there; her soul itself had revolted against it; but she had dared to do nothing else. And all through that night, huddled on the edge of the cot bed, her fingers clinging tenaciously to her revolver as though afraid for even an instant to relinquish it from her grasp, listening, listening, always listening for a footstep that might come up from that dark hall below, the footstep that would climax all the terrors that had surged upon her, her mind had kept on reiterating, always reiterating those words of the Adventurer--"Gypsy Nan is Danglar's wife."

And they were still with her, those words. Daylight had come again, and passed again, and it was evening once more; but those words remained, insensible to change, immutable in their foreboding. And Rhoda Gray, as Gypsy Nan, shuddered now as she scuffled along a shabby street deep in the heart of the East Side. She was Danglar's wife--by proxy. At dawn that morning when the gray had come creeping into the miserable attic through the small and dirty window panes, she had fallen on her knees and thanked God she had been spared that footstep. It was strange! She had poured out her soul in passionate thankfulness then that Danglar had not come--and now she was deliberately on her way to seek Danglar himself! But the daylight had done more than disperse the actual, physical darkness of the past night; it had brought, if not a measure of relief, at least a sense of guidance, and the final decision, perilous though it was, which she meant now to put into execution.

There was no other way--unless she were willing to admit defeat, to give up everything, her own good name, her father's name, to run from it all and live henceforth in hiding in some obscure place far away, branded in the life she would have left behind her as a despicable criminal and thief. And she could not, would not, do this while her intuition, at least, inspired her with the faith to believe that there was still a chance of clearing herself. It was the throw of the dice, perhaps--but there was no other way. Danglar, and those with him, were at the bottom of the crime of which she was held guilty. She could not go on as she had been doing, merely in the hope of stumbling upon some clew that would serve to exonerate her. There was not time enough for that. Danglar's trap set for herself and the Adventurer last night in old Nicky Viner's room proved that. And the fact that the woman who had originally masqueraded as Gypsy Nan--as she, Rhoda Gray, was masquerading now--was Danglar's wife, proved it a thousandfold more. She could no longer remain passive, arguing with herself that it took all her wits and all her efforts to maintain herself in the role of Gypsy Nan, which temporarily was all that stood between her and prison bars. To do so meant the certainty of disaster sooner or later, and if it meant that, the need for immediate action of an offensive sort was imperative.

And so her mind was made up. Her only chance was to find her way into the full intimacy of the criminal band of which Danglar was apparently the head; to search out its lair and its personnel; to reach to the heart of it; to know Danglar's private movements, and to discover where he lived so that she might watch him. It surely was not such a hopeless task! True, she knew by name and sight scarcely more than three of this crime clique, but at least she had a starting point from which to work. There was Shluker's junk shop where she had turned the tables on Danglar and Skeeny on the night they had planned to make the Sparrow their pawn. It was obvious, therefore, that Shluker himself, the proprietor of the junk shop, was one of the organization. She was going to Shluker's now.

Rhoda Gray halted suddenly, and stared wonderingly a little way up the block ahead of her. As though by magic a crowd was collecting around the doorway of a poverty-stricken, tumble-down frame house that made the corner of an alleyway. And where but an instant before the street's jostling humanity had been immersed in its wrangling with the push-cart men who lined the curb, the carts were now deserted by every one save their owners, whose caution exceeded their curiosity-- and the crowd grew momentarily larger in front of the house.

She drew Gypsy Nan's black, greasy shawl a little more closely around her shoulders, and moved forward again. And now, on the outskirts of the crowd, she could see quite plainly. There were two or three low steps that led up to the door- way, and a man and woman were standing there. The woman was wretchedly dressed, but with most strange incongruity she held in her hand, obviously subcon- sciously, obviously quite oblivious of it, a huge basket full to overflowing with, as nearly as Rhoda Gray could judge, all sorts of purchases, as though out of the midst of abject poverty a golden shower had suddenly descended upon her. And she was gray, and well beyond middle age, and crying bitterly; and her free hand, whether to support herself or with the instinctive idea of supporting her companion, was clutched tightly around the man's shoulders. And the man rocked unsteadily upon his feet. He was tall and angular, and older than the woman, and cadaverous of fea- ture, and miserably thin of shoulder, and blood trickled over his forehead and down one ashen, hollow cheek--and above the excited exclamations of the crowd Rhoda Gray heard him cough.

Rhoda Gray glanced around her. Where scarcely a second before she had been on the outer fringe of the crowd, she now appeared to be in the very center of it. Women were pushing up behind her, women who wore shawls as she did, only the shawls were mostly of gaudy colors; and men pushed up behind her, mostly men of swarthy countenance, who wore circlets of gold in their ears; and, brushing her skirts, seeking vantage points, ragged, ill-clad children wriggled and wormed their way deeper into the press. It was a crowd composed almost entirely of the foreign element which inhabited that quarter--and the crowd chattered and gesticulated with ever-increasing violence. She did not understand. And she could not see so well now. That pitiful tableau in the doorway was being shut out from her by a man, directly in front of her, who had hoisted a half-naked tot of three or four to a reserved seat upon his head.

And then a young man, one whom, from her years in the Bad Lands as the White Moll, she recognized as a hanger-on at a gambling hell in the Chatham Square district, came toward her, plowing his way, contemptuous of obstructions, out of the crowd.

Rhoda Gray, as Gypsy Nan, hailed him out of the corner of her mouth.

"Say, wot's de row?" she demanded.

The young man grinned.

"Somebody pinched a million from de old guy!" He shifted his cigarette with a deft movement of his tongue from one side of his mouth to the other, and grinned again. "Can youse beat it! Accordin' to him, he had enough coin to annex de whole of Noo Yoik! De moll's his wife. He went out to hell-an'-gone somewhere for a few years huntin' gold while de old girl starved. Den back he comes an' blows in to-day wid his pockets full, an' de old girl grabs a handful, an' goes out to buy up all de grub in sight 'cause she ain't had none for so long. An' w'en she comes back she finds de old geezer gagged an' tied in a chair, an' some guy's hit him a crack on de bean an' flown de coop wid de mazuma. But youse had better get out of here before youse gets run over! Dis ain't no place for an old skirt like youse. De bulls'll be down here on de hop in a minute, an' w'en dis mob starts sprinklin' de street wid deir fleetin' footsteps, youse are likely to get hurt. See?" The young man started to force his way through the crowd again. "Youse had better cut loose, mother!" he warned over his shoulder.

It was good advice. Rhoda Gray took it. She had scarcely reached the next block when the crowd behind her was being scattered pell-mell and without ceremony in all directions by the police, as the young man had predicted. She went on. There was nothing that she could do. The man's face and the woman's face haunted her. They had seemed stamped with such abject misery and despair. But there was nothing that she could do. It was one of those sore and grievous cross-sections out of the lives of the swarming thousands down here in this quarter which she knew so intimately and so well. And there were so many, many of those cross-sections! Once, in a small, pitifully meager and restricted way, she had been able to help some of these hurt lives, but now--Her lips tightened a little. She was going to Shluker's junk shop.

Her forehead gathered in little furrows as she walked along. She had weighed the pros and cons of this visit a hundred times already during the day; but even so, instinctively to reassure herself lest some apparently minor, but nevertheless fatally vital, point might have been overlooked, her mind reverted to it again. From Shluker's viewpoint, whether Gypsy Nan was in the habit of mingling with or visiting the other members of the gang or not--a matter upon which she could not even hazard a guess--her visit to-night must appear entirely logical. There was last night--and, a natural corollary, her equally natural anxiety on her supposed husband's account, providing, of course, that Shluker was aware that Gypsy Nan was Danglar's wife. But even if Shluker did not know that, he knew at least that Gypsy Nan was one of the gang, and, as such, he must equally accept it as natural that she should be anxious and disturbed over what had happened. She would be on safe ground either way. She would pretend to know only what had appeared in the papers; in other words, that the police, attracted to the spot by the sound of revolver shots, had found Danglar handcuffed to the fire escape of a well-known thieves' resort in an all too well-known and questionable locality.

A smile came spontaneously. It was quite true. That was where the Adventurer had left Danglar--handcuffed to the fire escape! The smile vanished. The humor of the situation was not long-lived; it ended there. Danglar was as cunning as the proverbial fox; and Danglar, at that moment, in desperate need of explaining his predicament in some plausible way to the police, had, as the expression went, run true to form. Danglar's story, as reported by the papers, even rose above his own high-water mark of vicious cunning, because it played upon a chord that appealed instantly to the police; and it rang true, not only because what the police could find out about him made it likely, but also because it contained a modicum of truth in itself; and, furthermore, Danglar had scored on still another count in that his story must stimulate the police into renewed activities as his unsuspecting allies in the one thing, the one aim and object that, at that moment, must obsess him above all others--the discovery of herself, the White Moll.

It was ingeniously simple, Danglar's smooth and oily lie! He had been walking along the street, he had stated, when he saw a woman, as she passed under a street lamp, who he thought resembled the White Moll. To make sure, he followed her--at a safe distance, as he believed. She entered the tenement. He hesitated. He knew the reputation of the place, which bore out his first impression that the woman was the one he thought she was; but he did not want to make a fool of himself by calling in the police until he was positive of her identity, so he finally followed her inside, and heard her go upstairs, and crept up after her in the dark. And then, suddenly, he was set upon and hustled into a room. It was the White Moll, all right; and the shots came from her companion, a man whom he described minutely--the description being that of the Adventurer, of course. They seemed to think that he, Danglar, was a plain-clothes man, and tried to sicken him of his job by frightening him. And then they forced him through the window and down the fire escape, and fastened him there with handcuffs to mock the police, and the White Moll's companion had deliberately fired some more shots to make sure of bringing the police to the scene, and then the two of them had run for it.

Rhoda Gray's eyes darkened angrily. The newspapers said that Danglar had been temporarily held by the police, though his story was believed to be true, for certainly the man would make no mistake as to the identity of the White Moll, since his life, what the police could find out about it, coincided with his own statements, and he would naturally therefore have seen her many times in the Bad Lands when she was working there under cover of her despicable role of sweet and innocent charity. Danglar had made no pretensions to self-righteousness--he was too cute for that. He admitted that he had no "specific occupation," that he hung around the gambling hells a good deal, that he followed the horses--that, frankly, he lived by his wits. He had probably given some framed-up address to the police, but, if so, the papers had not stated where it was. Rhoda Gray's face, under the grime of Gypsy Nan's disguise, grew troubled and perplexed. Neither had the papers, even the evening papers, stated whether Danglar had as yet been released--they had devoted the rest of their space to the vilification of the White Moll. They had demanded in no uncertain tones a more conclusive effort on the part of the authorities to bring her, and with her now the man in the case, as they called the Adventurer, to justice, and...

The thought of the Adventurer caused her mind to swerve sharply off at a tangent. Where he had piqued and aroused her curiosity before, he now, since last night, seemed more complex a character than ever. It was strange, most strange, the way their lives, his and hers, had become interwoven! She had owed him much; but last night she had repaid him and squared accounts. She had told him so. She owed him nothing more. If a sense of gratitude had once caused her to look upon him with--with--She bit her lips. What was the use of that? Had it become so much a part of her life, so much a habit, this throwing of dust in the eyes of others, this constant passing of herself off for some one else, this constant deception, warranted though it might be, that she must now seek to deceive herself! Why not frankly admit to her own soul, already in the secret, that she cared in spite of herself--for a thief? Why not admit that a great hurt had come, one that no one but herself would ever know, a hurt that would last for always because it was a wound that could never be healed?

A thief! She loved a thief. She had fought a bitter, stubborn battle with her common sense to convince herself that he was not a thief. She had snatched hungrily at the incident that centered around those handcuffs, so opportunely produced from the Adventurer's pocket. She had tried to argue that those handcuffs not only suggested, but proved, he was a police officer in disguise, working on some case in which Danglar and the gang had been mixed up; and, as she tried to argue in this wise, she tried to shut her eyes to the fact that the same pocket out of which the handcuffs came was at exactly the same moment the repository of as many stolen banknotes as it would hold. She had tried to argue that the fact that he was so insistently at work to defeat Danglar's plans was in his favor; but that argument, like all others, came quickly and miserably to grief. Where the "leak" was, as Danglar called it, that supplied the Adventurer with foreknowledge of the gang's movements, she had no idea, save that perhaps the Adventurer and some traitor in the gang were in collusion for their own ends--and that certainly did not lift the Adventurer to any higher plane, or wash from him the stigma of thief.

She clenched her hands. It was all an attempt at argument without the basis of a single logical premise. It was silly and childish! Why hadn't the man been an ordinary, plain, common thief and criminal--and looked like one? She would never have been attracted to him then even through gratitude! Why should he have all the graces and ear-marks of breeding? Why should he have all the appearances of gentleman? It seemed a needlessly cruel and additional blow that fate had dealt her, when already she was living through days and nights of fear, of horror, of trepidation, so great that at times it seemed she would literally lose her reason. If he had not looked, yes, and at times, acted, so much like a thorough-bred gentleman, there would never have come to her this hurt, this gulf between them that could not now be spanned, and in a personal way she would never have cared because he was--a thief.

Her mental soliloquy ended abruptly. She had reached the narrow driveway that led in, between the two blocks of down-at-the-heels tenements, to the court-yard at the rear that harbored Shluker's junk shop. And now, unlike that other night when she had first paid a visit to the place, she made no effort at conceal-ment as she entered the driveway. She walked quickly, and as she emerged into the courtyard itself she saw a light in the window of the junk shop.

Rhoda Gray nodded her head. It was still quite early, still almost twilight--not more than eight o'clock. Back there, on that squalid doorstep where the old woman and the old man had stood, it had still been quite light. The long summer evening had served at least to sear, somehow, those two faces upon her mind. It was singular that they should intrude themselves at this moment! She had been thinking, hadn't she, that at this hour she might naturally expect to find Shluker still in his shop? That was why she had come so early--since she had not cared to come in full day-light. Well, if that light meant anything, he was there.

She felt her pulse quicken perceptibly as she crossed the courtyard, and reached the shop. The door was open, and she stepped inside. It was a dingy place, filthy, and littered, without the slightest attempt at order, with a heterogeneous collection of, it seemed, every article one could think of, from scraps of old iron and bundles of rags to cast-off furniture that was in an appalling state of dissolution. The light, that of a single and dim incandescent, came from the interior of what was appar-ently the "office" of the establishment, a small, glassed-in partition affair, at the far end of the shop.

Her first impression had been that there was no one in the shop, but now, from the other side of the glass partition, she caught sight of a bald head, and became aware that a pair of black eyes were fixed steadily upon her, and that the occupant was beckoning to her with his hand to come forward.

She scuffled slowly, but without hesitation, up the shop. She intended to em-ploy the vernacular that was part of the disguise of Gypsy Nan. If Shluker, for that was certainly Shluker there, gave the slightest indication that he took it amiss, her explanation would come glibly and logically enough--she had to be careful; how was she supposed to know whether there was any one else about, or not!

"'Ello!" she said curtly, as she reached the doorway of the little office, and paused on the threshold. Shifty little black eyes met hers, as the bald head fringed with untrimmed gray hair, was lifted from a battered desk, and the wizened face of an old man was disclosed under the rays of the tin-shaded lamp. He grinned suddenly, showing discolored teeth--and instinctively she drew back a little. He was an uninviting and exceedingly disreputable old creature.

"You, eh, Nan!" he grunted. "So you've come to see old Jake Shluker, have you? 'Tain't often you come! And what's brought you, eh?"

"I can read, can't I?" Rhoda Gray glanced furtively around her, then leaned toward the other. "Say, wot's de lay? I been scared stiff all day. Is dat straight wot de papers said about youse-know-who gettin' pinched?"

A scowl settled over Shluker's features as he nodded.

"Yes; it's straight enough," he answered. "Damn 'em, one and all! But they let him out again."

"Dat's de stuff!" applauded Rhoda Gray earnestly. "Where is he, den?"

Shluker shook his head.

"He didn't say," said Shluker.

"He didn't say?" echoed Rhoda Gray, a little tartly. "Wot d'youse mean, he didn't say? Have youse seen him?"

Shluker jerked his hand toward the telephone instrument on the desk.

"He was talkin' to me a little while ago."

"Well, den"--Rhoda Gray risked a more peremptory tone--"where is he?"

Shluker shook his head again.

"I dunno," he said. "I'm tellin' you, he didn't say."

Rhoda Gray studied the wizened and repulsive old creature, that, huddled in his chair in the dirty, boxed-in little office, made her think of some crafty old spider lurking in its web for unwary prey. Was the man lying to her? Was he in any degree suspicious? Why should he be? He had given not the slightest sign that her uncouth language was either unexpected or unnecessary. Perhaps to Shluker, and perhaps to all the rest of the gang--except Danglar!--Gypsy Nan was accepted at face value as just Gypsy Nan; and, if that were so, the idea of playing up a natural wifely anxiety on Danglar's behalf could not be used unless Shluker gave her a lead in that direction. But, all that apart, she was getting nowhere. She bit her lips in disappointment. She had counted a great deal on this Shluker here, and Shluker was not proving the fount of information, far from it, that she had hoped he would.

She tried again-even more peremptorily than before.

"Aw, open up!" she snapped. "Wot's de use bein' a clam! Youse heard me, didn't youse? Where is he?"

Shluker leaned abruptly forward, and looked at her in a suddenly perturbed way.

"Is there anything wrong?" he asked in a tense, lowered voice. "What makes you so anxious to know?"

Rhoda Gray laughed shortly.

"Nothin'!" she answered coolly. "I told youse once, didn't I? I got a scare readin' dem papers--an' I ain't over it yet. Dat's wot I want to know for, an' youse seem afraid to open up!"

Shluker sank back again in his chair with an air of relief.

"Oh!" he ejaculated. "Well, that's all right, then. You were beginning to give me a scare, too. I ain't playin' the clam, and I dunno where he is; but I can tell you there's nothing to worry you any more about the rest of it. He was after the White Moll last night, and it didn't come off. They pulled one on him instead, and fastened him to the fire escape the way the papers said. Skeeny and the Cricket, who were in on the play with him, didn't have time to get him loose before the bulls got there. So Danglar told them to beat it, and he handed the cops the story that was in the papers. He got away with it, all right, and they let go him to-day; but he phoned a little while ago that they were still stickin' around kind of close to him, and that I was to pass the word that the lid was to go down tight for the next few days, and--"

Shluker stopped abruptly as the telephone rang, and reached for the instrument.

Rhoda Gray fumbled unnecessarily with her shawl, as the other answered the call. Failure! A curious bitterness came to her. Her plan then, for to-night it least, was a failure. Shluker did not know where Danglar was. She was quite convinced of that. Shluker was--She glanced suddenly at the wizened little old man. From an ordinary tone, Shluker's voice had risen sharply in protest about something. She listened now:

"No, no; it does not matter what it is!"

"What?...No! I tell you, no! Nothing! Not to-night! Those are the orders....No, I don't know! Nan is here now....Eh?....You'll pay for it if you do!" Shluker was snarling threateningly now. "What?....Well, then, wait! I'll come over....No, you can bet I won't be long! You wait! Understand?"

He banged the receiver on the hook, and got up from his chair hurriedly.

"Fools!" he muttered savagely. "No, I won't be long gettin' there!" He grabbed Rhoda Gray's arm. "Yes, and you come, too! You will help me put a little sense into their heads, if it is possible--eh? The fools!"

The man was violently excited. He half pulled Rhoda Gray down the length of the shop to the front door. Puzzled, bewildered, a little uneasy, she watched him lock the door, and then followed him across the courtyard, while he continued to mutter constantly to himself.

"Wot's de matter?" she asked him twice.

But it was not until they had reached the street, and Shluker was hurrying along as fast as he could walk, that he answered her.

"It's the Pug and Pinkie Bonn!" he jerked out angrily. "They're in the Pug's room. Pinkie went back there after telephonin'. They've nosed out something they want to put through. The fools! And after last night nearly havin' finished everything! I told 'em--you heard me--that everybody's to keep under cover now. But they think they've got a soft thing, and they say they're goin' to it. I've got to put a crimp in it, and you've got to help me. Y'understand, Nan?"

"Yes," she said mechanically.

Her mind was working swiftly. The night, after all, perhaps, was not to be so much of a failure! To get into intimate touch with all the members of the clique was equally one of her objects, and, failing Danglar himself to-night, here was an "open sesame" to the re-treat of two of the others. She would never have a better chance, or one in which risk and danger, under the chaperonage, as it were, of Shluker here, were, if not entirely eliminated, at least reduced to an apparently negligible minimum. Yes; she would go. To refuse was to turn her back on her own proposed line of action, and on the decision which she had made herself.

XII. CROOKS Vs. CROOKS

It was not far. Shluker, hastening along, still muttering to himself, turned into a cross street some two blocks away, and from there again into a lane; and, a moment later, led the way through a small door in the fence that hung, battered and half open, on sagging and broken hinges. Rhoda Gray's eyes traveled sharply around her in all directions. It was still light enough to see fairly well, and she might at some future time find the bearings she took now to be of inestimable worth. Not that there was much to remark! They crossed a diminutive and disgustingly dirty backyard, whose sole reason for existence seemed to be that of a receptacle for old tin cans, and were confronted by the rear of what appeared to be a four-story tenement. There was a back door here, and, on the right of the door, fronting the yard, a single window that was some four or five feet from the level of the ground.

Shluker, without hesitation, opened the back door, shut it behind them, led the way along a black, unlighted hall, and halting before a door well toward the front of the building, knocked softly upon it--giving two raps, a single rap, and then two more in quick succession. There was no answer. He knocked again in precisely the same manner, and then a footstep sounded from within, and the door was flung open. "Fools!" growled Shluker in greeting, as they stepped inside and the door was closed again. "A pair of brainless fools!"

There were two men there. They paid Shluker scant attention. They both grinned at Rhoda Gray through the murky light supplied by a wheezy and wholly inadequate gas-jet.

"Hello, Nan!" gibed the smaller of the two. "Who let you out?"

"Aw, forget it!" croaked Rhoda Gray.

Shluker took up the cudgels.

"You close your face, Pinkie!" he snapped. "Get down to cases! Do you think I got nothing else to do but chase you two around like a couple of puppy dogs that haven't got sense enough to take care of themselves? Wasn't what I told you over the phone enough without me havin' to come here?"

"Nix on that stuff!" returned the one designated as Pinkie imperturbably. "Say, you'll be glad you come when we lets you in on a little piece of easy money. We ain't askin' your advice; all we're askin' you to do is frame up the alibi, same as usual, for me an' the Pug here in case we wants it."

Shluker shook his fist.

"Frame nothing!" he spluttered angrily. "Ain't I tellin' you that the orders are not to make a move, that everything is off for a few days? That's the word I got a little while ago, and the Seven-Three-Nine is goin' out now. Nan'll tell you the same thing."

"Sure!" corroborated Rhoda Gray, picking up the obvious cue. "Dat's de straight goods."

The two men were lounging beside a table that stood at the extreme end of the room, and now for a moment they whispered together. And, as they whispered, Rhoda Gray found her first opportunity to take critical stock both of her surroundings and of the two men themselves. Pinkie, a short, slight little man, she dismissed with hardly a glance; he was the common type, with low, vicious cunning stamped all over his face--an ordinary rat of the underworld. But her glance rested longer on his companion. The Pug was indeed entitled to his moniker! His face made her think of one. It seemed to be all screwed up out of shape. Perhaps the eye-patch over the right eye helped a little to put the finishing touch of repulsiveness upon a countenance already most unpleasant. The celluloid eye-patch, once flesh-colored, was now so dirty and smeared that its original color was discernible only in spots, and the once white elastic cord that circled his head and kept the patch in place was in equal disrepute. A battered slouch hat came to the level of the eye-patch in a forbidding sort of tilt. His left eyelid drooped until it was scarcely open at all, and fluttered continually. One nostril of his nose was entirely closed; and his mouth seemed to be twisted out of shape, so that, even when in repose, the lips never entirely met at one corner. And his ears, what she could see of them in the poor light, and on account of the slouch hat, seemed to bear out the low-type criminal impression the man gave her, in that they lay flat back against his head.

She turned her eyes away with a little shudder of repulsion, and gave her attention to an inspection of the room. There was no window, except a small one high up in the right-hand partition wall. She quite understood what that meant. It was common enough, and all too unsanitary enough, in these old and cheap tenements; the window gave, not on the out-of-doors, but on a light-well. For the rest, it was a room she had seen a thousand times before--carpetless, unfurnished save for the barest necessities, dirt everywhere, unkempt.

Pinkie Bonn broke in abruptly upon her inspection.

"That's all right!" he announced airily. "We'll let Nan in on it, too. The Pug an' me figures she can give us a hand."

Shluker's wizened little face seemed suddenly to go purple.

"Are you tryin' to make a fool of me?" he half screamed. "Or can't you understand English? D'ye want me to keep on tellin' you till I'm hoarse that there ain't nobody goin' in with you, because you am't goin' in yourself! See? Understand that? There's nothing doin' to-night for anybody--and that means you!"

"Aw, shut up, Shluker!" It was the Pug now, a curious whispering sibilancy in his voice, due no doubt to the disfigurement of his lips. "Give Pinkie a chance to shoot his spiel before youse injure yerself throwin' a fit! Go on, Pinkie, spill it."

"Sure!" said Pinkie eagerly. "Listen, Shluk! It ain't any crib we're wantin' to crack, or nothin' like that. It's just a couple of crooks that won't dare open their yaps to the bulls, 'cause what we're after 'll be what they'll have pinched themselves. See?"

Shluker's face lost some of its belligerency, and in its place a dawning interest came.

"What's that?" he demanded cautiously. "What crooks?"

"French Pete an' Marny Day," said Pinkie--and grinned.

"Oh!" Shluker's eyebrows went up. He looked at the Pug, and the Pug winked knowingly with his half-closed left eyelid. Shluker reached out for a chair, and, finding it suspiciously wobbly, straddled it warily. "Mabbe I've been in wrong," he admitted. "What's the lay?"

"Me," said Pinkie, "I was down to Charlie's this afternoon havin' a little lay-off, an'--"

"One of these days," interrupted Shluker sharply, "you'll go out like"--he snapped his fingers--"that!" "Can't you leave the stuff alone?"

"I got to have me bit of coke," Pinkie answered, with a shrug of his shoulders. "An', anyway, I'm no pipe-hitter.

"It's all the same whatever way you take it!" retorted Shluker. "Well, go on with your story. You went down to Charlie's dope parlors, and jabbed a needle into yourself, or took it some other old way. I get you! What happened then?"

"It was about an hour ago," resumed Pinkie Bonn with undisturbed complacency. "Just as I was beatin' it out of there by the cellar, I hears some whisperin' as I was passin' one of the end doors. Savvy? I hadn't made no noise, an' they hadn't heard me. I gets a peek in, 'cause the door's cracked. It was French Pete an' Marny Day. I listens. An' after about two seconds I was goin' shaky for fear some one would come along an' I wouldn't get the whole of it. Take it from me, Shluk, it was some goods!"

Shluker grunted noncommittingly.

"Well, go on!" he prompted.

"I didn't get all the fine points," grinned Pinkie; "but I got enough. There was a guy by the name of Dainey who used to live somewhere on the East Side here, an' he used to work in some sweat-shop, an' he worked till he got pretty old, an' then his lungs, or something, went bad on him, an' he went broke. An' the doctor said he had to beat it out of here to a more salubrious climate. Some nut filled his ear full 'bout gold huntin' up in Alaska, an' he fell for it. He chewed it over with his wife, an' she was for it too, 'cause the doctor 'd told her her old man would bump off if he stuck around here, an' they hadn't any money to get away together. She figured she could get along workin' out by the day till he came back a millionaire; an' old Dainey started off.

"I dunno how he got there. I'm just fillin' in what I hears French Pete an' Marny talkin' about. I guess mostly he beat his way there ridin' the rods; but, anyway, he got there. See? An' then he goes down sick there again, an' a hospital, or some outfit, has to take care of him for a couple of years; an' back here the old woman got kind of feeble an' on her uppers, an there was hell to pay, an'--"

"Wot's bitin' youse, Nan?" The Pug's lisping whisper broke sharply in upon Pinkie Bonn's story.

Rhoda Gray started. She was conscious now that she had been leaning forward, staring in a startled way at Pinkie as he talked; conscious now that for a moment she had forgotten--that she was Gypsy Nan. But she was mistress of herself on the instant, and she scowled blackly at the Pug.

"Mabbe it's me soft heart dat's touched!" she flung out acidly. "Youse close yer trap, an' let Pinkie talk!"

"Yes, shut up!" said Pinkie. "What was I sayin'? Oh, yes! An' then the old guy makes a strike. Can you beat it! I dunno nothing about the way they pull them things, but he's off by his lonesome out somewhere, an' he finds gold, an' stakes out his claim, but he takes sick again an' can't work it, an' it's all he can do to get back alive to civilization. He keeps his mouth shut for a while, figurin' he'll get strong again, but it ain't no good, an' he gets a letter from the old woman tellin' how bad she is, an' then he shows some of the stuff he'd found. After that there's nothing to it! Everybody's beatin' it for the place; but, at that, old Dainey comes out of it all right, an' goes crazy with joy 'cause some guy offers him twenty-five thousand bucks for his claim, an' throws in the expenses home for good luck. He gets the money in cash, twenty-five one-thousand-dollar bills, an' the chicken feed for the expenses, an' starts for back here an' the old woman. But this time he don't keep his mouth shut about it when he'd have been better off if he had. See? He was tellin' about it on the train. I guess he was tellin' about it all the way across. But, anyway, he tells about it comm' from Philly this afternoon, an' French Pete an' Marny Day happens to be on the train, an' they hears it, an' frames it up to annex the coin before morning, 'cause he's got in too late to get the money into any bank to-day."

Pinkie Bonn paused, and stuck his tongue significantly in his cheek.

Shluker was rubbing his hands together now in a sort of unctuous way.

"It sounds pretty good," he murmured; "only there's Danglar--"

"Youse leave Danglar to me!" broke in the Pug. "As soon as we hands one to dem two boobs an' gets de cash, Pinkie can beat it back here wid de coin an wait fer me while I finds Danglar an' squares it wid him. He ain't goin' to put up no holler at dat. We ain't runnin' de gang into nothin'. Dis is private business--see? So youse just take a sneak wid yerself, an' fix a nice little alibi fer us so's we won't be takin' any chances."

Shluker frowned.

"But what's the good of that?" he demurred. "French Pete and Marny Day 'll see you anyway."

"Will dey!" scoffed the Pug. "Guess once more! A coupla handkerchiefs over our mugs is good enough fer dem, if youse holds yer end up. An' dey wouldn't talk fer publication, anyway, would dey?"

Shluker smiled now-almost ingratiatingly.

"And how much is my end worth?" he inquired softly.

"One of dem thousand-dollar engravin's," stated the Pug promptly. "An' Pinkie'll run around an' slip it to youse before mornin'."

"All right," said Shluker, after a moment. "It's half past eight now. From nine o'clock on, you can beat any jury in New York to it that you were both at the same old place--as long as you keep decently under cover. That'll do, won't it? I'll fix it. But I don't see--"

Rhoda Gray, as Gypsy Nan, for the first time projected herself into the discussion. She cackled suddenly in jeering mirth.

"I t'ought something was wrong wid her!" whispered the Pug with mock anxiety. "Mabbe she ain't well! Tell us about it, Nan!"

"When I do," she said complacently, "mabbe youse'll smile out of de other corner of dat mouth of yers!" She turned to Shluker. "Youse needn't lay awake waitin' fer dat thousand, Shluker, 'cause youse'll never see it. De little game's all off--'cause it's already been pulled. See? Dere was near a riot as I passes along a street goin' to yer place, an' I gets piped off to wot's up, an' it's de same story dat Pinkie's told, an' de crib's cracked, an' de money's gone--dat's all."

Shluker's face fell.

"I said you were fools when I first came in here!" he burst out suddenly, wheeling on Pinkie Bonn and the Pug. "I'm sure of it now. I was wonderin a minute ago how you were goin' to keep your lamps on Pete and Marny from here, or know when they were goin' to pull their stunt, or where to find 'em."

Pinkie Bonn, ignoring Shluker, leaned toward Rhoda Gray.

"Say, Nan, is that straight?" he inquired anxiously. "You sure?"

"Sure, I'm sure!" Rhoda Gray asserted tersely. The one thought in her head now was that her information would naturally deprive these men here of any further interest in the matter, and that she would get away as quickly as possible, and, in some way or other, see that the police were tipped off to the fact that it was French Pete and Marny Day who had taken the old couple's money. Those two old faces rose before her again now--blotting out most curiously the face of Pinkie Bonn just in front of her. She felt strangely glad--glad that she had heard all of old Dainey's story, because she could see now an ending to it other than the miserable, hopeless one of despair that she had read in the Daineys' faces just a little while ago. "Sure, I'm sure!" she repeated with finality.

"How long ago was it?" prodded Pinkie.

"I dunno," she answered. "I just went to Shluker's, an' den we comes over here. Youse can figure it fer yerself."

And then Rhoda Gray stared at the other--with sudden misgiving. Pinkie Bonn's face was suddenly wreathed in smiles.

"I'll answer you now, Shluk," he grinned. "What do you think? That we're nuts, me an' Pug? Well, forget it! We didn't have to stick around watchin' Pete an' Marny; we just had to wait until they had collected the dough. That was the most trouble we had--wonderin' when that would be. Well, we don't have to wonder any more. We know now that the cherries are ripe. See? An' now we'll go an' pick 'em! Where? Where d'ye suppose? Down to Charlie's, of course! I hears 'em talkin' about that, too. They ain't so foolish! They're out for an alibi themselves. Get the idea? They was to sneak out of Charlie's without anybody seem' 'em, an' if everything broke right for 'em, they was to sneak back again an' spend the night there. No, they ain't so foolish--I guess they ain't! There ain't no place in New York you can get in an' out of without nobody knowin' it like Charlie's, if you know the way, an--"

"Aw, write de rest of it down in yer memoirs!" interposed the Pug impatiently--and moved toward the door. "It's all right, Shluker--all de way. Now, everybody beat it, an' get on de job. Nan, youse sticks wid Pinkie an' me."

Rhoda Gray, her mind in confusion, found herself being crowded hurriedly through the doorway by the three men. Still in a mentally confused condition, she found herself, a few minutes later--Shluker having parted company with them--walking along the street between Pinkie Bonn and the Pug. She was fighting desperately to obtain a rip upon herself. The information she had volunteered had had an effect diametrically opposite to that which she had intended. She seemed terribly impotent; as though she were being swept from her feet and borne onward by some swift and remorseless current, whether she would or no.

The Pug, in his curious whisper, was talking to her: "Pinkie knows de way in. We don't want any row in dere, on account of Charlie. We ain't fer puttin' his place on de rough, an' gettin' him raided by de bulls. Charlie's all to de good. See? Well, dat's wot 'd likely happen if me an' Pinkie busts in on Pete an' Marny widout sendin' in our visitin'-cards first, polite-like. Dey would pull deir guns, an' though we'd get de coin just de same, dere'd be hell to pay fer Charlie, an' de whole place 'd go up in fireworks right off de bat. Well, dis is where youse come in. Youse are de visitin'-card. Youse gets into deir bunk room, pretendin' youse have made a mistake, an' youse leaves de door open behind youse. Dey don't know youse, an', bein' a woman, dey won't pull no gun on youse. An' den youse breaks it gently to dem dat dere's a coupla gents outside, an' just about den dey looks up an' sees me an' Pinkie an' our guns-an' I guess dat's all. Get it?"

"Sure!" mumbled Rhoda Gray.

The Pug talked on. She did not hear him. It seemed as though her brain ached literally with an acute physical pain. What was she to do? What could she do? She must do something! There must be some way to save herself from being drawn into the very center of this vortex toward which she was being swept closer with every second that passed. Those two old faces, haggard in their despair and misery, rose before her again. She felt her heart sink. She had counted, only a few moments before, on getting their money back for them--through the police. The police! How could she get any word to the police now, without first getting away from these two men here? And suppose she did get away, and found some means of communicating with the authorities, it would be Pinkie Bonn here, and the Pug, who would fall into the meshes of the law quite as much as would French Pete and Marny Day; and to have Pinkie and the Pug apprehended now, just as they seemed to be opening the gateway for her into the inner secrets of the gang, meant ruin to her own hopes and plans. And to refuse to go on with them now, as one of them, would certainly excite their suspicions--and suspicion of Gypsy Nan was the end of everything for her.

Her hands, under her shawl, clenched until the nails bit into her palms. Couldn't she do anything? And there was the money, too, for those two old people. Wasn't there any--She caught her breath. Yes, yes! Perhaps there was a way to save the money; yes, and at the same time to place herself on a firmer footing of intimacy with these two men here--if she went on with this. But--She shook her head. She could not afford "buts" now; they must take care of themselves afterwards. She would play Gypsy Nan now without reservation. These two men here, like Shluker, were obviously ignorant that Gypsy Nan was Danglar's wife; so she was--Pinkie Bonn's hand was on her arm. She had stumbled.

"Look out for yourself!" he cautioned under his breath. "Don't make a sound!"

They had drawn into a very dark and narrow area way between two buildings, and now Pinkie kept his touch upon her as he led the way along. What was this "Charlie's"? She did not know, except that, from what had been said, it was a drug dive of some kind, patronized extensively by the denizens of the underworld. She did not know where she was now, save that she had suddenly left one of the out-of-the--way East Side streets.

Pinkie halted suddenly, and, bending down, lifted up what was evidently a half section of the folding trapdoor to a cellar entrance.

"There's only a few of us regulars wise to this," whispered Pinkie. "Watch yourself! There's five steps. Count 'em, so's you won't trip. Keep hold of me all the way. An' nix on the noise, or we won't get away with it inside. Leave the trap open, Pug, for our getaway. We ain't goin' to be long. Come on!"

It was horribly dark. Rhoda Gray, with her hand on Pinkie Bonn's shoulder, descended the five steps. She felt the Pug keeping touch behind by holding the corner of her shawl. They went forward softly, slowly, stealthily. She felt her knees shake a little, and suddenly panic seized her, and she wanted to scream out. What was she doing? Where was she going? Was she mad, that she had ventured into this trap of blackness? Blackness! It was hideously black. She looked behind her. She could not see the Pug, close as he was to her; and dark as she had thought it outside there at the cellar entrance, it appeared by contrast to have been light, for she could even distinguish now the opening through which they had come.

They were in a cellar that was damp underfoot, and the soft earth deadened all sound as they walked upon it--and they seemed to be walking on interminably. It was too far--much too far! She felt her nerve failing her. She looked behind her again. That opening, still discernible to her straining eyes, beckoned her, lured her. Better to...

Pinkie had halted again. She bumped into him. And then she felt his lips press against her ear.

"Here we are!" he breathed. "They got the end room on the right, so's they could get in an' out with out bein' seen, an so's even Charlie'd swear they was here all the time. You're too old a bird to fall down, Nan. If the door's locked, knock--an' give 'em any old kind of a song an' dance till you gets 'em off their guard. The Pug an' me 'll see you through. Go it!"

Before Rhoda Gray could reply, Pinkie had stepped suddenly to one side. A door in front of her, a sliding door it seemed to be, opened noiselessly, and she could see a faintly lighted, narrow, and very short passage ahead of her. It appeared to make a right-angled turn just a few yards in, and what light there was seemed to filter in from around the corner. And on each side of the passage, before it made the turn, there was a door, and from the one on the right, through a cracked panel, a tiny thread of light seeped out.

Her lips moved silently. After all, it was not so perilous. Nobody would be hurt. Pinkie and the Pug would cover those two men in there--and take the money--and run for it--and...

The Pug gave her an encouraging push from behind.

She moved forward mechanically. There were many sounds now, but they came muffled and indeterminate from around that corner ahead--all save a low murmuring of voices from the door with the cracked panel on the right.

It was only a few feet. She found herself crouched before the door--but she did not knock upon it. Instead, her blood seemed suddenly to run cold in her veins, and she beckoned frantically to her two companions. She could see through the crack in the panel. There were two men in there, French Pete and Marny Day undoubtedly, and they sat on opposite sides of a table, and a lamp burned on the table, and one of the men was counting out a sheaf of crisp yellow-back banknotes--but the other, while apparently engrossed in the first man's occupation, and while he leaned forward in apparent eagerness, was edging one hand stealthily toward the lamp, and his other hand, hidden from his companion's view by the table, was just drawing a revolver from his pocket. There was no mistaking the man's murderous intentions. A dull horror, that numbed her brain, seized upon Rhoda Gray; the low-type brutal faces under the rays of the lamp seemed to assume the aspect of two monstrous gargoyles, and to spin around and around before her vision; and then--it could only have been but the fraction of a second since she had begun to beckon to Pinkie and the Pug--she felt herself pulled unceremoniously away from the door, and the Pug leaned forward in her place, his eyes to the crack in the panel.

She heard a low, quick-muttered exclamation from the Pug; and then suddenly, as the lamp was obviously extinguished, that crack of light in the panel had vanished. But in an instant, curiously like a jagged lightning flash, light showed through the crack again--and vanished again. It was the flash of a revolver shot from within, and the roar of the report came now like the roll of thunder on its heels.

Rhoda Gray was back against the opposite wall. She saw the Pug fling himself against the door. It was a flimsy affair. It crashed inward. She heard him call to Pinkie:

"Shoot yer flash on de table, an' grab de coin! I'll fix de other guy!"

Were eternities passing? Her eyes were fascinated by the interior beyond that broken door. It was utterly dark inside there, save that the ray of a flashlight played now on the table, and a hand reached out and snatched up a scattered sheaf of banknotes; and on the outer edge of the ray two shadowy forms struggled and one went down. Then the flashlight went out She heard the Pug speak:

"Beat it!"

Commotion came now; cries and footsteps from around that corner in the passage. The Pug grasped her by the shoulders, and rushed her back into the cellar. She was conscious, it seemed, only in a dazed and mechanical way. There were men in the passage running toward them--and then the passage had disappeared. Pinkie Bonn had shut the connecting door.

"Hop it like blazes!" whispered the Pug, as they ran for the faint glimmer of light that located the cellar exit. "Separate de minute we're outside!" he ordered. "Dere's murder in dere. Pete shot Marny. I put Pete to sleep wid a punch on de jaw; but de bunch knows now some one else was dere, an' Pete'll swear it was us, though he don't know who we was dat did de shootin'. I gotta make dis straight right off de bat wid Danglar." His whispering voice was labored, panting; they were climbing up the steps now. "Youse take de money to my room, Pinkie, an' wait fer me. I won't be much more'n half an hour. Nan, youse beat it fer yer garret, an' stay dere!"

They were outside. The Pug had disappeared in the darkness. Pinkie was clos-ing, and evidently fastening, the trap-door.

"The other way, Nan!" he flung out, as she started to run. "That takes you to the other street, an' they can't get around that way without goin' around the whole block. Me for a fence I knows about, an' we gives 'em the merry laugh! Go on!"

She ran--ran breathlessly, stumbling, half falling, her hands stretched out be-fore her to serve almost in lieu of eyes, for she could make out scarcely anything in front of her. She emerged upon a street. It seemed abnormal, the quiet, the lack of commotion, the laughter, the unconcern in the voices of the passers-by among whom she suddenly found herself. She hurried from the neighborhood.

XIII. THE DOOR ACROSS THE HALL

It was many blocks away before calmness came again to Rhoda Gray, and before it seemed, even, that her brain would resume its normal functions; but with the numbed horror once gone, there came in its place, like some surging tide, a fierce virility that would not be denied. The money! The old couple on that doorstep, stripped of their all! Wasn't that one reason why she had gone on with Pinkie Bonn and the Pug? Hadn't she seen a way, or at least a chance, to get that money back?

Rhoda Gray looked quickly about her. On the corner ahead she saw a drug store, and started briskly in that direction. Yes, there was a way! The idea had first come to her from the Pug's remark to Shluker that, after they had secured the money, Pinkie would return with it to the Pug's room, while the Pug would go and square things with Danglar. And also, at the same time, that same remark of the Pug's had given rise to a hope that she might yet trace Danglar to night through the Pug--but the circumstances and happenings of the last few minutes had shattered that hope utterly. And so there remained the money. And, as she had walked with Pinkie and the Pug a little while ago, knowing that Pinkie would, if they were successful, carry the money back to the Pug's room, just as was being done now precisely in accordance with the Pug's original intentions, she had thought of the Adventurer. It had seemed the only way then; it seemed the only way now--despite the fact that she would be hard put to it to answer the Adventurer if he thought to ask her how, or by what means, she was in possession of the information that enabled her to communicate with him. But she must risk that--put him off, if necessary, through the plea of haste, and on the ground that there was not time to-night for an unnecessary word. He had given her, believing her to be Gypsy Nan, his telephone number, which she, in turn, was to transmit to the White Moll--in other words, herself! But the White Moll, so he believed, had never received that message--and it must of necessity be as the White Moll that she must communicate with him to-night! It would be hard to explain--she meant to evade it. The one vital point was that she remembered the telephone number he had given her that night when he and Danglar had met in the garret. She was not likely to have forgotten it!

Rhoda Gray, alias Gypsy Nan, scuffled along. Was she inconsistent? The Adventurer would be in his element in going to the Pug's room, and in relieving Pinkie Bonn of that money; but the Adventurer, too, was a thief-wasn't he? Why, then, did she propose, for her mind was now certainly made up as to her course of action, to trust a thief to recover that money for her?

She smiled a little wearily as she reached the drug store, stepped into the telephone booth, and gave central her call. Trust a thief! No, it wasn't because her heart prompted her to believe in him; it was because her head assured her she was safe in doing so. She could trust him in an instance such as this because--well, because once before, for her sake he had foregone the opportunity of appropriating a certain diamond necklace worth a hundred times the sum that she would ask him--yes, if necessary, for her sake--to recover to-night. There was no...

She was listening in a startled way now at the instrument. Central had given her "information"; and "information" was informing her that the number she had asked for had been disconnected.

She hung up the receiver, and went out again to the street in a dazed and bewildered way. And then suddenly a smile of bitter self-derision crossed her lips. She had been a fool! There was no softer word--a fool! Why had she not stopped to think? She understood now! On the night the Adventurer had confided that telephone number to her as Gypsy Nan, he had had every reason to believe that Gypsy Nan would, as she had already apparently done, befriend the White Moll even to the extent of accepting no little personal risk in so doing. But since then things had taken a very different turn. The White Moll was now held by the gang, of which Gypsy Nan was supposed to be a member, to be the one who had of late profited by the gang's plans to the gang's discomfiture; and the Adventurer was ranked but little lower in the scale of hatred, since they counted him to be the White Moll's accomplice. Knowing this, therefore, the first thing the Adventurer would naturally do would be to destroy the clew, in the shape of that telephone number, that would lead to his whereabouts, and which he of course believed he had put into the gang's hands when he had confided in Gypsy Nan. Had he not told her, no later than last night, that Gypsy Nan was her worst enemy? He did not know, did he, that Gypsy Nan and the White Moll were one! And so that telephone had been disconnected--and to-night, now, just when she needed help at a crucial moment, when she had counted upon the Adventurer to supply it, there was no Adventurer, no means of reaching him, and no means any more of knowing where he was!

Rhoda Gray walked on along the street, her lips tight, her face drawn and hard. Failing the Adventurer, there remained--the police. If she telephoned the police and sent them to the Pug's room, they would of a certainty recover the money, and with equal certainty restore it to its rightful owners. She had already thought of that when she had been with Pinkie and the Pug, and had been loath even then to take such a step because it seemed to spell ruin to her own personal plans; but now there was another reason, and one far more cogent, why she should not do so. There had been murder committed back there in that underground drug-dive, and of that murder Pinkie Bonn was innocent; but if Pinkie were found in possession of that money, and French Pete, to save his own skin from the consequences of a greater crime, admitted to its original theft, Pinkie would be convicted out of hand, for there were the others in that dive, who had come running along the passage, to testify that an attack had been made on the door of French Pete and Marny Day's room, and that the thieves and murderers had fled through the cellar and escaped.

Her lips pressed harder together. And so there was no Adventurer upon whom she could call, and no police, and no one in all the millions in this great pulsing city to whom she could appeal; and so there remained only--herself.

Well, she could do it, couldn't she? Not as Gypsy Nan, of course--but as the White Moll. It would be worth it, wouldn't it? If she were sincere, and not a moral hypocrite in her sympathy for those two outraged old people in the twilight of their lives, and if she were not a moral coward, there remained no question as to what her decision should be.

Her mind began to mull over the details. Subconsciously, since the moment she had made her escape from that cellar, she found now that she had been walking in the direction of the garret that sheltered her as Gypsy Nan. In another five minutes she could reach that deserted shed in the lane behind Gypsy Nan's house where her own clothes were hidden, and it would take her but a very few minutes more to effect the transformation from Gypsy Nan to the White Moll. And then, in another ten minutes, she should be back again at the Pug's room. The Pug had said he would not be much more than half an hour, but, as nearly as she could calculate it, that would still give her from five to ten minutes alone with Pinkie Bonn. It was enough--more than enough. The prestige of the White Moll would do the rest. A revolver in the hands of the White Moll would insure instant and obedient respect from Pinkie Bonn, or any other member of the gang under similar conditions. And so--and so--it--would not be difficult. Only there was a queer fluttering at her heart now, and her breath came in hard, short little inhalations. And she spoke suddenly to herself:

"I'm glad," she whispered, "I'm glad I saw those two old faces on that doorstep, because--because, if I hadn't, I--I would be afraid."

The minutes passed. The dissolute figure of an old hag disappeared, like a deeper shadow in the blackness of a lane, through the broken door of a deserted shed; presently a slim, neat little figure, heavily veiled, emerged. Again the minutes passed. And now the veiled figure let herself in through the back door of the Pug's lodging house, and stole softly down the dark hall, and halted before the Pug's door. It was the White Moll now.

From under the door, at the ill-fitting threshold, there showed a thin line of light. Rhoda Gray, with her ear against the door panel, listened. There was no sound of voices from within. Pinkie Bonn, then, was still alone, and still waiting for the Pug. She glanced sharply around her. There was only darkness. Her gloved right hand was hidden in the folds of her skirt; she raised her left hand and knocked softly upon the door-two raps, one rap, two raps. She repeated it. And as it had been with Shluker, so it was now with her. A footstep crossed the floor within, the key turned in the lock, and the door was flung open.

"All right, Pug," said Pinkie Bonn, "I--"

The man's words ended in a gasp of surprised amazement. With a quick step forward, Rhoda Gray was in the room. Her revolver, suddenly outflung, covered the other; and her free hand, reaching behind her, closed and locked the door again.

There was an almost stupid look of bewilderment on Pinkie Bonn's face.

Rhoda Gray threw back her veil.

"My Gawd!" mumbled Pinkie Bonn--and licked his lips. "The White Moll!"

"Yes!" said Rhoda Gray tersely. "Put your hands up over your head and go over there and stand against the wall--with your face to it!"

Pinkie Bonn, like an automaton moved purely by mechanical means, obeyed.

Rhoda Gray followed him, and with the muzzle of her revolver pressed into the small of the man's back, felt rapidly over his clothes with her left hand for the bulge of his revolver. She found and possessed herself of the weapon, and, stepping back, ordered him to turn around again.

"I haven't much time," she said icily. "I'll trouble you now for the cash you took from Marny Day and French Pete."

"My Gawd!" he mumbled again. "You know about that!"

"Quick!" she said imperatively. "Put it on the table there, and then go back again to the wall!"

Pinkie Bonn fumbled in his pocket. His face was white, almost chalky white, and it held fear; but its dominant expression was one of helpless stupefaction. He placed the sheaf of banknotes on the table, and shuffled back again to the wall.

Rhoda Gray picked up the money, and retreated to the door. Still facing the man, working with her left hand behind her back, she unlocked the door again, and this time removed the key from the lock.

"You are quite safe here," she observed evenly, "since there appears to be no window through which you could get out; but you might make it a little unpleasant for me if you gave the alarm and aroused the other occupants of the house before I had got well away. I dare say that was in your mind, but"--she opened the door slightly, and inserted the key on the outer side--"I am quite sure you will reconsider any such intentions--Pinkie. It would be a very disastrous thing for you if I were caught. Somebody is 'wanted' for the murder of Marny Day at Charlie's a little while ago, and a jury would undoubtedly decide that the guilty man was the one who broke in the door there and stole the money. And if I were caught and were obliged to confess that I got it from you, and French Pete swore that it was whoever broke into the room that shot his pal, it might go hard with you, Pinkie--don't you think so?" She smiled coldly at the man's staring eyes and dropped jaw. "Goodnight, Pinkie; I know you won't make any noise," she said softly--and suddenly opened the door, and in a flash stepped back into the hall, and closed and locked the door, and whipped out the key from the lock.

And inside Pinkie Bonn made no sound.

It was done now. Rhoda Gray drew in her breath in a great choking gasp of relief. She found herself trembling violently. She found her limbs were bearing her none too steadily, as she began to grope her way now along the black hall toward the back door. But it was done now, and--No, she was not safe away, even yet! Some one was coming in through that back door just ahead of her; or, at least, she heard voices out there.

She was just at the end of the hall now. There was no time to go back and risk the front entrance. She darted across the hall to the opposite side from that of the Pug's room, because on that side the opening of the door would not necessarily expose her, and crouched down in the corner. It was black here, perhaps black enough to escape observation. She listened, her heart beating wildly. The voices outside continued. Why were they lingering there? Why didn't they do one thing or the other--either go away, or come in? There wasn't any too much time! The Pug might be back at any minute now. Perhaps one of those people out there was the Pug! Perhaps it would be better after all to run back and go out by the front door, risky as that would be. No, her escape in that direction now was cut off, too!

She shrank as far back into the corner as she could. The door of the end room on this side of the hall had opened, and now a man stepped out and closed the door behind him. Would he see her? She held her breath. No! It--it was all right. He was walking away from her toward the front of the hall. And now for a moment it seemed as though she had lost her senses, as though her brain were playing some mad, wild trick upon her. Wasn't that the Pug's door before which the man had stopped? Yes, yes! And he seemed to have a key to it, for he did not knock, and the door was opening, and now for an instant, just an instant, the light fell upon the man as he stepped with a quick, lightning-like movement inside, and she saw his face. It was the Adventurer.

She stifled a little cry. Her brain was in turmoil. And now the back door was opening. They--they might see her here! And--yes--it was safer--safer to act on the sudden inspiration that had come to her. The door of the room from which the Adventurer had emerged was almost within reach; and he had not locked it as he had gone out--she had subconsciously noted that fact. And she understood why he had not now--that he had safeguarded himself against the loss of even the second or two it would have taken him to unlock it when he ran back for cover again from the Pug's room. Yes-that room! It was the safest thing she could do. She could even get out that way, for it must be the room with the low window, which she remembered gave on the back yard, and--She darted silently forward, and, as the back door opened, slipped into the room the Adventurer had just vacated.

It was pitch black. She must not make a sound; but, equally, she must not lose a second. What was taking place in the Pug's room between Pinkie Bonn and the Adventurer she did not know. But the Adventurer was obviously on one of his marauding expeditions, and he might stay there no more than a minute or two once he found out that he had been forestalled. She must hurry--hurry!

She felt her way forward in what she believed to be the direction of the window. She ran against the bed. But this afforded her something by which to guide herself. She kept her touch upon it, her hand trailing along its edge. And then, halfway down its length, what seemed to be a piece of string caught in her extended, groping fingers. It seemed to cling, but also to yield most curiously, as she tried to shake it off; and then something, evidently from under the mattress, came away with a little jerk, and remained, suspended, in her hand.

It didn't matter, did it? Nothing mattered except to reach the window. Yes, here it was now! And the roller shade was drawn down; that was why the room was so dark. She raised the shade quickly--and suddenly stood there as though transfixed, her face paling, as in the faint light by the window she gazed, fascinated, at the object that still dangled by a cord from her hand.

And it seemed as if an inner darkness were suddenly riven as by a bolt of lightning--a hundred things, once obscure and incomprehensible, were clear now, terribly clear. She understood now how the Adventurer was privy to all the inner workings of the organization; she understood now how it was, and why, the Adventurer had a room so close to that other room across the hall. That dangling thing on an elastic cord was a smeared and dirty celluloid eye-patch that had once been flesh-colored! The Adventurer and the Pug were one!

Her wits! Quick! He must not know! In a frenzy of haste she ran for the bed, and slipped the eye-patch in under the mattress again; and then, still with frenzied speed, she climbed to the window sill, drew the roller shade down again behind her, and dropped to the ground.

Through the back yard and lane she gained the street, and sped on along the street--but her thoughts outpaced her hurrying footsteps. How minutely every detail of the night now seemed to explain itself and dovetail with every other one! At the time, when Shluker had been present, it had struck her as a little forced and unnecessary that the Pug should have volunteered to seek out Danglar with explanations after the money had been secured. But she understood now the craft and guile that lay behind his apparently innocent plan. The Adventurer needed both time and an alibi, and also he required an excuse for making Pinkie Bonn the custodian of the stolen money, and of getting Pinkie alone with that money in the Pug's room. Going to Danglar supplied all this. He had hurried back, changed in that room from the Pug to the Adventurer, and proposed in the latter character to relieve Pinkie of the money, to return then across the hall, become the Pug again, and then go back, as though he had just come from Danglar, to find his friend and ally, Pinkie Bonn, robbed by their mutual arch-enemy--the Adventurer!

The Pug-the Adventurer! She did not quite seem to grasp its significance as applied to her in a personal way. It seemed to branch out into endless ramifications. She could not somehow think logically, coolly enough now, to decide what this meant in a concrete way to her, and her to-morrow, and the days after the to-morrow.

She hurried on. To-night, as she would lay awake through the hours that were to come, for sleep was a thing denied, perhaps a clearer vision would be given her. For the moment there--there was something else--wasn't there? The money that belonged to the old couple.

She hurried on. She came again to the street where the old couple lived. It was a dirty street, and from the curb she stooped and picked up a dirty piece of old newspaper. She wrapped the banknotes in the paper.

There were not many people on the street as she neared the mean little frame house, but she loitered until for the moment the immediate vicinity was deserted; then she slipped into the alleyway, and stole close to the side window, through which, she had noted from the street, there shone a light. Yes, they were there, the two of them--she could see them quite distinctly even through the shutters.

She went back to the front door then, and knocked. And presently the old woman came and opened the door.

"This is yours," Rhoda said, and thrust the package into the woman's hand. And as the woman looked from her to the package uncomprehendingly, Rhoda Gray flung a quick "good-night" over her shoulder, and ran down the steps again.

But a few moments later she stole back, and stood for an instant once more by the shuttered window in the alleyway. And suddenly her eyes grew dim. She saw an old man, white and haggard, with bandaged head, sitting in a chair, the tears streaming down his face; and on the floor, her face hidden on the other's knees, a woman knelt--and the man's hand stroked and stroked the thin gray hair on the woman' s head.

And Rhoda Gray turned away. And out in the street her face was lifted and she looked upward, and there were myriad stars. And there seemed a beauty in them that she had never seen before, and a great, comforting serenity. And they seemed to promise something--that through the window of that stark and evil garret to which she was going now, they would keep her dreaded vigil with her until morning came again.

XIV. THE LAME MAN

Another night--another day! And the night again had been without rest, lest Danglar's dreaded footstep come upon her unawares; and the day again had been one of restless, abortive activity, now prowling the streets as Gypsy Nan, now returning to the garret to fling herself upon the cot in the hope that in daylight, when she might risk it, sleep would come, but it had been without avail, for, in spite of physical weariness, it seemed to Rhoda Gray as though her tortured mind would never let her sleep again. Danglar's wife! That was the horror that was in her brain, yes, and in her soul, and that would not leave her.

And now night was coming upon her once more. It had even begun to grow dark here on the lower stairway that led up to that wretched, haunted garret above where in the shadows stark terror lurked. Strange! Most strange! She feared the night--and yet she welcomed it. In a little while, when it grew a little darker, she would steal out again and take up her work once more. It was only during the night, under the veil of darkness, that she could hope to make any progress in reaching to the heart and core of this criminal clique which surrounded her, whose members accepted her as Gypsy Nan, and, therefore, as one of themselves, and who would accord to her, if they but even suspected her to be the White Mall, less mercy than would be shown to a mad dog.

She climbed the stairs. Fear was upon her now, because fear was always there, and with it was abhorrence and loathing at the frightful existence fate had thrust upon her; but, somehow, to-night she was not so depressed, not so hopeless, as she had been the night before. There had been a little success; she had come a little farther along the way; she knew a little more than she had known before of the inner workings of the gang who were at the bottom of the crime of which she herself was accused. She knew now the Adventurer's secret, that the Pug and the Adventurer were one; and she knew where the Adventurer lived, now in one character, now in the other, in those two rooms almost opposite each other across that tenement hall.

And so it seemed that she had the right to hope, even though there were still so many things she did not know, that if she allowed her mind to dwell upon that phase of it, it staggered her--where those code messages came from, and how; why Rough Rorke of headquarters had never made a sign since that first night; why the original Gypsy Nan, who was dead now, had been forced into hiding with the death penalty of the law hanging over her; why Danglar, though Gypsy Nan's husband, was comparatively free. These, and a myriad other things! But she counted now upon her knowledge of the Adventurer's secret to force from him everything he knew; and, with that to work on, a confession from some of the gang in corroboration that would prove the authorship of the crime of which she had seemingly been caught in the act of committing.

Yes, she was beginning to see the way at last--through the Adventurer. It seemed a sure and certain way. If she presented herself before him as Gypsy Nan, whom he believed to be not only one of the gang, but actually Danglar's wife, and let him know that she was aware of the dual role he was playing, and that the information he thus acquired as the Pug he turned to his own account and to the undoing of the gang, he must of necessity be at her mercy. Her mercy! What exquisite irony! Her mercy! The man her heart loved; the thief her common sense abhorred! What irony! When she, too, played a double role; when in their other characters, that of the Adventurer and the White Moll, he and she were linked together by the gang as confederates, whereas, in truth, they were wider apart than the poles of the earth!

Her mercy! How merciful would she be--to the thief she loved? He knew, he must know, all the inner secrets of the gang. She smiled wanly now as she reached the landing. Would he know that in the last analysis her threat would be only an idle one; that, though her future, her safety, her life depended on obtaining the evidence she felt he could supply, her threat would be empty, and that she was powerless--because she loved him. But he did not know she loved him--she was Gypsy Nan. If she kept her secret, if he did not penetrate her disguise as she had penetrated his, if she were Gypsy Nan and Danglar's wife to him, her threat would be valid enough, and--and he would be at her mercy!

A flush, half shamed, half angry, dyed the grime that was part of Gypsy Nan's disguise upon her face. What was she saying to herself? What was she thinking? That he did not know she loved him! How would he? How could he? Had a word, an act, a single look of hers ever given him a hint that, when she had been with him as the White Moll, she cared! It was unjust, unfair, to fling such a taunt at herself. It seemed as though she had lost nearly everything in life, but she had not yet lost her womanliness and her pride.

She had certainly lost her senses, though! Even if that word, that look, that act had passed between them, between the Adventurer and the White Moll, he still did not know that Gypsy Nan was the White Moll--and that was the one thing now that he must not know, and...

Rhoda Gray halted suddenly, and stared along the hallway ahead of her, and up the short, ladder-like steps that led to the garret. Her ears--or was it fancy?--had caught what sounded like a low knocking up there upon her door. Yes, it came again now distinctly. It was dusk outside; in here, in the hall, it was almost dark. Her eyes strained through the murk. She was not mistaken. Something darker than the surrounding darkness, a form, moved up there.

The knocking ceased, and now the form seemed to bend down and grope along the floor; and then, an instant later, it began to descend the ladder-like steps--and abruptly Rhoda Gray, too, moved forward. It wasn't Danglar. That was what had instantly taken hold of her mind, and she knew a sudden relief now. The man on the stairs--she could see that it was a man now--though he moved silently, swayed in a grotesquely jerky way as though he were lame. It wasn't Danglar! She would go to any length to track Danglar to his lair; but not here--here in the darkness--here in the garret. Here she was afraid of him with a deadly fear; here alone with him there would be a thousand chances of exposure incident to the slightest intimacy he might show the woman whom he believed to be his wife--a thousand chances here against hardly one in any other environment or situation. But the man on the stairs wasn't Danglar.

She halted now and uttered a sharp exclamation, as though she had caught sight of the man for the first time.

The other, too, had halted--at the foot of the stairs. A plaintive drawl reached her:

"Don't screech, Bertha! It's only your devoted brother-in-law. Curse your infernal ladder, and my twisted back!"

Danglar's brother! Bertha! She snatched instantly at the cue with an inward gasp of thankfulness. She would not make the mistake of using the vernacular behind which Gypsy Nan sheltered herself. Here was some one who knew that Gypsy Nan was but a role. But she had to remember that her voice was slightly hoarse; that her voice, at least, could not sacrifice its disguise to any one. Danglar had been a little suspicious of it until she had explained that she was suffering from a cold.

"Oh!" she said calmly. "It's you, is it? And what brought you here?"

"What do you suppose?" he complained irritably. "The same old thing, all I'm good for--to write out code messages and deliver them like an errand boy! It's a sweet job, isn't it? How'd you like to be a deformed little cripple?"

She did not answer at once. The night seemed suddenly to be opening some strange, even premonitory, vista. The code messages! Their mode of delivery! Here was the answer!

"Maybe I'd like it better than being Gypsy Nan!" she flung back significantly.

He laughed out sharply.

"I'd like to trade with you," he said, a quick note of genuine envy in his voice. "You can pitch away your clothes; I can't pitch away a crooked spine. And, anyway, after to-night, you'll be living swell again."

She leaned toward him, staring at him in the semi-darkness. That premonitory vista was widening; his words seemed suddenly to set her brain in tumult. After to-night! She was to resume, after to-night, the character that was supposed to lay behind the disguise of Gypsy Nan! She was to resume her supposedly true character--that of Pierre Danglar's wife!

"What do you mean?" she demanded tensely.

"Aw, come on!" he said abruptly. "This isn't the place to talk. Pierre wants you at once. That's what the message was for. I thought you were out, and I left it in the usual place so you'd get it the minute you got back and come along over. So, come on now with me."

He was moving down the hallway, blotching like some misshapen toad in the shadowy light, lurching in his walk, that was, nevertheless, almost uncannily noiseless. Mechanically she followed him. She was trying to think; striving frantically to bring her wits to play on this sudden and unexpected denouement. It was obvious that he was taking her to Danglar. She had striven desperately last night to run Danglar to earth in his lair. And here was a self-appointed guide! And yet her emotions conflicted and her brain was confused. It was what she wanted, what through bitter travail of mind she had decided must be her course; but she found herself shrinking from it with dread and fear now that it promised to become a reality. It was not like last night when of her own initiative she had sought to track Danglar, for then she had started out with a certain freedom of action that held in reserve a freedom to retreat if it became necessary. To-night it was as though she were deprived of that freedom, and being led into what only too easily might develop into a trap from which she could not retreat or escape.

Suppose she refused to go?

They had reached the street now, and now she obtained a better view of the misshapen thing that lurched jerkily along beside her. The man was deformed, miserably deformed. He walked most curiously, half bent over; and one arm, the left, seemed to swing helplessly, and the left hand was like a withered thing. Her eyes sought the other's face. It was an old face, much older than Danglar's, and it was white and pinched and drawn; and in the dark eyes, as they suddenly darted a glance at her, she read a sullen, bitter brooding and discontent. She turned her head away. It was not a pleasant face; it struck her as being both morbid and cruel to a degree.

Suppose she refused to go?

"What did you mean by 'after to-night'?" she asked again.

"You'll see," he answered. "Pierre'll tell you. You're in luck, that's all. The whole thing that has kept you under cover has bust wide open your way, and you win. And Pierre's going through for a clean-up. To-morrow you can swell around in a limousine again. And maybe you'll come around and take me for a drive, if I dress up, and promise to hide in a corner of the back seat so's they won't see your handsome friend!"

The creature flung a bitter smile at her, and lurched on.

He had told her what she wanted to know--more than she had hoped for. The mystery that surrounded the character of Gypsy Nan, the evidence of the crime at which the woman who had originated that role had hinted on the night she died, and which must necessarily involve Danglar, was hers, Rhoda Gray's, now for the taking. As well go and give herself up to the police as the White Moll and have done with it all, as to refuse to seize the opportunity which fate, evidently in a kindlier mood toward her now, was offering her at this instant. It promised her the hold upon Danglar that she needed to force an avowal of her own innocence, the very hold that she had but a few minutes before been hoping she could obtain through the Adventurer.

There was no longer any question as to whether she would go or not.

Her hand groped down under the shabby black shawl into the wide, voluminous pocket of her greasy skirt. Yes, her revolver was there. She knew it was there, but the touch of her fingers upon it seemed to bring a sense of reassurance. She was perhaps staking her all in accompanying this cripple here to-night--she did not need to be told that--but there was a way of escape at the last if she were cornered and caught. Her fingers played with the weapon. If the worst came to the worst she would never be at Danglar's mercy while she possessed that revolver and, if the need came, turned it upon herself.

They walked on rapidly; the lurching figure beside her covering the ground at an astounding rate of speed. The man made no effort to talk. She was glad of it. She need not be so anxiously on her guard as would be the case if a conversation were carried on, and she, who knew so much and yet so pitifully little, must weigh her every word, and feel her way with every sentence. And besides, too, it gave her time to think. Where were they going? What sort of a place was it, this headquarters of the gang? For it must be the headquarters, since it was from there the code messages would naturally emanate, and this deformed creature, from what he had said, was the "secretary" of the nefarious clique that was ruled by his brother. And was luck really with her at last? Suppose she had been but a few minutes later in reaching Gypsy Nan's house, and had found, instead of this man here, only the note instructing her to go and meet Danglar! What would she have done? What explanation could she have made for her nonappearance? Her hands would have been tied. She would have been helpless. She could not have answered the summons, for she could have had no idea where this gang-lair was; and the note certainly would not contain such details as street and number, which she was obviously supposed to know. She smiled a little grimly to herself. Yes, it seemed as though fortune were beginning to smile upon her again--fortune, at least, had supplied her with a guide.

The twisted figure walked on the inside of the sidewalk, and curiously seemed to seek as much as possible the protecting shadows of the buildings, and invariably shrank back out of the way of the passers-by they met. She watched him narrowly as they went along. What was he afraid of? Recognition? It puzzled her for a time, and then she understood: It was not fear of recognition; the sullen, almost belligerent stare with which he met the eyes of those with whom he came into close contact belied that. The man was morbidly, abnormally sensitive of his deformity.

They turned at last into one of the East Side cross streets, and her guide halted finally on a corner in front of a little shop that was closed and dark. She stared curiously as the man unlocked the door. Perhaps, after all, she had been woefully mistaken. It did not look at all the kind of place where crimes that ran the gamut of the decalogue were hatched, at all the sort of place that was the council chamber of perhaps the most cunning, certainly the most cold-blooded and unscrupulous, band of crooks that New York had ever harbored. And yet--why not? Wasn't there the essence of cunning in that very fact? Who would suspect anything of the sort from a ramshackle, two-story little house like this, whose front was a woe-begone little store, the proceeds of which might just barely keep the body and soul of its proprietor together?

The man fumbled with the lock. There was not a single light showing from the place, but in the dwindling rays of a distant street lamp she could see the meager window display through the filthy, unwashed panes. It was evidently a cheap and tawdry notion store, well suited to its locality. There were toys of the cheapest variety, stationery of the same grade, cheap pipes, cigarettes, tobacco, candy--a package of needles.

"Go on in!" grunted the man, as he pushed the door--which seemed to shriek out unduly on its hinges--wide open. "If anybody sees the door open, they'll be around wanting to buy a paper of pins--curse 'em!--and I ain't open to-night." He snarled as he shut and locked the door. "Pierre says you're grouching about your garret. How about me, and this job? You get out of yours to-night for keeps. What about me? I can't do anything but act as a damned blind for the rest of you with this fool store, just because I was born a freak that every gutter-snipe on the street yells at!"

Rhoda Gray did not answer.

"Well, go on!" snapped the man. "What are you standing there for? One would think you'd never been here before!"

Go on! Where? She had not the faintest idea. It was quite dark inside here in the shop. She could barely make out the outline of the other's figure.

"You're in a sweet temper to-night, aren't you?" she said tartly. "Go on, yourself! I'm waiting for you to get through your speech."

He moved brusquely past her, with an angry grunt. Rhoda Gray followed him. They passed along a short, narrow space, evidently between a low counter and a shelved wall, and then the man opened a door, and, shutting it again behind them, moved forward once more. She could scarcely see him at all now; it was more the sound of his footsteps than anything else that guided her. And then suddenly another door was opened, and a soft, yellow light streamed out through the doorway, and she found that she was standing in an intervening room between the shop and the room ahead of her. She felt her pulse quicken, and it seemed as though her heart began to thump almost audibly. Danglar! She could see Danglar seated at a table in there. She clenched her hands under her shawl. She would need all her wits now. She prayed that there was not too much light in that room yonder.

XV. IN THE COUNCIL CHAMBER

The man with the withered hand had passed through into the other room. She heard them talking together, as she followed. She forced herself to walk with as nearly a leisurely defiant air as she could. The last time she had been with Danglar--as Gypsy Nan--she had, in self-protection, forbidding intimacy, played up what he called her "grouch" at his neglect of her.

She paused in the doorway. Halfway across the room, at the table, Danglar's gaunt, swarthy face showed under the rays of a shaded oil lamp. Behind her spectacles, she met his small, black ferret eyes steadily.

"Hello, Bertha!" he called out cheerily. "How's the old girl to-night?" He rose from his seat to come toward her. "And how's the cold?"

Rhoda Gray scowled at him.

"Worse!" she said curtly-and hoarsely. "And a lot you care! I could have died in that hole, for all you knew!" She pushed him irritably away, as he came near her. "Yes, that's what I said! And you needn't start any cooing game now! Get down to cases!" She jerked her hand toward the twisted figure that had slouched into a chair beside the table. "He says you've got it doped out to pull something that will let me out of this Gypsy Nan stunt. Another bubble, I suppose!" She shrugged her shoulders, glanced around her, and, locating a chair--not too near the table--seated herself indifferently. "I'm getting sick of bubbles!" she announced insolently. "What's this one?"

He stood there for a moment biting at his lips, hesitant between anger and tolerant amusement; and then, the latter evidently gaining the ascendency, he too shrugged his shoulders, and with a laugh returned to his chair.

"You're a rare one, Bertha!" he said coolly. "I thought you'd be wild with delight. I guess you're sick, all right--because usually you're pretty sensible. I've tried to tell you that it wasn't my fault I couldn't go near you, and that I had to keep away from--"

"What's the use of going over all that again?" she interrupted tartly. "I guess I--"

"Oh, all right!" said Danglar hurriedly. "Don't start a row! After to-night I've an idea you'll be sweet enough to your husband, and I'm willing to wait. Matty maybe hasn't told you the whole of it."

Matty! So that was the deformed creature's name. She glanced at him. He was grinning broadly. A family squabble seemed to afford him amusement. Her eyes shifted and made a circuit of the room. It was poverty-stricken in appearance, bare-floored, with the scantiest and cheapest of furnishings, its one window tightly shuttered.

"Maybe not," she said carelessly.

"Well, then, listen, Bertha!" Danglar's voice was lowered earnestly. "We've uncovered the Nabob's stuff! Do you get me? Every last one of the sparklers!"

Rhoda Gray's eyes went back to the deformed creature at Danglar's side, as the man laughed out abruptly.

"Yes," grinned Matty Danglar, "and they weren't in the empty money-belt that you beat it with like a scared cat after croaking Deemer!"

How queer and dim the light seemed to go suddenly--or was it a blur before her own eyes? She said nothing. Her mind seemed to be groping its way out of darkness toward some faint gleam of light showing in the far distance. She heard Danglar order his brother savagely to hold his tongue. That was curious, too, because she was grateful for the man's gibe. Gypsy Nan, in her proper person, had murdered a man named Deemer in an effort to secure--Danglar's voice came again:

"Well, to-night we'll get that stuff, all of it--it's worth a cool half million; and to-night we'll get Mr. House-Detective Cloran for keeps--bump him off. That cleans everything up. How does that strike you, Bertha?"

Rhoda Gray's hands under her shawl locked tightly together. Her premonition had not betrayed her. She was face to face to-night with the beginning of the end.

"It sounds fine!" she said derisively.

Danglar's eyes narrowed for an instant; and then he laughed.

"You're a rare one, Bertha!" he ejaculated again. "You don't seem to put much stock in your husband lately."

"Why should I?" she inquired imperturbably. "Things have been breaking fine, haven't they?--only not for us!" She cleared her throat as though it were an effort to talk. "I'm not going crazy with joy till I've been shown."

Danglar leaned suddenly over the table.

"Well, come and look at the cards, then," he said impressively. "Pull your chair up to the table, and I'll tell you."

Rhoda Gray tilted her chair, instead, nonchalantly back against the wall--it was quite light enough where she was!

"I can hear you from here," she said coolly. "I'm not deaf, and I guess Matty's suite is safe enough so that you won't have to whisper all the time!"

The deformed creature at the table chortled again.

Danglar scowled.

"Damn you, Bertha!" he flung out savagely. "I could wring that neck of yours sometimes, and--"

"I know you could, Pierre," she interposed sweetly. "That's what I like about you--you're so considerate of me! But suppose you get down to cases. What's the story about those sparklers? And what's the game that's going to let me shed this Gypsy Nan stuff for keeps?"

"I'll tell her, Pierre," grinned the deformed one. "It'll keep you two from spitting at one another; and neither of you have got all night to stick around here." He swung his withered hand suddenly across the table, and as suddenly all facetiousness was gone both from his voice and manner. "Say, you listen hard, Bertha! What Pierre's telling you is straight. You and him can kiss and make up to-morrow or the next day, or whenever you damned please; but to-night there ain't any more time for scrapping. Now, listen! I handed you a rap about beating it with the empty money-belt the night you croaked Deemer with an overdose of knockout drops in the private dining-room up at the Hotel Marwitz, but you forget that! I ain't for starting any argument about that. None of us blames you. We thought the stuff was in the belt, too. And none of us blames you for making a mistake and going too strong with the drops, either; anybody might do that. And I'll say now that I take my hat off to you for the way you locked Cloran into the room with the dead man, and made your escape when Cloran had you dead to rights for the murder; and I'll say, too, that the way you've played Gypsy Nan and saved your skin, and ours too, is as slick a piece of work as has ever been pulled in the underworld. That puts us straight, you and me, don't it, Bertha?"

Rhoda Gray blinked at the man through her spectacles; her brain was whirling in a mad turmoil. "I always liked you, Matty," she whispered softly.

Danglar was lolling back in his chair, blowing smoke rings into the air. She caught his eyes fixed quizzically upon her.

"Go on, Matty!" he prompted. "You'll have her in a good humor, if you're not careful!"

"We were playing more or less blind after that." The withered hand traced an aimless pattern on the table with its crooked and half-closed fingers, and the man's face was puckered into a shrewd, reminiscent scowl. "The papers couldn't get a lead on the motive for the murder, and the police weren't talking for publication. Not a word about the Rajah's jewels. Washington saw to that! A young potentate's son, practically the guest of the country, touring about in a special for the sake of his education, and dashed near 'ending it in the river out West if it hadn't been for the rescue you know about, wouldn't look well in print; so there wasn't anything said about the slather of gems that was the reward of heroism from a grateful nabob, and we didn't get any help that way. All we knew was that Deemer came East with the jewels, presumably to cash in on them, and it looked as though Deemer were pretty clever; that he wore the money-belt for a stall, and that he had the sparklers safe somewhere else all the time. And I guess we all got to figuring it that way, because the fact that nothing was said about any theft was strictly along the lines the police were working anyway, and a was a toss-up that they hadn't found the stuff among his effects. Get me?"

Get him! This wasn't real, was it, this room here; those two figures sitting there under that shaded lamp? Something cold, an icy grip, seemed to seize at her heart, as in a surge there swept upon her the full appreciation of her peril through these confidences to which she was listening. A word, in act, some slightest thing, might so easily betray her; and then--Her fingers under the shawl and inside the wide pocket of her greasy skirt, clutched at her revolver. Thank God for that! It would at least be merciful! She nodded her head mechanically.

"But the police didn't find the jewels--because they weren't there to be found.

Somebody got in ahead of us. Pinched 'em, understand, may be only a few hours before you got in your last play, and, from the way you say Deemer acted, before he was wise to the fact that he'd been robbed."

Rhoda Gray let her chair come sharply down to the floor. She must play her role of "Bertha" now as she never had before. Here was a question that she could not only ask with safety, but one that was obviously expected.

"Who was it?" she demanded breathlessly.

"She's coming to life!" murmured Danglar, through a haze of cigarette smoke. "I thought you'd wake up after a while, Bertha. This is the big night, old girl, as you'll find out before we're through."

"Who was it?" she repeated with well-simulated impatience.

"I guess she'll listen to me now," said Danglar, with a little chuckle. "Don't over-tax yourself any more, Matty. I'll tell you, Bertha; and it will perhaps make you feel better to know it took the slickest dip New York ever knew to beat you to the tape. It was Angel Jack, alias the Gimp."

"How do you know?" Rhoda Gray demanded.

"Because," said Danglar, and lighted another cigarette, "he died yesterday afternoon up in Sing Sing."

She could afford to show her frank bewilderment. Her brows knitted into furrows, as she stared at Danglar.

"You--you mean he confessed?" she said.

"The Angel? Never!" Danglar laughed grimly, and shook his head. "Nothing like that! It was a question of playing one 'fence' against another. You know that Witzer, who's handled all our jewelry for us, has been on the look-out for any stones that might have come from that collection. Well, this afternoon he passed the word to me that he'd been offered the finest unset emerald he'd ever seen, and that it had come to him through old Jake Luertz's runner, a very innocent-faced young man who is known to the trade as the Crab."

Danglar paused--and laughed again. Unconsciously Rhoda Gray drew her shawl a little closer about her shoulders. It seemed to bring a chill into the room, that laugh. Once before, on another night, Danglar had laughed, and, with his parted lips, she had likened him to a beast showing its fangs. He looked it now more than ever. For all his ease of voice and manner, he was in deadly earnest; and if there was merriment in his laugh, it but seemed to enhance the menace and the promise of unholy purpose that lurked in the cold glitter of his small, black eyes.

"It didn't take long to get hold of the Crab"--Danglar was rubbing his hands together softly--"and the emerald with him. We got him where we could put the screws on without arousing the neighborhood."

"Another murder, I suppose!" Rhoda Gray flung out the words crossly.

"Oh, no," said Danglar pleasantly. "He squealed before it came to that. He's none the worse for wear, and he'll be turned loose in another hour or so, as soon as we're through at old Jake Luertz's. He's no more good to us. He came across all right--after he was properly frightened. He's been with old Jake as a sort of familiar for the last six years, and--"

"He'd have sold his soul out, he was so scared!" The withered hand on the table twitched; the deformed creature's face was twisted into a grimace; and the man was chuckling with unhallowed mirth, as though unable to contain himself at, presumably, the recollection of a scene which he had witnessed himself. "He was down on his knees and clawing out with his hands for mercy, and he squealed like a rat. 'It's the sixth panel in the bedroom upstairs,' he says; 'it's all there. But for God's sake don't tell Jake I told. It's the sixth panel. Press the knot in the sixth panel that--'" He stopped abruptly.

Danglar had pulled out his watch and with exaggerated patience was circling the crystal with his thumb.

"Are you all through, Matty?" he inquired monotonously. "I think you said something a little while ago about wasting time. Bertha's looking bored; and, besides, she's got a little job of her own on for to-night." He jerked his watch back into his pocket, and turned to Rhoda Gray again. "The only one who knew all the details Angel Jack, and he'll never tell now because he's dead. Whether he came down from the West with Deemer or not, or how he got wise to the stones, I don't know. But he got the stones, all right. And then he tumbled to the fact that the police were pushing him hard for another job he was 'wanted' for, and he had to get those stones out of sight in a hurry. He made a package of them and slipped them to old Luertz, who had always done his business for him, to keep for him; and before he could duck, the bulls had him for that other job. Angel Jack went up the river. See? Old Jake didn't know what was in that package; but he knew better than to monkey with it, because he always thought something of his own skin. He knew Angel Jack, and he knew what would happen if he didn't have that package ready to hand back the day Angel Jack got out of Sing Sing. Understand? But yesterday Angel Jack died-without a will; and old Jake appointed himself sole executor-without bonds! He opened that package, figured he'd begin turning it into money--and that's how we get our own back again. Old Jake will get a fake message to-night calling him out of the house on an errand uptown; and about ten o'clock Pinkie Bonn and the Pug will pay a visit there in his absence, and--well, it looks good, don't it, Bertha, after two years?"

Rhoda Gray was crouched down in her chair. She shrugged her shoulders now, and infused a sullen note into her voice.

"Yes, it's fine!" she sniffed. "I'll be rolling in wealth in my garret--which will do me a lot of good! That doesn't separate me from these rags, and the hell I've lived, does it--after two years?"

"I'm coming to that," said Danglar, with his short, grating laugh. "We've as good as got the stones now, and we're going through to-night for a clean-up of all that old mess. We stake the whole thing. Get me, Bertha--the whole thing! I'm showing my hand for the first time. Cloran's the man that's making you wear those clothes; Cloran's the only one who could go into the witness box and swear that you were the woman who murdered Deemer; and Cloran's the man who has been working his head off for two years to find you. We've tried a dozen times to bump him off in a way that would make his death appear to be due purely to an accident, and we didn't get away with it; but we can afford to leave the 'accident' out of it to-night, and go through for keeps--and that's what we're going to do. And once he's out of the way--by midnight--you can heave Gypsy Nan into the discard."

It seemed to Rhoda Gray that horror had suddenly taken a numbing hold upon her sensibilities. Danglar was talking about murdering some man, wasn't he, so that she could resume again the personality of a woman who was dead? Hysterical laughter rose to her lips. It was only by a frantic effort of will that she controlled herself. She seemed to speak involuntarily, doubtful almost that it was her own voice she heard.

"I'm listening," she said; "but I wouldn't be too sure. Cloran's a wary bird, and there's the White Moll."

She caught her breath. What suicidal inspiration had prompted her to say that! Had what she had been listening to here, the horror of it, indeed turned her brain and robbed her of her wits to the extent that she should invite exposure? Danglar's face had gone a mottled purple; the misshapen thing at Danglar's side was leering at her most curiously.

It was a moment before Danglar spoke; and then his hand, clenched until the white of the knuckles showed, pounded upon the table to punctuate his words.

"Not to-night!" he rasped out with an oath. "There's not a chance that she's in on this to-night--the she-devil! But she's next! With this cleaned up, she's next! If it takes the last dollar of to-night's haul, and five years to do it, I'll get her, and get--"

"Sure!" mumbled Rhoda Gray hurriedly. "But you needn't get excited! I was only thinking of her because she's queered us till I've got my fingers crossed, that's all. Go on about Cloran."

Danglar's composure did not return on the instant. He gnawed at his lips for a moment before he spoke.

"All right!" he jerked out finally. "Let it go at that! I told you the other night in the garret that things were beginning to break our way, and that you wouldn't have to stay there much longer, but I didn't tell you how or why--you wouldn't give me a chance. I'll tell you now; and it's the main reason why I've kept away from you lately. I couldn't take a chance of Cloran getting wise to that garret and Gypsy Nan." He grinned suddenly. "I've been cultivating Cloran myself for the last two weeks. We're quite pals! I'm for playing the luck every time! When the jewels showed up to-day, I figured that to-night's the night--see? Cloran and I are going to supper together at the Silver Sphinx at about eleven o'clock--and this is where you shed the Gypsy Nan stuff, and show up as your own sweet self. Cloran'll be glad to meet you!"

She stared at him in genuine perplexity and amazement.

"Show myself to Cloran!" she ejaculated heavily. "I don't get you!"

"You will in a minute," said Danglar softly. "You're the bait--see? Cloran and I will be at supper and watching the fox-trotters. You blow in and show yourself--I don't need to tell you how, you're clever enough at that sort of thing yourself--and the minute he recognizes you as the woman he's been looking for that murdered Deemer, you pretend to recognize him for the first time too, and then you beat it like you had the scare of your life for the door. He'll follow you on the jump. I don't know what it's all about, and I sit tight, and that lets me out. And now get this! There'll be two taxicabs outside. If there's more than two, it's the first two I'm talking about. You jump into the one at the head of the line. Cloran won't need any invitation to grab the second one and follow you. That's all! It's the last ride he'll take. It'll be our boys, and not chauffeurs, who'll be driving those cars to-night, and they've got their orders where to go. Cloran won't come back. Understand, Bertha'?"

There was only one answer to make, only one answer that she dared make. She made it mechanically, though her brain reeled. A man named Cloran was to be murdered; and she was to show herself as this--this Bertha--and...

"Yes," she said.

"Good!" said Danglar. He pulled out his watch again. "All right, then! We've been here long enough." He rose briskly. "It's time to make a move. You hop it back to the garret, and get rid of that fancy dress. I've got to meet Cloran uptown first. Come on, Matty, let us out."

The place stifled her. She got up and moved quickly through the intervening room. She heard Danglar and his crippled brother talking earnestly together as they followed her. And then the cripple brushed by her in the darkness, and opened the front door--and Danglar had drawn her to him in a quick embrace. She did not struggle; she dared not. Her heart seemed to stand still. Danglar was whispering in her ear:

"I promised I'd make it up to you, Bertha, old girl. You'll see--after to-night. We'll have another honey-moon. You go on ahead now--I can't be seen with Gypsy Nan. And don't be late--the Silver Sphinx at eleven."

She ran out on the street. Her fingers mechanically clutched at her shawl to loosen it around her throat. It seemed as though she were choking, that she could not breathe. The man's touch upon her had seemed like contact with some foul and loathsome thing; the scene in that room back there like some nightmare of horror from which she could not awake.

XVI. THE SECRET PANEL

Rhoda Gray hurried onward, back toward the garret, her mind in riot and dismay. It was not only the beginning of the end; it was very near the end! What was she to do? The Silver Sphinx--at eleven! That was the end--after eleven--wasn't it? She could impersonate Gypsy Nan; she could not, if she would, impersonate the woman who was dead! And then, too, there were the stolen jewels at old Jake Luertz's! She could not turn to the police for help there, because then the Pug might fall into their hands, and--and the Pug was--was the Adventurer.

And then a sort of fatalistic calm fell upon her. If the masquerade was over, if the end had come, there remained only one thing for her to do. There were no risks too desperate to take now. It was she who must strike, and strike first. Those jewels in old Luertz's bedroom became suddenly vital to her. They were tangible evidence. With those jewels in her possession she should be able to force Danglar to his knees. She could get them--before Pinkie Bonn and the Pug--if she hurried. Afterward she would know where to find Danglar--at the Silver Sphinx. Nothing would happen to Cloran, because, through her failure to cooperate, the plan would be abortive; but, veiled, as the White Moll, she could pick up Danglar's trail again there. Yes, it would be the end--one way or the other--between eleven o'clock and daylight!

She quickened her steps. Old Luertz was to be inveigled away from his home about ten o'clock. At a guess, she made it only a little after nine now. She would need the skeleton keys in order to get into old Luertz's place, and, yes, she would need a flashlight, too. Well, she would have time enough to get them, and time enough, then, to run to the deserted shed in the lane behind the garret and change her clothes.

Rhoda Gray, as Gypsy Nan, went on as speedily as she dared without inviting undue attention to herself, reached the garret, secured the articles she sought, hurried out again, and went down the lane in the rear to the deserted shed. She remained longer here than in the attic, perhaps ten minutes, working mostly in the darkness, risking the flashlight only when it was imperative; and then, the metamorphosis complete, a veiled figure, in her own person, as Rhoda Gray, the White Moll, she was out on the street again, and hastening back in the same general direction from which she had just come.

She knew old Jake Luertz's place, and she knew the man himself very intimately by reputation. There were few such men and such places that she could have escaped knowing in the years of self-appointed service that she had given to the worst, and perhaps therefore the most needy, element in New York. The man ostensibly conducted a little secondhand store; in reality he probably "shoved" more stolen goods for his clientele, which at one time or another undoubtedly embraced nearly every crook in the underworld, than any other "fence" in New York. She knew him for an oily, cunning old fox who lived alone in the two rooms over his miserable store--unless, of late, his young henchman, the Crab, had taken to living with him; though, as far as that was concerned, it mattered little to-night, since the Crab, for the moment, thanks to the gang, was eliminated from consideration.

She reached the secondhand store--and walked on past it. There was a light upstairs in the front window. Old Luertz therefore had not yet gone out in response to the gang's fake message. She knew old Luertz's reputation far too well for that; the man would never go out and leave a gas jet burning--which he would have to pay for!

There was nothing to do but wait. Rhoda Gray sought the shelter of a doorway across the street. She was nervously impatient now. The minutes dragged along. Why didn't 'the man hurry and go out? "About ten o'clock," Danglar had said-- but that was very indefinite. Pinkie Bonn and the Pug might be as late as that; but, equally, they might be earlier!

It seemed an interminable time. And then, her eyes strained across the street upon that upper window, she drew still farther back into the protecting shadows of the doorway. The light had gone out.

A moment more passed. The street door of the house opposite to her--a door separate from that of the secondhand store-opened, and a bent, gray-bearded man, stepped out, peered around, locked the door behind him, and scuffled down the street.

Rhoda Gray scanned the dingy and ill-lighted little street. It was virtually deserted. She crossed the road, and stepped into the doorway from which the old "fence" had just emerged. It was dark here, well out of the direct radius of the nearest street lamp, and, with luck, there was no reason why she should be observed--if she did not take too long in opening the door! She had never actually used a skeleton key in her life before, and...

She inserted one of her collection of keys in the lock. It would not work. She tried another, and still another-with mounting anxiety and perplexity. Suppose that--yes! The door was open now! With a quick glance over her shoulder, scanning the street in both directions to make sure that she was not observed, she stepped inside, closed the door, and locked it again.

Her flashlight stabbed through the darkness. Narrow stairs immediately in front of her led upward; at her right was a connecting door to the secondhand shop. Without an instant's hesitation she ran up the stairs. There was no need to observe caution since the place was temporarily untenanted; there was need only of haste. She opened the door at the head of the stairs, and, with a quick, eager nod of satisfaction, as the flashlight swept the interior, stepped over the threshold. It was the room she sought--old Luertz's bedroom.

And now the flashlight played inquisitively about her. The bed occupied a position by the window; across one corner of the room was a cretonne hanging, that evidently did service as a wardrobe; across another corner was a large and dilapidated washstand; there were a few chairs, and a threadbare carpet; and, opposite the bed, another door, closed, which obviously led into the front room.

Rhoda Gray stepped to this door, opened it, and peered in. She was not concerned that it was evidently used for kitchen, dining-room and the stowage of everything that overflowed from the bedroom; she was concerned only with the fact that it offered no avenue through which any added risk or danger might reach her. She closed the door as she had found it, and gave her attention now to the walls of old Luertz's bedroom.

She smiled a little whimsically. The Crab had used a somewhat dignified term when he had referred to "panels." True, the walls were of stained wood, but the wood was of the cheapest variety of matched boards, and the stain was of but a single coat, and a very meager one at that! The smile faded. There were a good many knots; and there were four corners to the room, and therefore eight boards, each one of which would answer to the description of being the "sixth panel."

She went to the corner nearest her, and dropped down on her knees. As well start with this one! She had not dared press Danglar, or Danglar's deformed brother, for more definite directions, had she? She counted the boards quickly from the corner to her right; and then, the flashlight playing steadily, she began to press first one knot after another, in the board before her, working from the bottom up. There were many knots; she went over each one with infinite care. There was no result.

She turned then to the sixth board from the corner to her left. The result was the same. She stood up, her brows puckered, a sense of anxious impatience creeping upon her. She had been quite a while over even these two boards, and it might be any one of the remaining six!

Her eyes traversed the room, following the ray of the flashlight. If she only knew which one, it would--Was it an inspiration? Her eyes had fixed on the cretonne hanging across one of the far corners from the door, and she moved toward it now quickly. The hanging might very well serve for an other purpose than that of merely a wardrobe! It seemed suddenly to be the most likely of the four corners because it was ingeniously concealed.

She parted the hanging. A heterogeneous collection of clothing hung from pegs and nails. Eagerly, hastily now, she brushed these aside, and, close to the wall, dropped down on her knees again. The minutes passed. Twice she went over the sixth board from the corner to her right. She felt so sure now that it was this corner. And then, still eagerly, she turned to the corresponding board at her left.

It was warm and close here. The clothing hanging from the pegs and nails enveloped her, and, with the cretonne hanging itself, shut out the air, what little of it there was, that circulated through the room.

Over the board, from the tiniest knot to the largest, her fingers pressed carefully. Had she missed one anywhere? She must have missed one! She was sure the panel in question was here behind this hanging. Well, she would try again, and...

What was that?

In an instant the flashlight in her hand was out, and she was listening tensely.

Yes, there was a footstep--two of them--not only on the stairs, but already just outside the door. It seemed as though a deadly fear, cold and numbing, settled upon her and robbed her of even the power of movement. She was caught! If it was Pinkie Bonn and the Pug, and if this corner hid the secret panel as she still believed it did, this was the first place to which they would come, and they would find her here amongst the clothing--which had evidently been the cause of deadening any sound on those stairs out there until it was too late.

She held her breath, her hands tight upon her bosom. There was no time to reach the sanctuary of the other room--the footsteps were already crossing the threshold from the head of the stairs. And then a voice reached her--the Pug's. It was the Pug and Pinkie Bonn.

"Strike a light, Pinkie! Dere's no use messin' around wid a flash. De old geezer'll be back on de hop de minute he finds out he's been bunked, an' de quicker we work de better."

A match crackled into flame. An air-choked gas jet, with a protesting hiss, was lighted. And then Rhoda Gray's drawn face relaxed a little, and a strange, mirthless smile came hovering over her lips. What was she afraid of? The Pug was the Adventurer, wasn't he? This was one of the occasions when he could not escape the entanglements of the gang, and must work for the gang instead of appropriating all the loot for his own personal and nefarious ends; but he was the Adventurer. The White Moll need not fear him, even though he appeared, linked with Pinkie Bonn, in the role of the Pug! So there was only Pinkie Bonn to fear.

Rhoda Gray took her revolver from her pocket. She was well armed--and in more than a material sense. The Adventurer did not know that she was aware of the Pug's identity. Her smile, still mirthless, deepened. She might even turn the tables upon them, and still secure the stolen stones. She had turned the tables upon Pinkie Bonn last night; to-night, if she used her wits, she could do it again!

And then, suddenly, she stifled an exclamation, as the Pug's voice reached her again:

"Wot are youse gapin' about? Dere ain't anything else worth pinchin' around here except wot's in de old gent's safety vault. Get a move on! We ain't got all night! It's de corner behind de washstand. Give us a hand to move de furniture!"

It wasn't here behind the cretonne hanging! Rhoda Gray bit her lips in a crestfallen little way. Well, her supposition had been natural enough, hadn't it? And she would have tried every corner before she was through if she had had the opportunity.

She moved now slightly, without a sound, parting the clothing away from in front of her, and moving the cretonne hanging by the fraction of an inch where it touched the side wall of the room. And now she could see the Pug, with his dirty and discolored celluloid eye-patch, and his ingeniously contorted face; and she could see Pinkie Bonn's pasty-white, drug-stamped countenance.

It was not a large room. The two men in the opposite corner along the wall from her were scarcely more than ten feet away. They swung the washstand out from the wall, and the Pug, going in behind it, began to work on one of the wall boards. Pinkie Bonn, an unlighted cigarette dangling from his lip, leaned over the washstand watching his companion.

A minute passed--another. It was still in the room, except only for the distant sounds of the world outside--a clatter of wheels upon the pavement, the muffled roar of the elevated, the clang of a trolley bell. And then the Pug began to mutter to himself. Rhoda Gray smiled a little grimly. She was not the only one, it would appear, who experienced difficulty with old Jake Luertz's crafty hiding place!

"Say, dis is de limit!" the Pug growled out suddenly. "Dere's more damned knots in dis board dan I ever save in any piece of wood in me life before, an'--" He drew back abruptly from the wall, twisting his head sharply around. "D'ye hear dat, Pinkie!" he whispered tensely. "Quick! Put out de light! Quick! Dere's some one down at de front door!"

Rhoda Gray felt the blood ebb from her face. She had heard nothing save the rattle and bump of a wagon along the street below; but she had had reason to appreciate on a certain occasion before that the Pug, alias the Adventurer, was possessed of a sense of hearing that was abnormally acute. If it was some one else--who was it? What would it mean to her? What complication here in this room would result? What...

The light was out. Pinkie Bonn had stepped silently across the room to the gas jet near the door. Her eyes, strained, she could just make out the Adventurer's form kneeling by the wall, and then--was she mad! Was the faint night-light of the city filtering in through the window mocking her? The Adventurer, hidden from his companion by the washstand, was working swiftly and without a sound--or else it was a phantasm of shadows that tricked her! A door in the wall opened; the Adventurer thrust in his hand, drew out a package, and, leaning around, slipped it quickly into the bottom of the washstand, where, with its little doors, there was a most convenient and very commodious apartment. He turned again then, seemed to take something from his pocket and place it in the opening in the wall, and then the panel closed.

It had taken scarcely more than a second.

Rhoda Gray brushed her hand across her eyes. No, it wasn't a phantasm! She had misjudged the Adventurer--quite misjudged him! The Adventurer, even with one of the gang present--to furnish an unimpeachable alibi for him!--was plucking the gang's fruit again for his own and undivided enrichment!

Pinkie Bonn's voice came in a guarded whisper from the doorway.

"I don't hear nothin'!" said Pinkie Bonn anxiously.

The Pug tiptoed across the room, and joined his companion. She could not see them now, but apparently they stood together by the door listening. They stood there for a long time. Occasionally she heard them whisper to each other; and then finally the Pug spoke in a less guarded voice.

"All right," he said. "I guess me nerves are gettin' de creeps. Shoot de light on again, an' let's get back on de job. An' youse can take a turn dis time pushin' de knots, Pinkie; mabbe youse'll have better luck."

The light went on again. Both men came back across the room, and now Pinkie Bonn knelt at the wall while the Pug leaned over the washstand watching him. Pinkie Bonn was not immediately successful; the Pug's nerves, of which he had complained, appeared shortly to get the better of him.

"Fer Gawd's sake, hurry up!" he urged irritably. "Or else lemme take another crack at it, Pinkie, an'..."

A low, triumphant exclamation came from Pinkie Bonn, as the small door in the wall swung suddenly open.

"There she is, my bucko!" he grinned. "Some nifty vault, eh? The old guy-" He stopped. He had thrust in his hand, and drawn it out again. His fingers gripped a sheet of notepaper--but he was seemingly unconscious of that fact. He was leaning forward, staring into the aperture. "It's empty!" he choked.

"Wot's dat?" cried the Pug, and sprang to his companion's side. "Youse're crazy, Pinkie!" He thrust his head toward the opening--and then turned and stared for a moment helplessly at Pinkie Bonn. "So help me!" he said heavily. "It's--it's empty." He shook his fist suddenly. "De Crab's handed us one, dat's wot! But de Crab'll get his fer--"

"It wasn't the Crab!" Pinkie Bonn was stuttering his words. He stood, jaws dropped, his eyes glued now on the paper in his hand.

The Pug, his face working, the personification of baffled rage and intolerance, leered at Pinkie Bonn. "Well, who was it, den?" he snarled.

Pinkie Bonn licked his lips.

"The White Moll!" He licked his lips again.

"De White Moll!" echoed the Pug incredulously.

"Yes," said Pinkie Bonn. "Listen to what's on this paper that I fished out of there I Listen! She's got all the nerve of the devil! 'With thanks, and my most grateful appreciation--the White Moll.'"

The Pug snatched the paper from Pinkie Bonn's hand, as though to assure himself that it was true. Rhoda Gray smiled faintly. It was good acting, very excellently done--seeing that the Pug had written the note and placed it in the hiding place himself!

"My God!" mumbled Pinkie Bonn thickly. "I ain't afraid of most things, but I'm gettin' scared of her. She ain't human. Last night you know what happened, and the night before, and--" He gulped suddenly. "Let's get out of here!" he said hurriedly. The Pug made no reply, except for a muttered growl of assent and a nod of his head.

The two men crossed the room. The light went out. Their footsteps echoed back as they descended the stairs, then died away.

And then Rhoda Gray moved for the first time. She brushed aside the cretonne hanging, ran to the washstand, possessed herself of the package she had seen the Pug place there, and then made her way, cautious now of the slightest sound, downstairs.

She tried the door that led into the secondhand shop from the hall, found it unlocked, and with a little gasp of relief slipped through, and closed it gently behind her. She did not dare risk the front entrance. Pinkie Bonn and the Pug were not far enough away yet, and she did not dare wait until they were. Too bulky to take the risk of attempting to conceal it about his person while with Pinkie Bonn, the Pug, it was obvious, would come back alone for that package, and it was equally obvious that he would not be long in doing so. There was old Luertz's return that he would have to anticipate. It would not take wits nearly so sharp as those possessed by the Pug to find an excuse for separating promptly from Pinkie Bonn!

Rhoda Gray groped her way down the shop, groped her way to a back door, unbolted it, working by the sense of touch, and let herself out into a back yard. Five minutes later she was blocks away, and hurrying rapidly back toward the deserted shed in the lane behind Gypsy Nan's garret.

Her lips formed into a tight little curve as she went along. There was still work to do to-night--if this package really contained the stolen legacy of gems left by Angel Jack. She had first of all to reach a place where she could examine the package with safety; then a place to hide it where it would be secure; and then--Danglar!

She gained the lane, stole along it, and disappeared into the shed through the broken door that hung, partially open, on sagging hinges. Here she sought a corner, and crouched down so that her body would smother any reflection from her flashlight. And now, eagerly, feverishly, she began to undo the package; and then, a moment later, she gazed, stupefied and amazed, at what lay before her. Precious stones, scores of them, nestled on a bed of cotton; they were of all colors and of all sizes--but each one of them seemed to pulsate and throb, and from some wondrous, glorious depth of its own to fling back from the white ray upon it a thousand rays in return, as though into it had been breathed a living and immortal fire.

And Rhoda Gray, crouched there, stared--until suddenly she grew afraid, and suddenly with a shudder she wrapped the package up again. These were the stones for whose fabulous worth the woman whose personality she, Rhoda Gray, had usurped, had murdered a man; these were the stones which were indirectly the instrumentality--since but for them Gypsy Nan would never have existed--that made her, Rhoda Gray, to-night, now, at this very moment, a hunted thing, homeless, friendless, fighting for her very life against police and underworld alike!

She rose abruptly to her feet. She had no longer any need of a flashlight. There was even light of a sort in the place--she could see the stars through the jagged holes in the roof, and through one of these, too, the moonlight streamed in. The shed was all but crumbling in a heap. Underfoot, what had once been flooring, was now but rotting, broken boards. Under one of these, beside the clothing of Gypsy Nan which she had discarded but a little while before, she deposited the package; then stepped out into the lane, and from there to the street again.

And now she became suddenly conscious of a great and almost overpowering physical weariness. She did not quite understand at first, unless it was to be attributed to the reaction from the last few hours--and then, smiling wanly to herself, she remembered. For two nights she had not slept. It seemed very strange. That was it, of course, though she was not in the least sleepy now--just tired, just near the breaking point.

But she must go on. To-night was the end, anyhow. To-night, failing to keep her appointment as "Bertha," the crash must come; but before it came, as the White Moll, armed with the knowledge of the crime that had driven Danglar's wife into hiding, and which was Danglar's crime too, and with the evidence in the shape of those jewels in her possession, she and Danglar would meet somewhere--alone. Before the law got him, when he would be close-mouthed and struggling with all his cunning to keep the evidence of other crimes from piling up against him and damning whatever meager chances he might have to escape the penalty for Deemer's murder, she meant--yes, even if she pretended to compound a felony with him--to force or to inveigle from him, it mattered little which, a confession of the authorship and details of the scheme to rob Skarbolov that night when she, Rhoda Gray, in answer to a dying woman's pleading, had tried to forestall the plan, and had been caught, apparently, in the very act of committing the robbery herself! With that confession in her possession, with the identity of the unknown woman who had died in the hospital that night established, her own story would be believed.

And so, if she were weary, what did it matter? It was only until morning. Danglar was at the Silver Sphinx now with the man he meant that she should help him murder, only--only that plan would fail, because there would be no "Bertha" to lure the man to his death, and she, Rhoda Gray, had only to keep track of Danglar until somewhere, where he lived perhaps, she should have that final scene, that final reckoning with him alone.

It was a long way to the Silver Sphinx, which she knew, as every one in the underworld, and every one in New York who was addicted to slumming knew, was a combination dance-hall and restaurant in the Chatham Square district. She tried to find a taxi, but with out avail. A clock in a jeweler's window which she passed showed her that it was ten minutes after eleven. She had had no idea that it was so late. At eleven, Danglar had said. Danglar would be growing restive! She took the elevated. If she could risk the protection of her veil in the Silver Sphinx, she could risk it equally in an elevated train!

But, in spite of the elevated, it was, she knew, well on towards half past eleven when she finally came down the street in front of the Silver Sphinx. From under her veil, she glanced, half curiously, half in a sort of grim irony, at the taxis lined up before the dancehall. The two leading cars were not taxis at all, though they bore the ear-marks, with their registers, of being public vehicles for hire; they were large, roomy, powerful, and looked, with their hoods up, like privately owned motors. Well, it was of little account! She shrugged her shoulders, as--she mounted the steps of the dance-hall. Neither "Bertha" nor Cloran would use those cars to-night!

XVII. THE SILVER SPHINX

A Bedlam of noise smote Rhoda Gray's ears as she entered the Silver Sphinx. A jazz band was in full swing; on the polished section of the floor in the center, a packed mass of humanity swirled and gyrated and wriggled in the contortions of the "latest" dance, and laughed and howled immoderately; and around the sides of the room, the waiters rushed this way and that amongst the crowded tables, mopping at their faces with their aprons. It seemed as though confusion itself held sway!

Rhoda Gray scanned the occupants of the tables. The Silver Sphinx was particularly riotous to-night, wasn't it? Yes, she understood! A great many of the men were wearing little badges. Some society or other was celebrating--and was doing it with abandon. Most of the men were half drunk. It was certainly a free-and-easy night! Everything went!

Danglar! Yes, 'there he was--quite close to her, only a few tables away--and beside him sat a heavy built, clean-shaven man of middle age. That would be Cloran, of course--the man who was to have been lured to his death. And Danglar was nervous and uneasy, she could see. His fingers were drumming a tattoo on the table; his eyes were roving furtively about the room; and he did not seem to be paying any but the most distrait attention to his companion, who was talking to him.

Rhoda Gray sank quickly into a vacant chair. Three men, linked arm in arm, and decidedly more than a little drunk, were approaching her. She turned her head away to avoid attracting their attention. It was too free and easy here to-night, and she began to regret her temerity at having ventured inside; she would better, perhaps, have waited until Danglar came out--only there were two exits, and she might have missed him--and...

A cold fear upon her, she shrank back in her chair. The three men had halted at the table, and were clustered around her. They began a jocular quarrel amongst themselves as to who should dance with her. Her heart was pounding. She stood up, and pushed them away.

"Oh, no, you don't!" hiccoughed one of the three. "Gotta see your--hic!--pretty face, anyhow!"

She put up her hands frantically and clutched at her veil--but just an instant too late to save it from being wrenched aside. Wildly her eyes flew to Danglar. His attention had been attracted by the scene. She saw him rise from his seat; she saw his eyes widen--and then, stumbling over his chair in his haste, he made toward her. Danglar had recognized the White Moll!

She turned and ran. Fear, horror, desperation, lent her strength. It was not like this that she had counted on her reckoning with Danglar! She brushed the roisterers aside, and darted for the door. Over her shoulder she glimpsed Danglar following her. She reached the door, burst through a knot of people there, and, her torn veil clutched in her hand, dashed down the steps. She could only run--run, and pray that in some way she might escape.

And then a mad exultation came upon her. She saw the man in the chauffeur's seat of the first car in the line lean out and swing the door open. And in a flash she grasped the situation. The man was waiting for just this--for a woman to come running for her life down the steps of the Silver Sphinx. She put her hand up to her face, hiding it with the torn veil, raced for the car, and flung herself into the tonneau.

The door slammed. The car leaped from the curb. Danglar was coming down the steps. She heard him shout. The chauffeur, in a startled way, leaned out, as he evidently recognized Danglar's voice--but Rhoda Gray was mistress of herself now. The tonneau of the car was not separated from the driver's seat, and bending forward, she wrenched her revolver from her pocket, and pressed the muzzle of her weapon to the back of the man's neck.

"Don't stop!" she gasped, struggling for her breath. "Go on! Quick!"

The man, with a frightened oath, obeyed. The car gained speed. A glance through the window behind showed Danglar climbing into the other car.

And then for a moment Rhoda Gray sat there fighting for her self-control, with the certain knowledge in her soul that upon her wits, and her wits alone, her life depended now. She studied the car's mechanism over the chauffeur's shoulder, even as she continued to hold her revolver pressed steadily against the back of the man's neck. She could drive a car--she could drive this one. The presence of this chauffeur, one of the gang, was an added menace; there were too many tricks he might play before she could forestall them, any one of which would deliver her into the hands of Danglar behind there--an apparently inadvertent stoppage due to traffic, for instance, that would bring the pursuing car alongside--that, or a dozen other things which would achieve the same end.

"Open the door on your side!" she commanded abruptly. "And get out--without slowing the car! Do you understand?"

He turned his head for a half incredulous, half frightened look at her. She met his eyes steadily--the torn veil, quite discarded now, was in her pocket. She did not know the man; but it was quite evident from the almost ludicrous dismay which spread over his face that he knew her.

"The--the White Moll!" he stammered. "It's the White Moll!"

"Jump!" she ordered imperatively--and her revolver pressed still more significantly against the man's flesh.

He seemed in even frantic haste to obey her. He whipped the door open, and, before she could reach to the wheel, he had leaped to the street. The car swerved sharply. She flung herself over into the vacated seat, and snatched at the wheel barely in time to prevent the machine from mounting the curb.

She looked around again through the window of the hood. The man had swung aboard Danglar's car, which was only a few yards behind.

Rhoda Gray drove steadily. Here in the city streets her one aim must be never to let the other car come abreast of her; but she could prevent that easily enough by watching Danglar's movements, and cutting across in front of him if he attempted anything of the sort. But ultimately what was she to do? How was she to escape? Her hands gripped and clenched in a sudden, almost panic-like desperation at the wheel. Turn suddenly around a corner, and jump from the car herself? It was useless to attempt it; they would keep too close behind to give her a chance to get out of sight. Well, then, suppose she jumped from the car, and trusted herself to the protection of the people on the street. She shook her head grimly. Danglar, she knew only too well, would risk anything, go to any length, to put an end to the White

Moll. He would not hesitate an instant to shoot her down as she jumped and he would be fairly safe himself in doing it. A few revolver shots from a car that speeded away in the darkness offered an even chance of escape. And yet, unless she forced an issue such as that, she knew that Danglar would not resort to firing at her here in the city. He would want to be sure that was the only chance he had of getting her, before he accepted the risk that he would run of being caught for it by the police.

She found herself becoming strangely, almost unnaturally, cool and collected now. The one danger, greater than all others, that menaced her was a traffic block that would cause her to stop, and allow those in the other car behind to rush in upon her as she sat here at the wheel. And sooner or later, if she stayed in the city, a block such as that was inevitable. She must get out of the city, then. It was only to invite another risk, the risk that Danglar was in the faster car of the two but there was no other way.

She drove more quickly, made her way to the Bridge, and crossed it. The car behind followed with immutable persistence. It made no effort to close the short gap between them; but, neither, on the other hand, did it permit that gap to widen.

They passed through Brooklyn; and then, reaching the outskirts, Rhoda Gray, with headlights streaming into the black, with an open Long Island road before her, flung her throttle wide, and the car leaped like a thing of life into the night. It was a sudden start, it gained her a hundred yards but that was all.

The wind tore at her and whipped her face; the car rocked and reeled as in some mad frenzy. There was not much traffic, but such as there was it cleared away from before her as if by magic, as, seeking shelter from the wild meteoric thing running amuck, the few vehicles, motor or horse, that she encountered hugged; the edge of the road, and the wind whisked to her ears fragments of shouts and execrations. Again and again she looked back two fiery balls of light blazed behind her always those same two fiery balls.

She neither gained nor lost. Rigid, like steel, her little figure was crouched over the wheel. She did not know the road. She knew nothing save that she was racing for her life. She did not know the end; she could not see the end. Perhaps there would be some merciful piece of luck for her that would win her through a breakdown to that roaring thing, with its eyes that were balls of fire, behind.

She passed through a town with lighted streets and lighted windows or was it only imagination? It was gone again, anyhow, and there was just black road ahead. Over the roar of the car and the sweep of the wind, then, she caught, or fancied she caught, a series of faint reports. She looked behind her. Yes, they were firing now. Little flashes leaped out above and at the sides of those blazing headlights.

How long was it since she had left the Silver Sphinx? Minutes or hours would not measure it, would they? But it could not last much longer! She was growing very tired; the strain upon her arms, yes, and upon her eyes, was becoming unbearable. She swayed a little in her seat, and the car swerved, and she jerked it back again into the straight. She began to laugh a little hysterically and then, suddenly, she straightened up, tense and alert once more.

That swerve was the germ of an inspiration! It took root swiftly now. It was desperate--but she was desperate. She could not drive much more, or much longer like this. Mind and body were almost undone. And, besides, she was not outdistancing that car behind there by a foot; and sooner or later they would hit her with one of their shots, or, perhaps what they were really trying to do, puncture one of her tires.

Again she glanced over her shoulder. Yes, Danglar was just far enough behind to make the plan possible. She began to allow the car to swerve noticeably at intervals, as though she were weakening and the car was getting beyond her control--which was, indeed, almost too literally the case. And now it seemed to her that each time she swerved there came an exultant shout from the car behind. Well, she asked for nothing better; that was what she was trying to do, wasn't it?--inspire them with the belief that she was breaking under the strain.

Her eyes searched anxiously down the luminous pathway made by her high-powered headlights. If only she could reach a piece of road that combined two things--an embankment of some sort, and a curve just sharp enough to throw those headlights behind off at a tangent for an instant as they rounded it, too, in following her.

A minute, two, another passed. And then Rhoda Gray, tight-lipped, her face drawn hard, as her own headlights suddenly edged away from the road and opened what looked like a deep ravine on her left, while the road curved to the right, flung a frenzied glance back of her. It was her chance--her one chance. Danglar was perhaps a little more than a hundred yards in the rear. Yes--now! His headlights were streaming out on her left as he, too, touched the curve. The right-hand side of her car, the right-hand side of the road were in blackness. She checked violently, almost to a stop, then instantly opened the throttle wide once more, wrenching the wheel over to head the machine for the ravine; and before the car picked up its momentum again, she dropped from the right-hand side, darted to the far edge of the road, and flung herself flat down upon the ground.

The great, black body of her car seemed to sail out into nothingness like some weird aerial monster, the headlights streaming uncannily through space--then blackness--and a terrific crash.

And now the other car had come to a stop almost opposite where she lay. Danglar and the two chauffeurs, shouting at each other in wild excitement, leaped out and rushed to the edge of the embankment. And then suddenly the sky grew red as a great tongue-flame shot up from below. It outlined the forms of the three men as they stood there, until, abruptly, as though with one accord, they rushed pell-mell down the embankment toward the burning wreckage. And as they disappeared from sight Rhoda Gray jumped to her feet, sprang for Danglar's car, flung herself into the driver's seat, and the car shot forward again along the road.

A shout, a wild chorus of yells, the reports of a fusillade of shots reached her; she caught a glimpse of forms running insanely after her along the edge of the embankment--then silence save for the roar of the speeding car.

She drove on and on. Somewhere, nearing a town, she saw a train in the distance coming in her direction. She reached the station first, and left the car standing there, and, with the torn veil over her face again, took the train.

She was weak, undone, exhausted. Even her mind refused its functions further. It was only in a subconscious way she realized that, where she had thought never to go to the garret again, the garret and the role of Gypsy Nan were, more than ever now, her sole refuge. The plot against Cloran had failed, but they could not blame that on "Bertha's" non-appearance; and since it had failed she would not now be expected to assume the dead woman's personality. True, she had not, as had been arranged, reached the Silver Sphinx at eleven, but there were a hundred excuses she could give to account for her being late in keeping the appointment so that she had arrived just in time, say, to see Danglar dash wildly in pursuit of a woman who had jumped into the car that she was supposed to take!

The garret! The garret again--and Gypsy Nan! Her surroundings seemed to become a blank to her; her actions to be prompted by some purely mechanical sense. She was conscious only that finally, after an interminable time, she was in New York again; and after that, long, long after that, dressed as Gypsy Nan, she was stumbling up the dark, ladder-like steps to the attic.

How her footsteps dragged! She opened the door, staggered inside, locked the door again, and staggered toward the cot, and dropped upon it; and the gray dawn came in with niggardly light through the grimy little window panes, as though timorously inquisitive of this shawled and dissolute figure prone and motionless, this figure who in other dawns had found neither sleep nor rest--this figure who lay there now as one dead.

XVIII. THE OLD SHED

Rhoda Gray opened her eyes, and, from the cot upon which she lay, stared with drowsy curiosity around the garret--and in another instant was sitting bolt upright, alert and tense, as the full flood of memory swept upon her.

There was still a meager light creeping in through the small, grimy window panes, but it was the light of waning day. She must have slept, then, all through the morning and the afternoon, slept the dead, heavy sleep of exhaustion from the moment she had flung herself down here a few hours before daybreak.

She rose impulsively to her feet. It was strange that she had not been disturbed, that no one had come to the garret! The recollection of the events of the night before were crowding themselves upon her now. In view of last night, in view of her failure to keep that appointment in the role of Danglar's wife, it was very strange indeed that she had been left undisturbed!

Subconsciously she was aware that she was hungry, that it was long since she had eaten, and, almost mechanically, she prepared herself something now from the store the garret possessed; but, even as she ate, her mind was far from thoughts of food. From the first night she had come here and self-preservation had thrust this miserable role of Gypsy Nan upon her, from that first night and from the following night when, to save the Sparrow, she had been whirled into the vortex of the gang's criminal activities, her mind raced on through the sequence of events that seemed to have spanned some vast, immeasurable space of time until they had brought her to--last night.

Last night! She had thought it was the end last night, but instead--The dark eyes grew suddenly hard and intent. Yes, she had counted upon last night, when, with the necessary proof in her possession with which to confront Danglar with the crime of murder, she could wring from the man all that now remained necessary to substantiate her own story and clear herself in the eyes of the law of that robbery at Skarbolov's antique store of which she was held guilty--and instead she had barely escaped with her life. That was the story of last night.

Her eyes grew harder. Well, the way was still open, wasn't it? Last night had changed nothing in that respect. To-night, as the White Moll, she had only to find and corner Danglar as she had planned to do last night. She had still only to get the man alone somewhere.

Rhoda Gray's hands clenched tightly. That was all that was necessary--just the substantiation of her own story that the plot to rob Skarbolov lay at the door of Danglar and his gang; or, rather, perhaps, that the plot was in existence before she had ever heard of Skarbolov. It would prove her own statement of what the dying woman had said. It would exonerate her from guilt; it would prove that, rather than having any intention of committing crime, she had taken the only means within her power of preventing one. The real Gypsy Nan, Danglar's wife, who had died that night, bad, even in eleventh-hour penitence, refused to implicate her criminal associates. There was a crime projected which, unless she, Rhoda Gray, would agree to forestall it in person and would give her oath not to warn the police about it and so put the actual criminals in jeopardy, would go on to its fulfillment!

She remembered that night in the hospital. The scene came vividly before her now. The woman's pleading, the woman's grim loyalty even in death to her pals. She, Rhoda Gray, had given her oath.

It became necessary only to substantiate those facts. Danglar could be made to do it. She had now in her possession the evidence that would convict him of complicity in the murder of Deemer, and for which murder the original Gypsy Nan had gone into hiding; she even had in her possession the missing jewels that had prompted that murder; she had, too, the evidence now to bring the entire gang to justice for their myriad depredations; she knew where their secret hoard of ill-gotten gains was hidden--here in this attic, behind that ingeniously contrived trap-door in the ceiling. She knew all this; and this information placed before the police, providing only it was backed by the proof that the scheme to rob Skarbolov was to be carried out by the gang, as she, Rhoda Gray, would say the dying woman had informed her, would be more than enough to clear her. She had not had this proof on that first night when she had snatched at the mantle of Gypsy Nan as the sole means of escape from Rough Rorke, of headquarters; she did not have it now--but she would have it, stake all and everything in life she had to have it, for it, in itself, literally meant everything and all--and Danglar would make a written confession, or else--or else--She smiled mirthlessly. That was all! Last night she had failed. To-night she would not fail. Before morning came, if it were humanly within her power, she and Danglar would have played out their game--to the end.

And now a pucker came and gathered her forehead into little furrows, and anxiety and perplexity crept into her eyes. Another thought tormented her. In the exposure that was to come the Adventurer, alias the Pug, was involved. Was there any way to save the man to whom she owed so much, the splendidly chivalrous, high-couraged gentleman she loved, the thief she abhorred?

She pushed the remains of her frugal meal away from her, stood up abruptly from the rickety washstand at which she had been seated, and commenced to pace nervously up and down the stark, bare garret. Where was the line of demarcation between right and wrong? Was it a grievous sin, or an infinitely human thing to do, to warn the man she loved, and give him a chance to escape the net she meant to furnish the police? He was a thief, even a member of the gang--though he used the gang as his puppets. Did ethics count when one who had stood again and again between her and peril was himself in danger now? Would it be a righteous thing, or an act of despicable ingratitude, to trap him with the rest?

She laughed out shortly. Warn him! Of course, she would warn him! But then--what? She shivered a little, and her face grew drawn and tired. It was the old, old story of the pitcher and the well. It was almost inevitable that sooner or later, for some crime or another, the man she loved would be caught at last, and would spend the greater portion of his days behind prison bars. That was what the love that had come into her life held as its promise to her! It was terrible enough without her agency being the means of placing him there!

She did not want to think about it. She forced her mind into other channels, though they were scarcely less disquieting. Why was it that during the day just past there had been not a sign from Danglar or any one of the gang, when every plan of theirs had gone awry last night, and she had failed to keep her appointment in the role of Danglar's wife? Why was it? What did it mean? Surely Danglar would never allow what had happened to pass unchallenged, and--was that some one now?

She halted suddenly by the door to listen, her hand going instinctively to the wide, voluminous pocket of her greasy skirt for her revolver. Yes, there was a footstep in the hall below, but it was descending now to the ground floor, not coming up. She even heard the street door close, but still she hung there in a strained, tense way, and into her face there came creeping a gray dismay. Her pocket was empty.

The revolver was gone! Its loss, pregnant with a hundred ominous possibilities, seemed to bring a panic fear upon her, holding her for a moment inert--and then she rushed frantically to the cot. Perhaps it had fallen out of her pocket during the hours she had lain there asleep. She searched the folds of the soiled and crumpled blanket, that was the cot's sole covering, then snatched the blanket completely off the cot and shook it; and then, down on her knees, she searched the floor under the cot. There was no sign of the revolver.

Rhoda Gray stood up, and stared in a stunned way about her. Was this, then, the explanation of her having seemingly been left undisturbed here all through the day? Had some one, after all, been here, and--? She shook her head suddenly with a quick, emphatic gesture of dissent. The door was still locked, she could see the key on the inside; and, besides, as a theory, it wasn't logical. They wouldn't have taken her revolver and left her placidly asleep!

The loss of the revolver was a vital matter. It was her one safeguard; the one means by which she could first gain and afterwards hold the whip-hand over Danglar in the interview she proposed to have with him; the one means of escape, the last resort, if she herself were cornered and fell into his power. It had sustained her more than once, that resolution to turn it against herself if she were in extremity. It meant everything to her, that weapon, and it was gone now; but the panic that had seized upon her was gone too, and she could think rationally and collectively again.

Last night, or rather this morning, when she had made her way back to the shed out there in the lane behind the garret, she had been in a state of almost utter exhaustion. She had changed from the clothes of the White Moll to those of Gypsy Nan, but she must have done so almost mechanically for she had no concrete recollection of it. It was quite likely then, even more than probable, that she had left the revolver in the pocket of her other clothes; for she had certainly had, not only her revolver, but her flashlight and her skeleton keys with her when she had visited old Luertz's place last night, and later on too, when she had jumped into that automobile in front of the Silver Sphinx, she had had her revolver, for she had used it to force the chauffeur out of the car--and she had no one of those articles now.

Of course! That was it! She stepped impulsively to the door, and, opening it, made her way quickly down the stairs to the street. The revolver was undoubtedly in the pocket of her other skirt, and she felt a surge of relief sweep upon her; but a sense of relief was far from enough. She would not feel safe until the weapon was again in her possession, and intuitively she felt that she had no time to lose in securing it. She had already been left too long alone not to make a break in that unaccountable isolation they had accorded her as something to be expected at any moment. She hurried now down the street to the lane that intervened between Gypsy Nan's house and the next corner, glanced quickly about her, and, seeing no one in her immediate vicinity, slipped into the lane. She gained the deserted shed some fifty yards along the lane, entered through the broken door that hung, half open, on sagging hinges, and, dropping on her knees, reached in under the decayed and rotting flooring. She pushed aside impatiently the package of jewels, at whose magnificence she had gazed awe-struck and bewildered the night before, and drew out the bundle that comprised her own clothing. Her hand sought the pocket eagerly. Yes, it was here--at least the flashlight was, and so were the skeleton keys. That was what had happened! She had been near utter collapse last night, and she had forgotten, and--Rhoda Gray, unconscious even that she still held the clothing in her hands, rose mechanically to her feet. There was a sudden weariness in her eyes as she stared unseeingly about her. Yes, the flashlight and the keys were here-- but the revolver was not! Her brain harked back in lightning flashes over the events of the preceding night. She must have lost it somewhere, then. Where? She had had it in the automobile, that she knew positively; but after that she did not remember, unless--yes, it must have been that! When she had jumped from the car and flung herself down at the roadside! It must have fallen out of her pocket then.

Her heart seemed to stand still. Suppose they had found it! They would certainly recognize it as belonging to Gypsy Nan! They were not fools. The deduction would be obvious--the identity of the White Moll would be solved. Was that why no one had apparently come near her? Were they playing at cat-and-mouse, watching her before they struck, so that she would lead them to those jewels under the flooring here that were worth a king's ransom? They certainly believed that the White Moll had them. The Adventurer's note, so ironically true, that he had intended as an alibi for himself, and which he had exchanged for the package in old Luertz's place, would have left no doubt in their minds but that the stones were in her possession. Was that it? Were they--She held her breath. It seemed as though suddenly her limbs were refusing to support her weight. In the soft earth outside she had heard no step, but she saw now a shadow fall athwart the half-open doorway. There was no time to move, even had she been capable of action. It seemed as though even her soul had turned to stone, and, with the White Moll's clothes in her hands, she stood there staring at the doorway, and something that was greater than fear, because it mingled horror, ugly and forbidding, fell upon her. It was still just light enough to see. The shadow moved forward and came inside. She wanted to scream, to rush madly in retreat to the farthest corner of the shed; but she could not move. It was Danglar who was standing there. He seemed to sway a little on his feet, and the dark, sinister face seemed blotched, and he seemed to smile as though possessed of some unholy and perverted sense of humor.

She was helpless, at his mercy, unarmed, saved for her wits. Her wits! Were wits any longer of avail? She could believe nothing else now except that he had been watching her--before he struck.

"What are you doing here, and what are those clothes you've got in your hands?" he rasped out.

She could only fence for time in the meager hope that some loophole would present itself. She forced an assumed defiance into her tones and manner, that was in keeping with the sort of armed truce, which, from her first meeting with Danglar, she had inaugurated as a barrier between them.

"You have asked me two questions," she said tartly. "Which one do you want me to answer first?"

"Look here," he snapped, "you cut that out! There's one or two things need explaining--see? What are those clothes?"

Her wits! Perhaps he did not know as much as she was afraid he did! She seemed to have become abnormally contained, her mind abnormally acute and active. It was not likely that the woman, his wife, whom he believed she was, had worn her own clothes in his presence since the day, some two years ago, when she had adopted the disguise of Gypsy Nan; and she, Rhoda Gray, remembered that on the night Gypsy Nan, re-assuming her true personality, had gone to the hospital, the woman's clothes, like these she held now, had been of dark material. It was not likely that a man would be able to differentiate between those clothes and the clothes of the White Moll, especially as the latter hung folded in her hands now, and even though he had seen them on her at the Silver Sphinx last night.

"What clothes do you suppose they are but my own?--though I haven't had a chance to wear them much lately!" she countered crisply.

He scowled at her speculatively.

"What are you doing with them out here in this hole, then?" he demanded.

"I had to wear them last night, hadn't I?" she retorted. "I'd have looked well coming out of Gypsy Nan's garret dressed as myself if any one had seen me!" She scowled at him in turn. She was beginning to believe that he had not even an inkling of her identity. Her safest play was to stake everything on that belief. "Say, what's the matter with you?" she inquired disdainfully. "I came out here and changed last night; and I changed into these rags I'm wearing now when I got back again; and I left my own clothes here because I was expecting to get word that I could put them on again soon for keeps--though I might have known from past experience that something would queer the fine promises you made at Matty's last night! And the reason I'm out here now is because I left some things in the pocket, amongst them"--she stared at him mockingly--"my marriage certificate."

Danglar's face blackened.

"Curse you!" he burst out angrily. "When you get your tantrums on, you've got a tongue, haven't you! You'd have been wearing your clothes now, if you'd have done as you were told. You're the one that queered things last night." His voice was rising; he was rocking even more unsteadily upon his feet. "Why in hell weren't you at the Silver Sphinx?"

Rhoda Gray squinted at him through Gypsy Nan's spectacles. She knew an hysterical impulse to laugh outright in the sure consciousness of supremacy over him now. The man had been drinking. He was by no means drunk; but, on the other hand, he was by no means sober--and she was certain now that, though she did not know how he had found her here in the shed, not the slightest suspicion of her had entered his mind.

"I was at the Silver Sphinx," she announced coolly.

"You lie!" he said hoarsely. "You weren't! I told you to be there at eleven, and you weren't. You lie! What are you lying to me for--eh? I'll find out, you--you--"

Rhoda Gray dashed the clothes down on the floor at her feet, and faced the man as though suddenly overcome in turn herself with passion, shaking both closed fists at him.

"Don't you talk to me like that, Pierre Danglar!" she shrilled. "I lie, do I? Well, I'll prove to you I don't! You said you were going to have supper with Cloran at about eleven o'clock, and perhaps I was a few minutes after that, but maybe you think it's easy to get all this Gypsy Nan stuff off me face and all, and rig up in my own clothes that I haven't seen for so long it's a wonder they hold together at all. I lie, do I? Well, just as I got to the Silver Sphinx, I saw a woman breaking her neck to get down the steps with you after her. She jumped into the automobile it was doped out I was to take, and you jumped into the other one, and both beat it down the street. I thought you'd gone crazy. I was afraid that Cloran would come out and recognize me, so I turned and ran, too. The safest thing I could do was to get back into the Gypsy Nan game again, and that's what I did. And I've been lying low ever since, waiting to get word from some of you, and not a soul came near me. You're a nice lot, you are! And now you come sneaking here and call me a liar! How'd you get to this shed, anyway?"

Danglar pushed his hand in a heavy, confused way across his eyes.

"My God!" he said heavily. "So that's it, is it?" His voice became suddenly conciliating in its tones. "Look here, Bertha, old girl, don't get sore. I didn't understand, see? And there was a whole lot that looked queer. We even lost the jewels at old Luertz's last night. Do you know who that woman was? It was the White Moll! She led us a chase all over Long Island, and--"

"The White Moll!" ejaculated Rhoda Gray. And then her laugh, short and jeering, rang out. The tables were turned. She had him on the defensive now. "You needn't tell me I She got away again, of course! Why don't you hire a detective to help you? You make me weary! So, it was the White Moll, was it? Well, I'm listening--only I'd like to know first how you got here to this shed."

"There's nothing in that!" he answered impatiently. "There's something more important to talk about. I was coming over to the garret, and just as I reached the corner I saw you go into the lane. I followed you; that's all there is to that."

"Oh!" she sniffed. She stared at him for a moment. There was something in which there was the uttermost of irony now, it seemed, in this meeting between them. Last night she had striven to meet him alone, and she had meant to devote to-night to the same purpose; and she was here with him now, and in a place than which, in her wildest hopes, she could have imagined one no better suited to the reckoning she would have demanded and forced. And she was helpless, powerless to make use of it. She was unarmed. Her revolver was gone. Without that to protect her, at an intimation that she was the White Moll she would never leave the shed alive. The spot would be quite as ideal under those circumstances for him, as it would have been under other circumstances for her. She shrugged her shoulders. Danglar's continued silence evidently invited further comment on her part. "Oh!" she sniffed again. "And I suppose, then, that you have been chasing the White Moll ever since last night at eleven, and that's why you didn't get around sooner to allay my fears, even though you knew I must be half mad with anxiety at the way things broke last night. She'll have us down and out for keeps if you haven't got brains enough to beat her. How much longer is this thing going on?"

Danglar's little black eyes narrowed. She caught a sudden glint of triumph in them. It was Danglar now who laughed.

"Not much longer!" His voice was arrogant with malicious satisfaction. "The luck had to turn, hadn't it? Well, it's turned! I've got the White Moll at last!"

She felt the color leave her face. It seemed as though something had closed with an icy clutch upon her heart. She had heard aright, hadn't she?--that he had said he had got the White Moll at last. And there was no mistaking the mans s sinister delight in making that announcement. Had she been premature, terribly premature, in assuring herself that her identity was still safe as far as he was concerned? Did it mean that, after all, he had been playing at cat-and-mouse with her, as she had at first feared?

"You--you've got the White Moll?" She forced the words from her lips, striving to keep her voice steady and in control, and to infuse into it an ironical incredulity.

"Sure!" he said complacently. "The showdown comes to-night. In another hour or so we'll have her where we want her, and--"

"Oh!" She laughed almost hysterically in relief. "I thought so! You haven't got her yet. You're only going to get her--in another hour or so! You make me tired! It's always in 'another hour or so' with you--and it never comes off!"

Danglar scowled at her under the taunt.

"It'll come off this time!" he snarled in savage menace. "You hold that tongue of yours! Yes, it'll come off! And when it does"--a sweep of fury sent the red into his working face--"I'll keep the promise I made her once--that she'd wish she had never been born! D'ye hear, Bertha?"

"I hear," she said indifferently. "But would you mind telling me how you are going to do it? I might believe you then--perhaps!"

"Damn you, Bertha!" he exploded. "Sometimes I'd like to wring that pretty neck of yours; and sometimes!"--he moved suddenly toward her--"I would sell my soul for you, and--"

She retreated from him coolly.

"Never mind about that! This isn't a love scene!" she purred caustically. "And as for the other, save it for the White Moll. What makes you think you've got her at last?"

"I don't think--I know." He stood gnawing at his lips, eying her uncertainly, half angrily, half hungrily. And then he shrugged his shoulders. "Listen!" he said. "I've got some one else, too! And I know now where the leak that's queered every one of our games and put the White Moll wise to every one of our plans beforehand has come from. I guess you'll believe me now, won't you? We've got that dude pal of hers fastened up tighter than the night he fastened me with his cursed handcuffs! Do you know who that same dude pal is?" He laughed in an ugly, immoderate way. "You don't, of course, so I'll tell you. It's the Pug!" Rhoda Gray did not answer. It was growing dark here in the shed now--perhaps that was why the man's form blended suddenly into the doorway and wall, and blurred before her. She tried to think, but there seemed to have fallen upon her a numbed and agonized stupefaction. There was no confusing this issue. Danglar had found out that the Adventurer was the Pug. And it meant--oh, what did it mean? They would kill him. Of course, they would kill him! The Adventurer, discovered, would be safer at the mercy of a pack of starved pumas, and...

"I thought that would hold you!" said Danglar with brutal serenity. "That's why I didn't get around till now. I didn't get back from that chase until daylight--the she-fiend stole our car--and then I went to bed to get a little sleep. About three o'clock this afternoon Pinkie Bonn woke me up. He was half batty with excitement. He said he was over in the tenement in the Pug's room. The Pug wasn't in, and Pinkie was waiting for him, and then all of a sudden he heard a woman screaming like mad from somewhere. He went to the door and looked out, and saw a man dash out of a room across the hall, and burst in the door of the next room. There was a woman in there with her clothes on fire. She'd upset a coal-oil stove, or something. The man Pinkie had seen beats the fire out, and everybody in the tenement begins to collect around the door. And then Pinkie goes pop-eyed. The man's face was the face of the White Moll's dude pal--but he had on the Pug's clothes. Pinkie's a wise guy. He slips away to me without getting himself in the limelight or spilling any beans. And I didn't ask him if he'd been punching the needle again overtime, either. It fitted like a glove with what happened at old Luertz's last night. You don't know about that. Pinkie and this double-crossing snitch went there--and only found a note from the White Moll. He'd tipped her off before, of course, and the note made a nice little play so's he'd be safe himself with us. Well, that's about all. We had to get him--where we wanted him--and we got him. We waited until he showed up again as the Pug, and then we put over a frame-up deal on him that got him to go over to that old iron plant in Harlem, you know, behind Jake Malley's saloon, where we had it fixed to hand Cloran his last night--and the Pug's there now. He's nicely gagged, and tied, and quite safe. The plant's been shut down for the last two months, and there's only the watchman there, and he's 'squared.' We gave the Pug two hours of solitary confinement to think it over and come across. We just asked him for the White Moll's address, so's we could get her and the sparklers she swiped at Old Luertz's place last night."

Still Rhoda Gray did not speak for a moment. She seemed to be held in thrall by both terror and a sickening dismay. It did not seem real, her surroundings here, this man, and the voice that was gloatingly pronouncing the death sentence upon the man who had come unbidden into her life, and into her heart, the man she loved. Yes, she understood! Danglar's words had been plain enough. The Adventurer had been trapped--not through Danglar's cunning, or lack of cunning on the Adventurer's own part, but through force of circumstances that had caused him to fling all thought of self-consideration to the winds in an effort to save another's life. Her hands, hidden in the folds of her skirt, clenched until they hurt. And it was another self, it seemed, subconsciously enacting the role of Gypsy Nan, alias Danglar's wife, who spoke at last.

"You are a fool! You are all fools!" she cried tempestuously. "What do you expect to gain by that? Do you imagine you can make the Pug come across with any information by a threat to kill him if he doesn't? You tried that once. You had him cold, or at least you thought you had, and so did he, that night in old Nicky Viner's room, and he laughed at you even when he expected you to fire the next second. He's not likely to have changed any since then, is he?"

"No," said Danglar, with a vicious chuckle; "and that's why I'm not trying the same game twice. That's why we've got him over in the old iron plant now."

There was something she did not like in Danglar's voice, something of ominous assurance, something that startled her.

"What do you mean?" she demanded sharply.

"It's a lonely place," said Danglar complacently. "There's no one around but the watchman, and he's an old friend of Shluker's; and it's so roomy over there that no one could expect him to be everywhere at once. See? That let's him out. He's been well greased, and he won't know anything. Don't you worry, old girl! That's what I came here for--to tell you that everything is all right, after all. The Pug will talk. Maybe he wouldn't if he just had his choice between that and the quick, painless end that a bullet would bring; but there are some things that a man can't stand. Get me? We'll try a few of those on the Pug, and, believe me, before we're through, there won't be any secrets wrapped up in his bosom."

Rhoda Gray stood motionless. Thank God it had grown dark--dark enough to hide the whiteness that she knew had crept over her face, and the horror that had crept into her eyes. "You mean"--her voice was very low--"you mean you're going to torture him into talking?"

"Sure!" said Danglar. "What do you think!"

"And after that?"

"We bump him off, of course," said Danglar callously. "He knows all about us, don't he? And I guess we'll square up on what's coming to him! He's put the crimp into us for the last time!" Danglar's voice pitched suddenly hoarse in fury. "That's a hell of a question to ask! What do you think we'd do with a yellow cur that's double-crossed us like that?"

Plead for the Adventurer's life? It was useless; it was worse than useless--it would only arouse suspicion toward herself. From the standpoint of any one of the gang, the Adventurer's life was forfeit. Her mind was swift, cruelly swift, in its workings now. There came the prompting to disclose her own identity to tell Danglar that he need not go to the Adventurer to discover the whereabouts of the White Moll, that she was here now before him; there came the prompting to offer herself in lieu of the man she loved. But that, too, was useless, and worse than useless; they would still do away with the Adventurer because he had been the Pug, and the only chance he now had, as represented by whatever she might be able to do, would be gone, since she would but have delivered herself into their hands.

She drew back suddenly. Danglar had stepped toward her. She was unable to avoid him, and his arm encircled her waist. She shivered as the pressure of his arm tightened.

"It's all right, old girl!" he said exuberantly. "You've been through hell, you have; but it's all right at last. You leave it to me! Your husband's got a kiss to make up for every drop of that grease you've had to put on the prettiest face in New York."

It seemed as though she must scream out. It was hideous. She could not force herself to endure it another instant even for safety's safe. She pushed him away. It was unbearable--at any risk, cost what it might. Mind, soul and body recoiled from the embrace.

"Leave me alone!" she panted. "You've been drinking. Leave me alone!"

He drew back, and laughed.

"Not very much," he said. "The celebration hasn't started yet, and you'll be in on that. I guess your nerves have been getting shaky lately, haven't they? Well, you can figure on the swellest rest-cure you ever heard of, Bertha. Take it from me! We're going down to keep the Pug company presently. You blow around to Matty's about midnight and get the election returns. We'll finish the job after that by getting Cloran out of the road some way before morning, and that will let you out for keeps--there won't be any one left to recognize the woman who was with

Deemer the night he shuffled out." He backed to the doorway. "Get me? Come over to Matty's and see the rajah's sparklers about midnight. We'll have 'em then--and the she-fiend, too. So long, Bertha!"

She scarcely heard him; she answered mechanically.

"Good-night," she said.

XIX. DREAD UPON THE WATERS

For a moment after Danglar had gone, Rhoda Gray stood motionless; and then, the necessity for instant action upon her, she moved quickly toward the doorway herself. There was only one thing she could do, just one; but she must be sure first that Danglar was well started on his way. She reached the doorway, looked out--and suddenly caught her breath in a low, quick inhalation, In the semi-darkness she could just make out Danglar's form, perhaps twenty-five yards away now, heading along the lane toward the street; but behind Danglar, at a well-guarded distance in the rear, hugging the shadows of the fence, she saw the form of another man. Her brows knitted in a perplexed and anxious frown. The second man was undoubtedly following Danglar. That was evident. But why? Who was it? What did it mean?

She retreated back into the shed, and commenced hastily to disrobe and dress again in her own clothes, which she had flung down upon the floor. In the last analysis, did it matter who it was that was following Danglar--even if it were one of the police? For, supposing that the man who was shadowing Danglar was a plain-clothes man, and suppose he even followed Danglar and the rest of the gang to the old iron plant, and suppose that with the necessary assistance he rounded them all up, and in that sense effected the Adventurer's rescue, it scarcely meant a better fate for the Adventurer! It simply meant that the Adventurer, as one of the gang, and against whom every one of the rest would testify as the sole means left to them of wreaking their vengeance upon one who had tricked and outwitted them again and again for his own ends, would stand his trial with the others, and with the others go behind prison bars for a long term of years.

She hurried now, completing the last touches that transformed her from Gypsy Nan into the veiled figure of the White Moll, stepped out into the lane, and walking rapidly, reached the street and headed, not in the direction of Harlem, but deeper over into the East Side. Even as Danglar had been speaking she had realized that, for the Adventurer's own sake, and irrespective of what any premature disclosure of her own identity to the authorities might mean to her, she could not call upon the police for aid. There was only one way, just one--to go herself, to reach the Adventurer herself before Danglar returned there and had an opportunity of putting his worse than murderous intentions into effect.

Well, she was going there, wasn't she? And if she lost no time she should be there easily ahead of them, and her chances would be excellent of releasing the Adventurer with very little risk. From what Danglar had said, the Adventurer was there alone. Once tied and gagged there had been no need to leave anybody to guard him, save that the watchman would ordinarily serve to keep any one off the premises, which was all that was necessary. But that he had been left at all worried her greatly. He had, of course, already refused to talk. What they had done to him she did not know, but the 'solitary confinement' Danglar had referred to was undoubtedly the first step in their efforts to break his spirit. Her lips tightened as she went along. Surely she could accomplish it! She had but to evade the watchman--only, first, the lost revolver, the one safeguard against an adverse turn of fortune, must be replaced, and that was where she was going now. She knew, from her associations with the underworld as the White Moll in the old days, where such things could be purchased and no questions asked, if one were known. And she was known in the establishment to which she was going, for evil days had once fallen upon its proprietor, one "Daddy" Jacques, in that he had incurred the enmity of certain of his own ilk in the underworld, and on a certain night, which he would not be likely to forget, she had stood between him and a manhandling that would probably have cost him his life, and--Yes, this was the place.

She entered a dirty-windowed, small and musty pawnshop. A little old man, almost dwarf-like in stature, with an unkempt, tawny beard, who wore a greasy and ill-fitting suit, and upon whose bald head was perched an equally greasy skull cap, gazed at her inquiringly from behind the counter.

"I want a gun, and a good one, please," she said, after a glance around her to assure herself that they were alone.

The other squinted at her through his spectacles, as he shook his head.

"I haven't got any, lady," he answered. "We're not allowed to sell them without--"

"Oh, yes, you have, Daddy," she contradicted quietly, as she raised her veil. "And quick, please; I'm in a hurry."

The little old man leaned forward, staring at her for a moment as though fascinated; and then his hand, in a fumbling way, removed the skull cap from his bead. There was a curious, almost wistful reverence in his voice as he spoke.

"The White Moll!" he said.

"Yes," she smiled. "But the gun, Daddy. Quick! I haven't an instant to lose."

"Yes, yes!" he said eagerly--and shuffled away.

He was back in a moment, an automatic in his hand.

"It's loaded, of course?" she said, as she took the weapon. She slipped it into her pocket as he nodded affirmatively. "How much, Daddy?"

"The White Moll!" He seemed still under the spell of amazement. "It is nothing. There is no charge. It is nothing, of course."

"Thank you, Daddy!" she said softly--and laid a bill upon the counter, and stepped back to the door. "Good-night!" she smiled.

She heard him call to her; but she was already on the street again, and hurrying along. She felt better, somehow, in a mental way, for that little encounter with the shady old pawnbroker. She was not so much alone, perhaps, as she had thought; there were many, perhaps, even if they were of the underworld, who had not swerved from the loyalty they had once professed to the White Moll.

It brought a new train of thought, and she paused suddenly in her walk. She might rally around her some of those underworld intimates upon whose allegiance she felt she could depend, and use them now, to-night, in behalf of the Adventurer; she would be sure then to be a match for Danglar, no matter what turn affairs took. And then, with an impatient shake of her head, she hurried on again. There was no time for that. It would take a great deal of time to find and pick her men; she had even wasted time herself, where there was no time to spare, in the momentary pause during which she had given the thought consideration.

She reached the nearest subway station, which was her objective, and boarded a Harlem train, satisfied that her heavy veil would protect her against recognition. Unobtrusively she took a window seat. No one paid her any attention. Hours passed, it seemed to her impatience, while the black walls rushed by, punctuated by occasional scintillating signal lights, and, at longer intervals, by the fuller glare from the station platforms.

In the neighborhood of 125th street she left the train, and, entering the first drug store she found, consulted a directory. She did not know this section of New York at all; she did not know either the location or the firm name of the iron plant to which Danglar, assuming naturally, of course, that she was conversant with it, had referred; and she did not care to ask to be directed to Jake Malley's saloon, which was the only clew she had to guide her. The problem, however, did not appear to be a very difficult one. She found the saloon's address, and, asking the clerk to direct her to the street indicated, left the drug store again.

But, after all, it was not so easy; no easier than for one unacquainted with any locality to find one's way about. Several times she found herself at fault, and several times she was obliged to ask directions again. She had begun to grow panicky with fear and dread at the time she had lost, before, finally, she found the saloon. She was quite sure that it was already more than half an hour since she had left the drug store; and that half an hour might easily mean the difference between safety and disaster, not only for the Adventurer, but for herself as well. Danglar might have been in no particular hurry, and he would probably have gone first to whatever rendezvous he had appointed for those of the gang selected to accompany him, but even to have done so in a leisurely way would surely not have taken more than that half hour!

Yes, that was Jake Malley's saloon now, across the road from her, but she could not recall the time that was already lost! They might be there now--ahead of her.

She quickened her steps almost to a run. There should be no difficulty in finding the iron plant now. "Behind Jake Malley's saloon," Danglar had said. She turned down the cross street, passed the side entrance to the saloon, and hastened along. The locality was lonely, deserted, and none too well lighted. The arc lamps, powerful enough in themselves, were so far apart that they left great areas of shadow, almost blackness, between them. And the street too was very narrow, and the buildings, such as they were, were dark and unlighted--certainly it was not a residential district!

And now she became aware that she was close to the river, for the sound of a passing craft caught her attention. Of course! She understood now. The iron plant, for shipping facilities, was undoubtedly on the bank of the river itself, and--yes, this was it, wasn't it?--this picket fence that began to parallel the right-hand side of the street, and enclose, seemingly, a very large area. She halted and stared at it-- and suddenly her heart sank with a miserable sense of impotence and dismay. Yes, this was the place beyond question. Through the picket fence she could make out the looming shadows of many buildings, and spidery iron structures that seemed to cobweb the darkness, and--and--Her face mirrored her misery. She had thought of a single building. Where, inside there, amongst all those rambling structures, with little time, perhaps none at all, to search, was she to find the Adventurer?

She did not try to answer her own question--she was afraid that her dismay would get the better of her if she hesitated for an instant. She crossed the street, choosing a spot between two of the arc lamps where the shadows were blackest. It was a high fence, but not too high to climb. She reached up, preparatory to pulling herself to the top--and drew back with a stifled cry. She was too late, then--already too late! They were here ahead of her--and on guard after all! A man's form, appearing suddenly out of the darkness but a few feet away, was making quickly toward her. She wrenched her automatic from her pocket. The touch of the weapon in her hand restored her self-control.

"Don't come any nearer!" she cried out sharply. "I will fire if you do!"

And then the man spoke.

"It's you, ain't it?" he called in guarded eagerness. "It's the White Moll, ain't it? Thank God, it's you!"

Her extended hand with the automatic fell to her side. She had recognized his voice. It wasn't Danglar, it wasn't one of the gang, or the watchman who was no better than an accomplice; it was Marty Finch, alias the Sparrow.

"Marty!" she exclaimed. "You! What are you doing here?"

"I'm here to keep you from goin' in there!" he answered excitedly. "And--and, say, I was afraid I was too late. Don't you go in there! For God's sake, don't you go! They're layin' a trap for you! They're goin' to bump you off! I know all about it!"

"You know? What do you mean?" she asked quickly. "How do you know?"

"I quit my job a few days after that fellow you called Danglar tried to murder me that night you saved me," said the Sparrow, with a savage laugh. "I knew he had it in for you, and I guess I had something comm' to him on my own account too, hadn't I? That's the job I've been on ever since--tryin' to find the dirty pup. And I found him! But it wasn't until to-night, though you can believe me there weren't many joints in the old town where I didn't look for him. My luck turned to-night. I spotted him comin' out of Italian Joe's bar. See? I followed him. After a while he slips into a lane, and from the street I saw him go into a shed there. I worked my way up quiet, and got as near as I dared without bein' heard and seen, and I listened. He was talkin' to a woman. I couldn't hear everything they said, and they quarreled a lot; but I heard him say something about framin' up a job to get somebody down to the old iron plant behind Jake Malley's saloon and bump 'em off, and I heard him say there wouldn't be any White Moll by morning, and I put two and two together and beat it for here."

Rhoda Gray reached out and caught the Sparrow's hand.

"Thank you, Marty! You haven't got it quite right--though, thank Heaven, you got it the way you did, since you are here now!" she said fervently. "It wasn't me, it wasn't the White Moll, they expected to get here; it's the man who helped me that night to clear you of the Hayden-Bond robbery that Danglar meant to make you shoulder. He risked his life to do it, Marty. They've got him a prisoner somewhere in there; and they're coming back to--to torture him into telling them where I am, and--and afterwards to do away with him. That's why I'm here, Marty--to get him away, if I can, before they come back."

The Sparrow whistled low under his breath.

"Well, then, I guess it's my hunt too," he said coolly. "And I guess this is where a prison bird horns in with the goods. Ever since I've been looking for that Danglar guy, I've been carryin' a full kit--because I didn't know what might break, or what kind of a mess I might want to get out of. Come on! We ain't got no time. There's a couple of broken pickets down there. We might be seen climbin' the fence. Come on!"

Bread upon the waters! With a sense of warm gratitude upon her, Rhoda Gray followed the ex-convict. They made their way through the fence. A long, low building, a storage shed evidently, showed a few yards in front of them. It seemed to be quite close to the river, for now she could see the reflection of lights from here and there playing on the black, mirror-like surface of the water. Farther on, over beyond the shed, the yard of the plant, dotted with other buildings and those spidery iron structures which she had previously noticed, stretched away until it was lost in the darkness. Here, however, within the radius of one of the street arc lamps it was quite light.

Rhoda Gray had paused in almost hopeless indecision as to how or where to begin her search, when the Sparrow spoke again.

"It looks like we got a long hunt," whispered the Sparrow; "but a few minutes before you came, a guy with a lantern comes from over across the yard there and nosed around that shed, and acted kind of queer, and I could see him stick his head up against them side doors there as though he was listenin' for something inside. Does that wise you up to anything?"

"Yes!" she breathed tensely. "That was the watchman. He's one of them. The man we want is in that shed beyond a doubt. Hurry, Marty--hurry!"

They ran together now, and reached the double side-door. It was evidently for freight purposes only, and probably barred on the inside, for they found there was no way of opening it from without.

"There must be an entrance," she said feverishly--and led the way toward the front of the building in the direction away from the river. "Yes, here it is!" she exclaimed, as they rounded the end of the shed.

She tried the door. It was locked. She felt in her pocket for her skeleton keys, for she had not been unprepared for just such an emergency, but the Sparrow brushed her aside.

"Leave it to me!" he said quickly. "I'll pick that lock like one o'clock! It won't take me more'n a minute."

Rhoda Gray did not stand and watch him. Minutes were priceless things, and she could put the minute he asked for to better advantage than by idling it away. With an added injunction to hurry and that she would be back in an instant, she was already racing around the opposite side of the shed. If they were pressed, cornered, by the arrival of Danglar, it might well mean the difference between life and death to all of them if she had an intimate knowledge of the surroundings.

She was running at top speed. Halfway down the length of the shed she tripped and fell over some object. She pushed it aside as she rose. It was an old iron casting, more bulky in shape than in weight, though she found it none too light to lift comfortably. She ran on. A wharf projected out, she found, from this end of the shed. At the edge, she peered over. It was quite light here again; away from the protecting shadows of the shed, the rays of the arc lamp played without hindrance on the wharf just as they did on the shed's side door. Below, some ten or twelve feet below, and at the corner of the wharf, a boat, or, rather, a sort of scow, for it was larger than a boat though oars lay along its thwarts, was moored. It was partly decked over, and she could see a small black opening into the forward end of it, though the opening itself was almost hidden by a heap of tarpaulin, or sailcloth, or something of the kind, that lay in the bottom of the craft. She nodded her head. They might all of them use that boat to advantage!

Rhoda Gray turned and ran back. The Sparrow, with a grunt of satisfaction, was just opening the door. She stepped through the doorway. The Sparrow followed.

"Close it!" said Rhoda Gray, under her breath. She felt her heart beat quicken, the blood flood her face and then recede. Her imagination had suddenly become too horribly vivid. Suppose they--they had already gone farther than...

With an effort she controlled herself--and the round, white ray of her flashlight swept the place. A moment more, and, with a low cry, she was running forward to where, on the floor near the wall of the shed opposite the side door, she made out the motionless form of a man. She reached him, and dropped on her knees beside him. It was the Adventurer. She spoke to him. He did not answer. And then she remembered what Danglar had said, and she saw that he was gagged. But--but she was not sure that was the reason why he did not answer. The flashlight in her hand wavered unsteadily as it played over him. Perhaps the whiteness of the ray itself exaggerated it, but his face held a deathly pallor; his eyes were closed; and his hands and feet were twisted cruelly and tightly bound.

"Give me your knife--quick--Sparrow!" she called. "Then go and keep watch just outside."

The Sparrow handed her his knife, and hurried back to the door.

She worked in the darkness now. She could not use both hands and still hold the flashlight; and, besides, with the door partially open now where the Sparrow was on guard there was always the chance, if Danglar and those of the gang with him were already in the vicinity, of the light bringing them all the more quickly to the scene.

Again she spoke to the Adventurer, as she removed the gag--and a fear that made her sick at heart seized up on her. There was still no answer. And now, as she worked, cutting at the cords on his hands and feet, the love that she knew for the man, its restraint broken by the sense of dread and fear at his condition, rose dominant within her, and impulse that she could not hold in least took possession of her, and in the darkness, since he would not know, and there was none to see, she bent her head, and, half crying, her lips pressed upon his forehead.

She drew back startled, a crimson in her face that the darkness hid. What had she done? Did he know? Had he returned to consciousness, if he really had been unconscious, in time to know? She could not see; but she knew his eyes had opened.

She worked frantically with the bonds. He was free now. She cast them off.

He spoke then--thickly, with great difficulty.

"It's you, the White Moll, isn't it?"

"Yes," she answered.

He raised himself up on his elbow, only to fall back with a suppressed groan.

"I don't know how you found me, but get away at once--for God's sake, get away!" he cried. "Danglar'll be here at any minute. It's you he wants. He thinks you know where some--some jewels are, and that I--I--"

"I know all about Danglar," she said hurriedly. "And I know all about the jewels, for I've got them myself."

He was up on his knees now, swaying there. She caught at his shoulder to support him.

"You!" he cried out incredulously. "You--you've got them? Say that again! You--you've--"

"Yes," she said, and with an effort steadied her voice. He--he was a thief. Cost her what it might, with all its bitter hurt, she must remember that, even--even if she had forgotten once. "Yes," she said. "And I mean to turn them over to the police, and expose every one of Danglar's gang. I--you are entitled to a chance; you once stood between me and the police. I can do no less by you. I couldn't turn the police loose on the gang without giving you warning, for, you see, I know you are the Pug."

"Good God!" he stammered. "You know that, too?"

"Try and walk," she said breathlessly. "There isn't any time. And once you are away from here, remember that when Danglar is in the hands of the police he will take the only chance for revenge he has left, and give the police all the information he can, so that they will get you too."

He stumbled pitifully.

"I can't walk much yet." He was striving to speak coolly. "They trussed me up a bit, you know--but I'll be all right in a little while when I get the cramps out of my joints and the circulation back. And so, Miss Gray, won't you please go at once? I'm free now, and I'll manage all right, and--"

The Sparrow came running back from the door.

"They're comm'!" he said excitedly. "They're comm' from a different way than we came in. I saw 'em sway up there across the yard for a second when they showed up under a patch of light from an arc lamp on the other street. There's three of 'em. We got about a couple of minutes, and--"

"Get those side doors open! Quick! And no noise!'" ordered Rhoda Gray tersely. And then to the Adventurer: "Try--try and walk! I'll help you."

The Adventurer made a desperate attempt at a few steps. It was miserably slow. At that rate Danglar would be upon them before they could even cross the shed itself.

"I can crawl faster," laughed the Adventurer with bitter whimsicality. "Give me your revolver, Miss Gray, and you two go--and God bless you!"

The Sparrow was opening the side door, but she realized now that even if they could carry the Adventurer they could not get away in time. Her mind itself seemed stunned for an instant--and then, in a lightning flash, inspiration came. She remembered that iron casting, and the wharf, and the other side of the shed in shadow. It was desperate, perhaps almost hopeless, but it was the only way that gave the Adventurer a chance for his life.

She spoke rapidly. The little margin of time they had must be narrowing perilously.

"Marty, help this gentleman! Crawl to the street, if you have to. The only thing is that you are not to make the slightest noise, and--"

"What are you going to do?" demanded the Adventurer hoarsely.

"I'm going to take the only chance there is for all of us," she answered.

She started toward the front door of the shed; but he reached out and held her back.

"You are going to take the only chance there is for me!" he cried brokenly. "You're going out there--where they are. Oh, my God! I know! You love me! I--I was only half conscious, but I am sure you kissed me a little while ago. And but for this you would never have known that I knew it, because, please God, whatever else I am, I am not coward enough to take that advantage of you. But I love you, too! Rhoda! I have the right to speak, the right our love gives me. You are not to go--that way. Run--run through the side door there--they will not see you."

She was trembling. Repudiate her love? Tell him there could be nothing between them because he was a thief? She might never live to see him again. Her soul was in riot, the blood flaming hot in her cheeks. He was clinging to her arm. She tore herself forcibly away. The seconds were counting now. She tried to bid him good-by, but the words choked in her throat. She found herself running for the front door.

"Sparrow--quick! Do as I told you!" she half sobbed over her shoulder--and opening the door, stepped out and dosed it behind her.

XX. A LONE HAND

And now Rhoda Gray was in the radius of the arc lamp, and distinctly visible to any one coming down the yard. How near were they? Yes, she saw them now--three forms-perhaps a little more than a hundred yards away. She moved a few steps deliberately toward them, as though quite unconscious of their presence; and then, as a shout from one of them announced that she was seen, she halted, hesitated as though surprised, terrified and uncertain, and, as they sprang forward, she turned and ran--making for the side of the shed away from the side door.

A voice rang out--Danglar's:

"By God, it's the White Moll!"

It was the only way! She had the pack in cry now. They would pay no attention to the Adventurer while the White Moll was seemingly almost within their grasp. If she could only hold them now for a little while--just a little while--the Adventurer wasn't hurt--only cramped and numbed--he would be all right again and able to take care of himself in a little while--and meanwhile the Sparrow would help him to get away.

She was running with all her speed. She heard them behind her--the pound, pound, pound of feet. She had gained the side of the shed. The light from the arc lamp was shut off from her now, and they would only be able to see her, she knew, as a dim, fleeting shadow. Where was that iron casting? Pray God, it was heavy enough; and pray God, it was not too heavy! Yes, here it was! She pretended to stumble--and caught the thing up in her arms. An exultant cry went up from behind her as she appeared to fall--oaths, a chorus of them, as she went on again.

They had not gained on her before; but with the weight in her arms, especially as she was obliged to carry it awkwardly in order to shield it from their view with her body, she could not run so fast now, and they were beginning to close up on her. But she was on the wharf now, and there was not much farther to go, and--and surely she could hold all the lead she needed until she reached the edge.

The light from the arc lamp held her in view again out here on the wharf where she was clear of the shed; but she knew they would not fire at her except as a last resort. They could not afford to sound an alarm that would attract notice to the spot--when they had, or believed they had, both the Adventurer and the White Moll within their grasp now.

She was running now with short, hard, panting gasps. There were still five yards to go-three-one! She looked around her like a hunted animal at bay, as she reached the end of the wharf and stood there poised at the edge. Yes, thank God, they were still far enough behind to give her the few seconds she needed! She cried out loudly as though in despair and terror--and sprang from the edge of the wharf. And as she sprang she dropped the casting; but even as it struck the water with a loud splash, Rhoda Gray, in frantic haste, was crawling in through the little locker-like opening under the decked-over bow of the half scow, half boat into which she had leaped. And quick as a flash, huddled inside, she reached out and drew the heap of what proved to be sailcloth nearer to her to cover the opening-and lay still.

A few seconds passed; then she heard them at the edge of the wharf, and heard Danglar s voice.

"Watch where she comes up! She can't get away!"

A queer, wan smile twisted Rhoda Gray's lips. The casting had served her well; the splash had been loud enough! She listened, straining her ears to catch every sound from above. It was miserably small this hiding place into which she had crawled, scarcely large enough to hold her--she was beginning to be painfully cramped and uncomfortable already.

Another voice, that she recognized as Pinkie Bonn's now, reached her:

"It's damned hard to spot anything out there; the water's blacker'n hell."

Came a savage and impatient oath from Danglar.

"She's got to come up, ain't she--or drown!" he rasped. "Maybe she's swum under the wharf, or maybe she's swum under water far enough out so's we can't see her from here. Anyway, jump into that boat there, and we'll paddle around till we get her."

Rhoda Gray held her breath. The boat rocked violently as, one after another, the men jumped into it. Her right hand was doubled under her, it was hard to reach her pocket and her automatic. She moved a little; they were cursing, splashing with their oars, making too much noise to hear any slight rustle that she might make.

A minute, two, went by. She had her automatic now, and she lay there, grim-lipped, waiting. Even if they found her now, she had her own way out; and by now, beyond any question, the Adventurer and the Sparrow would have reached the street, and, even if they had to hide out there somewhere until the Adventurer had recovered the use of his limbs, they would be safe.

She could not see, of course. Once the boat bumped, and again. They were probably searching around under the wharf. She could not hear what they said, for they were keeping quiet now, talking in whispers--so as not to give her warning of their whereabouts undoubtedly!

The time dragged on. Her cramped position was bringing her excruciating agony now. She could understand how the Adventurer, in far worse case in the brutal position in which they had bound him, had fainted. She was afraid she would faint herself--it was not only the pain, but it was terribly close in the confined space, and her head was swimming.

Occasionally the oars splashed; and then, after an interminable time, the men, as though hopeless of success, and as though caution were no longer of any service, began to talk louder.

The third man was Shluker. She recognized his voice, too.

"It's no use!" he snarled. "If she's a good swimmer, she could get across the river easy. She's got away; that's sure. What the hell's the good of this? We're playing the fool. Beat it back! She was nosing around the shed. How do we know she didn't let the Pug loose before we saw her?"

Pinkie Bonn whined:

"If he's gone too, we're crimped! The whole works is bust up! The Pug knows everything, where our money is, an' everything. They'll have us cold!"

"Close your face, Pinkie!" It was Danglar speaking, his voice hoarse with un-controllable rage. "Go on back, then, Shluker. Quick!"

Rhoda Gray heard the hurried splashing of the oars now; and presently she felt the bumping of the boat against the wharf, and its violent rocking as the men climbed out of it again. But she did not move--save with her hand to push the folds of sailcloth a cautious inch or two away from the opening. It did not ease the agony she was suffering from her cramped position, but it gave her fresher air, and she could hear better--the ring of their boot-heels on the wharf above, for instance.

The footsteps died away. There was silence then for a moment; and then, faintly, from the direction of the shed, there came a chorus of baffled rage and execration. She smiled a little wearily to herself. It was all right. That was what she wanted to know. The Adventurer had got away.

Still she lay there. She dared not leave the boat yet; but she could change her position now. She crawled half out from under the docking, and lay with her head on the sailcloth. It was exquisite relief! They could not come back along the wharf without her hearing them, and she could retreat under the decking again in an instant, if necessary.

Voices reached her now occasionally from the direction of the shed. Finally a silence fell. The minutes passed--ten--fifteen--twenty of them. And then Rhoda Gray climbed warily to the wharf, made her way warily past the shed, and gained the road--and three-quarters of an hour later, in another shed, in the lane behind the garret, she was changing quickly into the rags of Gypsy Nan again.

It was almost the end now. To-night, she would keep the appointment Danglar had given her--and keep it ahead of time. It was almost the end. Her lips set tightly. The Adventurer had been warned. There was nothing now to stand in the way of her going to the police, save only the substantiation of that one point in her own story which Danglar must supply.

Her transformation completed, she reached in under the flooring and took out the package of jewels--they would help very materially when she faced Danglar!--and, though it was somewhat large, tucked it inside her blouse. It could not be noticed. The black, greasy shawl hid it effectively.

She stepped out into the lane, and from there to the street, and began to make her way across town. She did not have to search for Danglar to-night. She was to meet him at Matty's at midnight, and it was not more than halfpast eleven now. Three hours and a half! Was that all since at eight o'clock, as nearly as she could place it, he had left her in the lane? It seemed as many years; but it was only twenty minutes after eleven, she had noticed, when she had left the subway on her return a few minutes ago. Her hand clenched suddenly. She was to meet him at Matty's--and, thereafter, if it took all night, she would not leave him until she had got him alone somewhere and disclosed herself. The man was a coward in soul. She could trust to the effect upon him of an automatic in the hands of the White Mall to make him talk.

Rhoda Gray walked quickly. It was not very far. She turned the corner into the street where Danglar's deformed brother, Matty, cloaked the executive activities of the gang with his cheap little notion store--and halted abruptly. The store was just ahead of her, and Danglar himself, coming out, had just closed the door.

He saw her, and stepping instantly to her side, grasped her arm roughly and wheeled her about.

"Come on!" he said--and a vicious oath broke from his lips.

The man was in a towering, ungovernable passion. She cast a furtive glance at his face. She had seen him before in anger; but now, with his lips drawn back and working, his whole face contorted, he seemed utterly beside himself.

"What's the matter?" she inquired innocently. "Wouldn't the Pug talk, or is it a case of 'another hour or so,' and--"

He swung on her furiously.

"Hold your cursed tongue!" he flared. "You'll snicker on the wrong side of your face this time!" He gulped, stared at her threateningly, and quickened his step, forcing her to keep pace with him. But he spoke again after a minute, savagely, bitterly, but more in control of himself. "The Pug got away. The White Moll queered us again. But it's worse than that. The game's up! I told you to be here at midnight. It's only half past eleven yet. I figured you would still be over in the garret, and I was going there for you. That's where we're going now. There's no chance at those rajah's jewels now; there's no chance of fixing Cloran so's you can swell it around in the open again--the only chance we've got is to save what we can and beat it!"

She did not need to simulate either excitement or disquiet.

"What is it? What's happened?" she asked tensely.

"The gang's thrown us down!" he said between his teeth. "They're scared; they've got cold feet--they're going to quit. Shluker and Pinkie were with me at the iron plant. We went back to Matty's from there. Matty's with them, too. They say the Pug knows every one of us, and every game we've pulled, and that in revenge for our trying to murder him he'll wise up the police--that he could do it easily enough without getting nipped himself, by sending them a letter, or even telephoning the names and addresses of the whole layout. They're scared--he curs! They say he knows where all our coin is too; and they're for splitting it up to-night, and ducking it out of New York for a while to get under cover." He laughed out suddenly, raucously. "They will--eh? I'll show them--the yellow-streaked pups! They wouldn't listen to me--and it meant that you and I were thrown down for fair. If we're caught, it's the chair. I'll show them! When I saw it wasn't any use trying to get them to stick, I pretended to agree with them. See? I said they could go around and dig up the rest of the gang, and if the others felt the same way about it, they were all to come over to the garret, and I'd be waiting for them,--and we'd split up the swag, and everybody'd be on his own after that." Again he laughed out raucously. "It'll take them half an hour to get together--but it won't take that long for us to grab all that's worth grabbing out of that trap-door, and making our getaway. See? I'll teach them to throw Pierre Danglar down! Come on, hurry!"

"Sure!" she mumbled mechanically.

Her mind was sifting, sorting, weighing what he had said. She was not surprised. She remembered Pinkie Bonn's outburst in the boat. She walked on beside Danglar. The man was muttering and cursing under his breath. Well, why shouldn't she appear to fall in with his plans? Under what choicer surroundings could she get him alone than in the garret? And half an hour would be ample time for her, too! Yes, yes, she began to see! With Danglar, when she had got what she wanted out of him herself, held up at the point of her automatic, she could back to the door and lock him in there--and notify the police--and the police would not only get Danglar and the ill-gotten hoard hidden in the ceiling behind that trap-door, but they would get all the rest of the gang as the latter in due course appeared on the scene. Yes, why not? She experienced an exhilaration creeping upon her; she even increased, unconsciously, the rapid pace which Danglar had set.

"That's the stuff!" he grunted in savage approval. "We need every minute we've got."

They reached the house where once--so long ago now, it seemed!--Rhoda Gray had first found the original Gypsy Nan; and, Danglar leading, mounted the dark, narrow stairway to the hall above, and from there up the short, ladder-like steps to the garret. He groped in the aperture under the partition for the key, opened the door, and stepped inside. Rhoda Gray, following, removed the key, inserted it on the inside of the door, and, as she too entered, locked the door behind her. It was pitch-black here in the attic. Her face was set now, her lips firm. She had been waiting for this, hadn't she? It was near the end at last. She had Danglar--alone. But not in the darkness! He was too tricky! She crossed the garret to where the candle-stub, stuck in the neck of the gin bottle, stood on the rickety washstand.

"Come over here and light the candle," she said. "I can't find my matches."

Her hand was in the pocket of her skirt now, her fingers tight-closed on the stock of her automatic, as he shuffled his way across the attic to her side. A match spurted into flame; the candle wick flickered, then steadied, dispersing little by little, as it grew brighter, the nearer shadows--and there came a startled cry from Danglar--and Rhoda Gray, the weapon in her pocket forgotten, was staring as though stricken of her senses across the garret. The Adventurer was sitting on the edge of the cot, and a revolver in his hand held a steady bead upon Danglar and herself..

XXI. THE RECKONING

I t was the Adventurer who spoke first.

"Both of you! What charming luck!" he murmured whimsically. "You'll forgive the intrusion won't you? A friend of mine, the Sparrow by name--I think you are acquainted with him, Danglar--was good enough to open the door for me, and lock it again on the outside. You see, I didn't wish to cause you any alarm through a premature suspicion that you might have a guest!" His voice hardened suddenly as he rose from the cot, and, though he limped badly, stepped quickly toward them. "Don't move, Danglar--or you, Mrs. Danglar!" he ordered sharply--and with a lightning movement of his hand felt for, and whipped Danglar's revolver from the latter's pocket. "Pardon me!" he said--and his hand was in and out of Rhoda Gray's pocket. He tossed the two weapons coolly over onto the cot. "Well, Danglar," he smiled grimly, "there's quite a change in the last few hours, isn't there?"

Danglar made no answer. His face was ashen; his little black eyes, like those of a cornered rat, and as though searching for some avenue of escape, were darting hunted glances all around the garret.

Rhoda Gray, the first shock of surprise gone, leaned back against the washstand with an air of composure that she did not altogether feel. What was the Adventurer going to do? True, she need have no fear of personal violence--she had only to disclose herself. But--but there were other considerations. She saw that reckoning of her own with Danglar at an end, though--yes!--perhaps the Adventurer would become her ally in that matter. But, then, there was something else. The Adventurer was a thief, and she could not let him get away with those packages of banknotes up there behind the trap-door in the ceiling, if she could help it. That was perhaps what he had come for, and--and--Her mind seemed to tumble into chaos. She did not know what to do. She stared at the Adventurer. He was still dressed as the Pug, though the eye-patch was gone, and there was no longer any sign of the artificial facial disfigurements.

The Adventurer spoke again.

"Won't you sit down--Mrs. Danglar?" He pushed the single chair the garret possessed toward her--and shrugged his shoulders as she remained motionless. "You'll pardon me, then, if I sit down myself." He appropriated the chair, and faced them, his revolver dangling with ominous carelessness in his hand. "I've had a rather upsetting experience this evening, and I am afraid I am still a little the worse for it--as perhaps you know, Danglar?"

"You damned traitor!" Danglar burst out wildly. "I--I--"

"Quite so!" said the Adventurer smoothly. "But we'll get to that in a minute. Do you mind if I inflict a little story on you? I promise you it won't take long. It's a little personal history which I think will be interesting to you both; but, in any case, as my hosts, I am sure you will be polite enough to listen. It concerns the murder of a man named Deemer; but in order that you may understand my interest in the matter, I must go back quite a little further. Perhaps I even ought to introduce myself. My name, my real name, you know, is David Holt. My father was in the American Consular service in India when I was about ten. He eventually left it and went into business there through the advice of a very warm friend of his, a certain very rich and very powerful rajah in the State of Chota Nagpur in the Province of Bengal, where we then lived. I became an equally intimate friend of the rajah's son, and--do I bore you, Danglar?"

Danglar was like a crouched animal, his head drawn into his shoulders, his hands behind him with fingers twisting and gripping at the edge of the washstand.

"What's your proposition?" he snarled. "Curse you, name your price, and have done with it! You're as big a crook as I am!"

"You are impatient!" The Adventurer's shoulders went up again. "In due time the rajah decided that a trip through Europe and back home through America would round out his son's education, and broaden and fit him for his future duties in a way that nothing else would. It was also decided, I need hardly say to my intense delight, that I should accompany him. We come now to our journey through the United States--you see, Danglar, that I am omitting everything but the essential details. In a certain city in the Middle West--I think you will remember it well,

Danglar--the young rajah met with an accident. He was out riding in the outskirts of the city. His horse took fright and dashed for the river-bank. He was an excellent horseman, but, pitched from his seat, his foot became tangled in the stirrup, and as he hung there head down, a blow from he horse's hoof rendered him unconscious, and he was being dragged along, when a man by the name of Deemer, at the risk of his own life, saved the rajah's son. The horse plunged over the bank and into the water with both of them. They were both nearly drowned. Deemer, let me say in passing, did one of the bravest things that any man ever did. Submerged, half drowned himself, he stayed with the maddened animal until he had succeeded in freeing the unconscious man. All this was some two years ago."

The Adventurer paused.

Rhoda Gray, hanging on his words, was leaning tensely forward--it seemed as though some great, dawning wonderment was lifting her out of herself, making her even unconscious of her surroundings.

"The rajah's son remained at the hotel there for several days to recuperate," continued the Adventurer deliberately; "and during that time he saw a great deal of Deemer, and, naturally, so did I. And, incidentally, Danglar, though I thought nothing much of it then, I saw something of you; and something of Mrs. Danglar there, too, though--if she will permit me to say it--in a more becoming costume than she is now wearing!" Once more he shrugged his shoulders as Danglar snarled. "Yes, yes; I will hurry. I am almost through. While it was not made public through-out the country, inasmuch as the rajah's son was more or less an official guest of the government, the details of the accident were of course known locally, as also was the fact that the young rajah in token of his gratitude had presented Deemer with a collection of jewels of almost priceless worth. We resumed our journey; Deemer, who was a man in very moderate circumstances, and who had probably never had any means in his life before, went to New York, presumably to have his first real holiday, and, as it turned out, to dispose of the stones, or at least a portion of them. When we reached the coast we received two advices containing very ill news. The first was an urgent message to return instantly to India on account of the old rajah's serious illness; the second was to the effect that Deemer had been murdered by a woman in New York, and that the jewels had been stolen."

Again the Adventurer paused, and, eying Danglar, smiled--not pleasantly.

"I will not attempt to explain to you," he went on, "the young rajah's feelings when he heard that the gift he had given Deemer in return for his own life had cost Deemer his. Nor will I attempt to explain the racial characteristics of the people of whom the young rajah was one, and who do not lightly forget or forgive. But an eye for an eye, Danglar--you will understand that. If it cost all he had, there should be justice. He could not stay himself; and so I stayed-because he made me swear I would, and because he made me swear that I would never allow the chase to lag until the murderers were found.

"And so I came East again. I remembered you, Danglar--that on several occasions when I had come upon Deemer unawares, you, sometimes accompanied by a woman, and sometimes not, had been lurking in the background. I went to Cloran, the house detective at the hotel here in New York where Deemer was murdered. He described the woman. She was the same woman that had been with you. I went to the authorities and showed my credentials, with which the young rajah had seen to it I was supplied from very high sources indeed. I did not wish to interfere with the authorities in their handling of the case; but, on the other hand, I had no wish to sit down idly and watch them, and it was necessary therefore that I should protect myself in anything I did. I also made myself known to one of New York's assistant district attorneys, who was an old friend of my father's. And then, Danglar, I started out after you.

"I discovered you after about a month; then I wormed myself into your gang as the Pug. That took about a year. I was almost another year with you as an accepted member of the gang. You know what happened during that period. A little while ago I found out that the woman we wanted--with you, Danglar--was your wife, living in hiding in this garret as Gypsy Nan. But the jewels themselves were still missing. To-night they are not. A--a friend of mine, one very much misjudged publicly, I might say, has them, and has told me they would be handed to the police.

"And so, Danglar, after coming here to-night, I sent the Sparrow out to gather together a few of the authorities who are interested in the case--my friend the assistant district attorney; Cloran, the house detective; Rough Rorke of headquarters, who on one occasion was very much interested in Gypsy Nan; and enough men to make the round of arrests. They should be conveniently hidden across the road now, and waiting for my signal. My idea, you see, was to allow Mrs. Danglar to enter here without having her suspicions aroused, and to see that she did not get away again if she arrived before those who are duly qualified--which I am not--to arrest her did; also, in view of what transpired earlier this evening, I must confess I was a little anxious about those several years' accumulation of stolen funds up there in the ceiling. As I said at the beginning, I hardly expected the luck to get you both at the same time; though we should have got you, Danglar, and every one of the rest of the gang before morning, and--"

"You," Rhoda Gray whispered, "you--are not a thief!" Brain and soul seemed on fire. It seemed as though she had striven to voice those words a dozen times since he had been speaking, but that she had been afraid--afraid that this was not true, this great, wonderful thing, that it could not be true. "You--you are not a--a thief!"

The Adventurer's face lost its immobility. He half rose from his chair, staring at her in a startled way--but it was Danglar now who spoke.

"It's a lie!" he screamed out. "It's a lie!" The man's reason appeared to be almost unhinged; a mad terror seemed to possess him. "It's all a lie! I never heard of this rajah bunk before in my life! I never heard of Deemer, or any jewels before. You lie! I tell you, you lie! You can't prove it; you can't--"

"But I can," said Rhoda Gray in a low voice. The shawl fell from her shoulders; from her blouse she took the package of jewels and held them out to the Adventurer. "Here are the stones. I got them from where you had put them in old Luertz's room. I was hidden there all the time last night." She was removing her spectacles and her wig of tangled gray hair as she spoke, and now she turned her face full upon Danglar. "I heard you discuss Deemer's murder with your brother last night, and plan to get rid of Cloran, who you thought was the only existing witness you need fear, and--"

"Great God!" The Adventurer cried out. "You--Rhoda! The White Moll! I--I don't understand, though I can see you are not the woman who originally masqueraded as Gypsy Nan, for I knew her, as I said, by sight."

He was on his feet now, his face aflame with a great light. He took a step toward her.

"Wait!" she said hurriedly. She glanced at Danglar. The man's face was blanched, his body seemed to have shriveled up, and there was a light in his eyes as they held upon her that was near to the borderland of insanity. "That night at Skarbolov's!"

she said, and tried to hold her voice in control. "Gypsy Nan, this man's wife, died that night in the hospital. I had found her here sick, and I had promised not to divulge her secret. I helped her get to the hospital. She was dying; she was penitent in a way; she wanted to prevent a crime that she said was to be perpetrated that night, but she would not inform on her accomplices. She begged me to forestall them, and return the money anonymously the next day. That was the choice I had--either to allow the crime to be carried out, or else swear to act alone in return for the information that would enable me to keep the money away from the thieves without bringing the police into it. I--I was caught. You--you saved me from Rough Rorke, but he followed me. I put on Gypsy Nan's clothes, and managed to outwit him. I had had no opportunity to return the money, which would have been proof of my innocence; the only way I could prove it, then, was to try and find the authors of the crime myself. I--I have lived since then as Gypsy Nan, fighting this hideous gang of Danglar's here to try and save myself, and--and to-night I thought I could see my way clear. I--I knew enough at last about this man to make him give me a written statement that it was a pre-arranged plan to rob Skarbolov. That would substantiate my story. And"--she looked again at Danglar; the man was still crouched there, eying her with that same mad light in his eyes--"and he must be made to--to do it now for--"

"But why didn't you ask me?" cried the Adventurer. "You knew me as the Pug, and therefore must have believed that I, too, know all about it."

"Yes," she said, and turned her head away to hide the color she felt was mounting to her cheeks. "I--I thought of that. But I thought you were a thief, and--and your testimony wouldn't have been much good unless, with it, I could have handed you, too, over to the police, as I intended to do with Danglar; and--and--I--I couldn't do that, and--Oh, don't you see?" she ended desperately.

"Rhoda! Rhoda!" There was a glad, buoyant note in the Adventurer's voice. "Yes, I see! Well, I can prove it for you now without any of those fears on my behalf to worry you! I went to Skarbolov's myself, knowing their plans, to do exactly what you did. I did not know you then, and, as Rough Rorke, who was there because, as I heard later, his suspicions had been aroused through seeing some of the gang lurking around the back door in the lane the night before, had taken the actual money from you, I contrived to let you get away, because I was afraid that you were some new factor in the game, some member of the gang that I did not know about, and that I must watch, too! Don't you understand? The jewels were still missing. I had not got the general warning that was sent out to the gang that night to lay low, for at the last moment it seems that Danglar here found out that Rough Rorke had suspicions about Skarbolov's place." He came close to her--and with the muzzle of his revolver he pushed Danglar's huddled figure back a little further against the washstand. "Rhoda--you are clear. The assistant district attorney who had your case is the one I spoke of a few minutes ago. That night at Hayden-Bond's, though I did not understand fully, I knew that you were the bravest, truest little woman into whom God had ever breathed the breath of life. I told him the next day there was some mistake, something strange behind it all. I told him what happened at Hayden-Bond's. He agreed with me. You have never been indicted. Your case has never come before the grand jury. And it never will now! Rhoda! Rhoda! Thank God for you! Thank God it has all come out right, and--"

A peal of laughter, mad, insane, horrible in its perverted mirth, rang through the garret. Danglar's hands were creeping queerly up to his temples. And then, oblivious evidently in his frenzy of the revolver in the Adventurer's hand, and his eye catching the weapons that lay upon the cot, he made a sudden dash in that di-rection--and Rhoda Gray, divining his intention, sprang for the cot, too, at the same time. But Danglar never reached his objective. As Rhoda Gray caught up the weap-ons and thrust them into her pocket, she heard Danglar's furious snarl, and whirling around, she saw the two men locked and struggling in each other's embrace.

The Adventurer's voice reached her, quick, imperative:

"Show the candle at the window, Rhoda! The Sparrow is waiting for it in the yard below. Then open the door for them."

A sudden terror and fear seized her. The Adventurer was not fit, after what he had been through to-night to cope with Danglar. He had been limping badly even a few minutes ago. It seemed to her, as she rushed across the garret and snatched up the candle, that Danglar was getting the best of it even now. And the Adventurer could have shot him down, and been warranted in doing it! She reached the win-dow, waved the candle frantically several times across the pane, then setting the candle down on the window ledge, she ran for the door.

She looked back again, as she turned the key in the lock. With a crash, pitching over the chair, both men went to the floor--and the Adventurer was underneath. She cried out in alarm, and wrenched the door open--and stood for an instant there on the threshold in a startled way.

They couldn't be coming already! The Sparrow hadn't had time even to get out of the yard. But there were footsteps in the hall below, many of them. She stepped out on the landing; it was too dark to see, but...

A sudden yell as she showed even in the faint light of the open garret door, the quicker rush of feet, reached her from below.

"The White Moll! That's her! The White Moll!" She flung herself flat down, wrenching both the automatic and the revolver from her pocket. She understood now! That was Pinkie Bonn's voice. It was the gang arriving to divide up the spoils, not the Sparrow and the police. Her mind was racing now with lightning speed. If they got her, they would get the Adventurer in there, too, before the police could intervene. She must hold this little landing where she lay now, hold those short, ladder-like steps that the oncoming footsteps from below there had almost reached.

She fired once--twice--again; but high, over their heads, to check the rush.

Yells answered her. A vicious tongue-flame from a revolver, another and another, leaped out at her from the black below; the spat, spat of bullets sounded from behind her as they struck the walls.

Again she fired. They were at least more cautious now in their rush--no one seemed anxious to be first upon the stairs. She cast a wild glance through the open door into the garret at her side. The two forms in there, on their feet again, were spinning around and around with the strange, lurching gyrations of automatons-- and then she saw the Adventurer whip a terrific blow to Danglar's face--and Danglar fall and lie still--and the Adventurer come leaping toward her.

But faces were showing now above the level of the floor, and there was suddenly an increased uproar from further back in the rear until it seemed that pandemonium itself were loosed.

"It's the police! The police behind us!" she heard Shluker's voice shriek out.

She jumped to her feet. Two of the gang had reached the landing and were smashing at the Adventurer. There seemed to be a swirling mob in riot there below. The Adventurer was fighting like a madman. It was hand to hand now.

"Quick! Quick!" she cried to the Adventurer. "Jump back through the door."

"Oh, no, you don't!" It was Skeeny--she could see the man's brutal face now. "Oh, no, you don't, you she-devil!" he shouted, and, over-reaching the Adventurer's guard, struck at her furiously with his clubbed revolver.

It struck her a glancing blow on the head, and she reeled and staggered, but recovered herself. And now it seemed as though it were another battle that she fought--and one more desperate; a battle to fight back a horrible giddiness from overpowering her, and with which her brain was swimming, to fight it back for just a second, the fraction of a second that was needed until--until--"Jump!" she cried again, and staggered over the threshold, and, as the Adventurer leaped backward beside her, she slammed the door, and locked it--and slid limply to the floor.

When she regained consciousness she was lying on the cot. It seemed very still, very quiet in the garret. She opened her eyes. It--it must be all right, for that was the Sparrow standing there watching her, and shifting nervously from foot to foot, wasn't it? He couldn't be there, otherwise. She held out her hand.

"Marty," she said, and smiled with trembling lips, "we--we owe you a great deal."

The Sparrow gulped.

"Gee, you're all right again! They said it wasn't nothin', but you had me scared worse'n down at the iron plant when I had to do the rough act with that gent friend of yours to stop him from crawlin' after you and fightin' it out, and queerin' the whole works. You don't owe me nothin', Miss Gray; and, besides, I'm gettin' a lot more than is comm' to me, 'cause that same gent friend of yours there says I'm goin' to horn in on the rewards, and I guess that's goin' some, for they got the whole out-fit from Danglar down, and the stuff up in the ceiling there, too."

She turned her head. The Adventurer was coming toward the cot.

"Better?" he called cheerily.

"Yes," she said. "Quite! Only I--I'd like to get away from here, from this--this horrible place at once, and back to--to my flat if they'll let me. Are--are they all gone?"

The Adventurer's gray eyes lighted with a whimsical smile.

"Nearly all!" he said softly. "And--er--Sparrow, suppose you go and find a taxi!"

"Me? Sure! Of course! Sure!" said the Sparrow hurriedly, and retreated through the door.

She felt the blood flood her face, and she tried to avert it.

He bent his head close to hers.

"Rhoda," his voice was low, passionate, "I--"

"Wait!" she said. "Your friend--the assistant district attorney--did he come?"

"Yes," said the Adventurer. "But I shooed them all out, as soon as we found you were not seriously hurt. I thought you had had enough excitement for one night. He wants to see you in the morning."

"To see me"--she rose up anxiously on her elbow--"in the morning?"

He was smiling at her. His hands reached out and took her face between them, and made her look at him.

"Rhoda," he said gently, "I knew to-night in the iron plant that you cared. I told him so. What he wants to see you for is to tell you that he thinks I am the luckiest man in all the world. You are clear, dear. Even Rough Rorke is singing your praises; he says you are the only woman who ever put one over on him."

She did not answer for a moment; and then with a little sob of glad surrender she buried her face on his shoulder.

"It--it is very wonderful," she said brokenly, "for--for even we, you and I, each thought the other a--a thief."

"And so we were, thank God!" he whispered--and lifted her head until now his lips met hers. "We were both thieves, Rhoda, weren't we? And, please God, we will be all our lives--for we have stolen each other's heart."

The Codes Of Hammurabi And Moses
W. W. Davies

QTY

The discovery of the Hammurabi Code is one of the greatest achievements of archaeology, and is of paramount interest, not only to the student of the Bible, but also to all those interested in ancient history...

Religion   **ISBN:** *1-59462-338-4*   **Pages:132**
MSRP $12.95

The Theory of Moral Sentiments
Adam Smith

QTY

This work from 1749. contains original theories of conscience amd moral judgment and it is the foundation for systemof morals.

Philosophy **ISBN:** *1-59462-777-0*   **Pages:536**
MSRP $19.95

Jessica's First Prayer
Hesba Stretton

QTY

In a screened and secluded corner of one of the many railway-bridges which span the streets of London there could be seen a few years ago, from five o'clock every morning until half past eight, a tidily set-out coffee-stall, consisting of a trestle and board, upon which stood two large tin cans, with a small fire of charcoal burning under each so as to keep the coffee boiling during the early hours of the morning when the work-people were thronging into the city on their way to their daily toil...

Childrens   **ISBN:** *1-59462-373-2*   **Pages:84**
MSRP $9.95

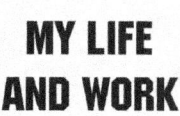

My Life and Work
Henry Ford

QTY

Henry Ford revolutionized the world with his implementation of mass production for the Model T automobile. Gain valuable business insight into his life and work with his own auto-biography... "We have only started on our development of our country we have not as yet, with all our talk of wonderful progress, done more than scratch the surface. The progress has been wonderful enough but..."

Biographies/   **ISBN:** *1-59462-198-5*   **Pages:300**
MSRP $21.95

The Art of Cross-Examination
Francis Wellman

QTY

I presume it is the experience of every author, after his first book is published upon an important subject, to be almost overwhelmed with a wealth of ideas and illustrations which could readily have been included in his book, and which to his own mind, at least, seem to make a second edition inevitable. Such certainly was the case with me; and when the first edition had reached its sixth impression in five months, I rejoiced to learn that it seemed to my publishers that the book had met with a sufficiently favorable reception to justify a second and considerably enlarged edition. ..

Pages:412

Reference   **ISBN: *1-59462-647-2***   *MSRP $19.95*

On the Duty of Civil Disobedience
Henry David Thoreau

QTY

Thoreau wrote his famous essay, On the Duty of Civil Disobedience, as a protest against an unjust but popular war and the immoral but popular institution of slave-owning. He did more than write—he declined to pay his taxes, and was hauled off to gaol in consequence. Who can say how much this refusal of his hastened the end of the war and of slavery ?

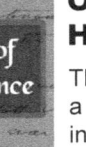

Law   **ISBN: *1-59462-747-9***   **Pages:48**

MSRP $7.45

Dream Psychology Psychoanalysis for Beginners
Sigmund Freud

QTY

Sigmund Freud, born Sigismund Schlomo Freud (May 6, 1856 - September 23, 1939), was a Jewish-Austrian neurologist and psychiatrist who co-founded the psychoanalytic school of psychology. Freud is best known for his theories of the unconscious mind, especially involving the mechanism of repression; his redefinition of sexual desire as mobile and directed towards a wide variety of objects; and his therapeutic techniques, especially his understanding of transference in the therapeutic relationship and the presumed value of dreams as sources of insight into unconscious desires.

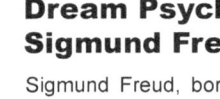

Dream Psychology
Psychoanalysis for Beginners

Sigmund Freud

Pages:196

Psychology   **ISBN: *1-59462-905-6***   *MSRP $15.45*

The Miracle of Right Thought
Orison Swett Marden

QTY

Believe with all of your heart that you will do what you were made to do. When the mind has once formed the habit of holding cheerful, happy, prosperous pictures, it will not be easy to form the opposite habit. It does not matter how improbable or how far away this realization may see, or how dark the prospects may be, if we visualize them as best we can, as vividly as possible, hold tenaciously to them and vigorously struggle to attain them, they will gradually become actualized, realized in the life. But a desire, a longing without endeavor, a yearning abandoned or held indifferently will vanish without realization.

Pages:360

Self Help   **ISBN: *1-59462-644-8***   *MSRP $25.45* www.**bookjungle**.com *email: sales@bookjungle.com fax: 630-214-0564 mail: Book Jungle PO Box 2226 Champaign, IL 61825*

QTY

The Rosicrucian Cosmo-Conception Mystic Christianity by *Max Heindel*   ISBN: *1-59462-188-8*   **$38.95**
The Rosicrucian Cosmo-conception is not dogmatic, neither does it appeal to any other authority than the reason of the student. It is: not controversial, but is: sent forth in the, hope that it may help to clear..   New Age/Religion Pages 646

Abandonment To Divine Providence by *Jean-Pierre de Caussade*   ISBN: *1-59462-228-0*   **$25.95**
"The Rev. Jean Pierre de Caussade was one of the most remarkable spiritual writers of the Society of Jesus in France in the 18th Century. His death took place at Toulouse in 1751. His works have gone through many editions and have been republished...   Inspirational/Religion Pages 400

Mental Chemistry by *Charles Haanel*   ISBN: *1-59462-192-6*   **$23.95**
Mental Chemistry allows the change of material conditions by combining and appropriately utilizing the power of the mind. Much like applied chemistry creates something new and unique out of careful combinations of chemicals the mastery of mental chemistry...   New Age Pages 354

The Letters of Robert Browning and Elizabeth Barret Barrett 1845-1846 vol II   ISBN: *1-59462-193-4*   **$35.95**
by *Robert Browning and Elizabeth Barrett*   Biographies Pages 596

Gleanings In Genesis (volume I) by *Arthur W. Pink*   ISBN: *1-59462-130-6*   **$27.45**
Appropriately has Genesis been termed "the seed plot of the Bible" for in it we have, in germ form, almost all of the great doctrines which are afterwards fully developed in the books of Scripture which follow...   Religion/Inspirational Pages 420

The Master Key by *L. W. de Laurence*   ISBN: *1-59462-001-6*   **$30.95**
In no branch of human knowledge has there been a more lively increase of the spirit of research during the past few years than in the study of Psychology, Concentration and Mental Discipline. The requests for authentic lessons in Thought Control, Mental Discipline and...   New Age/Business Pages 422

The Lesser Key Of Solomon Goetia by *L. W. de Laurence*   ISBN: *1-59462-092-X*   **$9.95**
This translation of the first book of the "Lernegton" which is now for the first time made accessible to students of Talismanic Magic was done, after careful collation and edition, from numerous Ancient Manuscripts in Hebrew, Latin, and French...   New Age/Occult Pages 92

Rubaiyat Of Omar Khayyam by *Edward Fitzgerald*   ISBN:*1-59462-332-5*   **$13.95**
Edward Fitzgerald, whom the world has already learned, in spite of his own efforts to remain within the shadow of anonymity, to look upon as one of the rarest poets of the century, was born at Bredfield, in Suffolk, on the 31st of March, 1809. He was the third son of John Purcell...   Music Pages 172

Ancient Law by *Henry Maine*   ISBN: *1-59462-128-4*   **$29.95**
The chief object of the following pages is to indicate some of the earliest ideas of mankind, as they are reflected in Ancient Law, and to point out the relation of those ideas to modern thought.   Religion/History Pages 452

Far-Away Stories by *William J. Locke*   ISBN: *1-59462-129-2*   **$19.45**
"Good wine needs no bush, but a collection of mixed vintages does. And this book is just such a collection. Some of the stories I do not want to remain buried for ever in the museum files of dead magazine-numbers an author's not unpardonable vanity..."   Fiction Pages 272

Life of David Crockett by *David Crockett*   ISBN: *1-59462-250-7*   **$27.45**
"Colonel David Crockett was one of the most remarkable men of the times in which he lived. Born in humble life, but gifted with a strong will, an indomitable courage, and unremitting perseverance...   Biographies/New Age Pages 424

Lip-Reading by *Edward Nitchie*   ISBN: *1-59462-206-X*   **$25.95**
Edward B. Nitchie, founder of the New York School for the Hard of Hearing, now the Nitchie School of Lip-Reading, Inc, wrote "LIP-READING Principles and Practice". The development and perfecting of this meritorious work on lip-reading was an undertaking...   How-to Pages 400

A Handbook of Suggestive Therapeutics, Applied Hypnotism, Psychic Science   ISBN: *1-59462-214-0*   **$24.95**
by *Henry Munro*   Health/New Age/Health/Self-help Pages 376

A Doll's House: and Two Other Plays by *Henrik Ibsen*   ISBN: *1-59462-112-8*   **$19.95**
Henrik Ibsen created this classic when in revolutionary 1848 Rome. Introducing some striking concepts in playwriting for the realist genre, this play has been studied the world over.   Fiction/Classics/Plays 308

The Light of Asia by *sir Edwin Arnold*   ISBN: *1-59462-204-3*   **$13.95**
In this poetic masterpiece, Edwin Arnold describes the life and teachings of Buddha. The man who was to become known as Buddha to the world was born as Prince Gautama of India but he rejected the worldly riches and abandoned the reigns of power when...   Religion/History/Biographies Pages 170

The Complete Works of Guy de Maupassant by *Guy de Maupassant*   ISBN: *1-59462-157-8*   **$16.95**
"For days and days, nights and nights, I had dreamed of that first kiss which was to consecrate our engagement, and I knew not on what spot I should put my lips..."   Fiction/Classics Pages 240

The Art of Cross-Examination by *Francis L. Wellman*   ISBN: *1-59462-309-0*   **$26.95**
Written by a renowned trial lawyer, Wellman imparts his experience and uses case studies to explain how to use psychology to extract desired information through questioning.   How-to/Science/Reference Pages 408

Answered or Unanswered? by *Louisa Vaughan*   ISBN: *1-59462-248-5*   **$10.95**
Miracles of Faith in China   Religion Pages 112

The Edinburgh Lectures on Mental Science (1909) by *Thomas*   ISBN: *1-59462-008-3*   **$11.95**
This book contains the substance of a course of lectures recently given by the writer in the Queen Street Hall, Edinburgh. Its purpose is to indicate the Natural Principles governing the relation between Mental Action and Material Conditions...   New Age/Psychology Pages 148

Ayesha by *H. Rider Haggard*   ISBN: *1-59462-301-5*   **$24.95**
Verily and indeed it is the unexpected that happens! Probably if there was one person upon the earth from whom the Editor of this, and of a certain previous history, did not expect to hear again...   Classics Pages 380

Ayala's Angel by *Anthony Trollope*   ISBN: *1-59462-352-X*   **$29.95**
The two girls were both pretty, but Lucy who was twenty-one who supposed to be simple and comparatively unattractive, whereas Ayala was credited, as her Bombwhat romantic name might show, with poetic charm and a taste for romance. Ayala when her father died was nineteen...   Fiction Pages 484

The American Commonwealth by *James Bryce*   ISBN: *1-59462-286-8*   **$34.45**
An interpretation of American democratic political theory. It examines political mechanics and society from the perspective of Scotsman James Bryce   Politics Pages 572

Stories of the Pilgrims by *Margaret P. Pumphrey*   ISBN: *1-59462-116-0*   **$17.95**
This book explores pilgrims religious oppression in England as well as their escape to Holland and eventual crossing to America on the Mayflower, and their early days in New England...   History Pages 268

QTY

The Fasting Cure *by Sinclair Upton*   ISBN: *1-59462-222-1*   **$13.95**
*In the Cosmopolitan Magazine for May, 1910, and in the Contemporary Review (London) for April, 1910, I published an article dealing with my experi-
ences in fasting. I have written a great many magazine articles, but never one which attracted so much attention... New Age/Self Help/Health Pages 164*

Hebrew Astrology *by Sepharial*   ISBN: *1-59462-308-2*   **$13.45**
*In these days of advanced thinking it is a matter of common observation that we have left many of the old landmarks behind and that we are now pressing
forward to greater heights and to a wider horizon than that which represented the mind-content of our progenitors...   Astrology Pages 144*

Thought Vibration or The Law of Attraction in the Thought World   ISBN: *1-59462-127-6*   **$12.95**

by William Walker Atkinson   *Psychology/Religion Pages 144*

Optimism *by Helen Keller*   ISBN: *1-59462-108-X*   **$15.95**
*Helen Keller was blind, deaf, and mute since 19 months old, yet famously learned how to overcome these handicaps, communicate with the world, and
spread her lectures promoting optimism. An inspiring read for everyone...   Biographies/Inspirational Pages 84*

Sara Crewe *by Frances Burnett*   ISBN: *1-59462-360-0*   **$9.45**
*In the first place, Miss Minchin lived in London. Her home was a large, dull, tall one, in a large, dull square, where all the houses were alike, and all the
sparrows were alike, and where all the door-knockers made the same heavy sound...   Childrens/Classic Pages 88*

The Autobiography of Benjamin Franklin *by Benjamin Franklin*   ISBN: *1-59462-135-7*   **$24.95**
*The Autobiography of Benjamin Franklin has probably been more extensively read than any other American historical work, and no other book of its kind
has had such ups and downs of fortune. Franklin lived for many years in England, where he was agent...   Biographies/History Pages 332*

Name

Email

Telephone

Address

City, State ZIP

☐ **Credit Card**   ☐ **Check / Money Order**

Credit Card Number

Expiration Date

Signature

*Please Mail to: Book Jungle
PO Box 2226
Champaign, IL 61825*
or Fax to: 630-214-0564

ORDERING INFORMATION
web: *www.bookjungle.com*
email: *sales@bookjungle.com*
fax: *630-214-0564*
mail: *Book Jungle PO Box 2226 Champaign, IL 61825*
or PayPal *to sales@bookjungle.com*

Please contact us for bulk discounts

DIRECT-ORDER TERMS

**20% Discount if You Order
Two or More Books**
Free Domestic Shipping!
Accepted: Master Card, Visa,
Discover, American Express